H.E.
Publish
College Bookshop Publishers
Edited by
Geoff Morley

Author Mike Nelson

Published by College Bookshop Publishers

I.S.B.N 9780956695024
Agent Nielsen
Published 2012
Copyright

Editor's notes
Please note
This book does not contain similarity or
resemblance to any references or opinions to any
charity services or characters are purely fictional,
and bearing no symmetry with opinions held by
the Author .

H.E.L.P

By Mike Nelson

Introducing the Charlie Becker / Lisa Baker

series

....The first Charlie Becker Novel.

Dedicated to; George Nelson, son, best friend &

constant joy x

Thanks to; Geoff Morley, who recognized my work and guided me through the process of publication so patiently. To: Toni McLaughlin-keen, Heather Murphy, Ben Marson, Rachel McGinnety, Hayley Arnold, Dave Doughty, Heidi Richards, Helen Munshi, Tobie Roffey, & Nina Prosser; some of my work colleagues. Without their collective support during the working week, I wouldn't have had enough brain cells left to complete this book in my free time. To my lovely Mum; Patricia Bates & beautiful sister Karen Bruce; for their endless words of encouragement and demonstrations of support. To my wonderful son George who had absolutely no doubt at all this book would be published and still keeps telling me to "keep at it".

CONTENTS

* * * *

PROLOGUE
The Place of Assembly

The Place of Assembly had been, up until this particular gathering, relatively peaceful. There were a few groups discussing strategy, others, debating unanticipated events upon the Earth. It wasn't always easy to react and plan for the unexpected events, which were constantly transpiring upon an increasingly volatile planet. Previous missions had generally been a great deal easier for spiritual messengers to navigate, especially when the assignment hadn't involved human beings. Each operation had varying degrees of complexity, although some, much more intricate in nature, there were few that involved such a violent indigenous species. Not many who had been assigned to humans through the ages had managed to survive their mission unscathed. A commission to guide and influence even a solitary mortal was very rarely coveted, as they are generally regarded, the most unpredictable of races. The onerous task of working with humans inevitably resulted in its fair share of confusion, not to mention the anxiety generated when the wisest of heavenly plans proved ineffective when faced with the destructive impulses of Earth creatures. If there was one thing the Power didn't appreciate, it was his plans being placed in constant jeopardy and so, to spar with humans was regarded at best, as rather precarious. Even for one as powerful as he.

Seven, quite agitated looking, beings, entered the Place of Assembly. The air was filled with angelic argument, agitation and no little amount of jostling for prominence and positions of power. All of the angelic beings involved were trying desperately not to dwell too long on what may result, after this mêlée of accusation and counter claim. These were desperate times and it was essential, when the chaos of the assembly had ceased, to remain among the innocent. The course of every individual human was constantly being revised by The Ultimate Power. The route and final destination was largely dictated by the choices they made in life. Directives would regularly proceed from The Ultimate Realm, via those named as special messengers who gained their intelligence from more esteemed spirits, directly serving and advising The Power. Once the edicts had gone forth from this chain of spiritual conduits, they would eventually arrive on the four winds, for the purpose of instructing the myriad of overseers, scattered among the living too implement. The leaders of this most esteemed breed of overseers would then pass on the orders to those who were simply known as, those who are assigned. Assigned to the living and in this case the living, were unfortunately human.

Nathanial- led such a group of Angel overseers. He took the stand majestically, even though is argument was weak. Regarding the life of Charlie

Becker! It had already been recognised that it was not going well!

The discussions had been conducted in a tense and testy environment. Motives had been questioned and certainly, the management of this particular group of guardian angels was questioned inexhaustibly.

The fact remained that sooner rather than later they would all be called to account and they had better make sure they got that account straight. Nathanial concluded the assembly with his closing remarks "We were all aware it was not progressing pleasingly. His diversion may eventually help him; it may eventually be his salvation, as it were. Surely when Charlie Becker attempted to kill himself those who worked in rebellion to the Power should have been alerted to this deviation, they'll do all they can to make the situation as damaging for us as they can. I would be very surprised if they hadn't already learned of our mistake.

* * * *

"Therefore, my beloved, as you have always obeyed, so now, not only as in my presence but much more in my absence, **work out your own salvation with fear and trembling"**
Philippians; 2:12 - The Holy Bible.

Chapter 1
Uninvited Guest

My name is Charlie Becker and believe it or not,
I didn't know that I was dead!

I can't remember waking up. I didn't feel
groggy. I didn't really feel anything! I knew
somehow however, that I hadn't been around here
long. I decided to roam around with just my eyes
for now and see what was happening. I had no
inclination to move at all, as the pain I could
vividly remember had subsided and I was
enjoying its absence. It was the first time in an
age I didn't remember feeling nauseous as I came
too. I thought I'd try and take it easy, as there
didn't appear to be anything pressing requiring
my attention. My thoughts drifted momentarily,
back to the time I used to wake up on a Sunday
morning, as a child, with no one shouting at me,
to get up and go to School. I could lie still,
perfectly warm and comfortable, for what
seemed like hours, no pressure on me to do
anything at all. I would snuggle down; scared to
move, just in case I wouldn't be able to get quite
as cosy again if I did. My gaze was met with,
well, not much really, just a very vague mauve
mist! No, the atmosphere was more like a sheen,
or, haze, than a vivid colour. In any event, it was
an atmosphere I hadn't experienced before, even
in my most alcohol soaked moments. All of a
sudden, I felt a wave of disappointment, as I
recalled some rather unsavoury memories. I came

to the conclusion; I must have fallen asleep in the bath. Awake again now, I have to concentrate hard on keeping as still as I can. If I moved, I was convinced it would surely kick in; sure, as day is day, it will kick in. The clawing, piercing, headache, along with the gut crippling nausea, I had come to know and loath over the years, as my own personal strain of hangover. Along with the sickness, came the overwhelming and utterly depressing realization, that I had once again abused myself to the point of oblivion. Yet, due to the miracle of the human spirit, I would always be able to overcome the feelings of utter shit and somehow find myself winding my way to work and just, well, just carrying on..........One day, I knew, I would stop! Stone dead; literally. I smiled inwardly as I remembered the old Woody Allen line, "I don't mind the idea of death. I just don't want to be around when it happens." However, this time I felt numb, nothing? I waited; waited, and even started to feel a little bored. But no, this time, there was no horrible gut retching, or, whimpering cries of, never, never again, as I began to convince myself of the ridicules deception, that I would definitely stop drinking tomorrow.

There was also, no sign at all, of the intense and inevitable feelings of unadulterated guilt and fear visiting me, this fateful day. How did I know it was even day time? It must be a dream. No, I don't remember dreams, but it definitely felt heavenly to feel okay.

"Heavenly, oh crap." I tried to say aloud, but the words wouldn't make themselves audible.

A voice broke my contemplations. Not loud nor booming, just very distinct, clear, crisp. Considering I had no idea what was coming my way, or if I was about to be brutally and maliciously abused by my new friends, I found the tones quite comforting. I hadn't felt comforted for as long as I could remember, it felt nice, very nice indeed. In addition, with the voice, they suddenly appeared. They joined me in a manner that somehow suggested to me that I had, up to that point, been an object of their observation.

"**It's not what you expected, right!**"

"Right!" I said. But when I say, I said. I found myself able somehow to communicate without words! But what isn't. What isn't what I expected?" I thought!

"**No, it never is.**" The voice that sounded like a thousand swallows getting ready to roost on a summers day, came back to me.

I was, for the first time in my entire adult existence, totally lost for anything intelligible to say. So I just mumbled - w - why - where am......? It took me the longest time to

10

concentrate on real words instead of thoughts and feelings. The sight of them was quite overwhelming and when they looked at me, I felt as if my soul was being dissected.

"Where am I?" **"You ask the wrong question son."** "Son?"You cannot possibly be my Dad! My Dad is still alive and well and living a self-indulgent life in some God forsaken middle class suburb in central England!

"Please help me." What could possibly "be" the right question at a time such as this? There were four of them – probably – I couldn't be entirely sure because it looked as if they almost blended into one another. I continued to stare into shadows and flickers of light and dark. I could make out vague pastel colours, but everything around me was strangely incomplete, real, but not solid or properly formed. I had absolutely no sense of where this place could be, or, what time of day or night it was. I couldn't feel my body in the traditional sense, but somehow, possessing a body as I used to understand it, didn't seem relevant. There didn't seem to be anywhere to go and I seemed to be able to communicate irrespective of the absence of a voice or physical expression. It was also the first time ever I had felt wonderfully light and dreamy, but at the same time, trapped inside my form. I did feel like I might burst eventually, because I couldn't physically express the myriad of emotions sweeping through me. As I waited for my new companions to make a move, it was as if I was waiting for permission to continue on with my very own existence. I was not the one in control here! My mind suddenly began to race and I thought of all the possible reasons why I might be experiencing such a surreal encounter with my heavenly hosts. Was I in a coma? I eventually came to the conclusion that I was experiencing some kind of psychosis. Don't be a dick, was the thought immediately afterward, along with the realization that it would be quite typical of me, to let my mind run to extremes, just because I didn't have a logical answer. I certainly couldn't come up with a rational response to this weird dreamlike state. I tried to remain patient; at least the ghostly figures weren't being hostile yet I had thought at one point they wanted to help me and to be honest, as they were locked in debate with each other, they seemed more anxious than I was. The one who seemed to be the leader was incredibly tall. I couldn't make out quite where he began at the top of his head or when he ended at his feet. Such was the hazy confusion of the misty atmosphere. I did get the distinct impression I was an inconvenience to him, a mistake. This wasn't a completely new experience for me. My ex wife had made me feel exactly the same for the last two years of our marriage. If the one I was assuming was in charge, if he had worn a watch, I'm pretty sure he would've been constantly looking at it, fidgeting and politely asking me to leave. The feelings of guilt were now my strongest emotion, yet I couldn't remember what, if anything, I had done wrong. I had spent a lot of time feeling guilty during what I could remember of my life so far. Somehow I sensed the cause of this particular guilt had cost me something drastic, I was sure of it. The shadowy figure to the left of the leader looked like he was about to make a suggestion. I had faith in this one. He seemed to radiate an altogether more sanguine energy than the other three. The two figures that seemed to be studying the giant and his lieutenant appeared to be listening intensely and were definitely adopting a subordinate position. It felt slightly surreal that I was furiously trying to work out what was going on in the minds of these, huge, silhouette like apparitions. Phantoms, from god knows where, who, could very well be my new captors. I attempted, once again, to get their attention. "Okay please, hello – HEEELLLOOO - please look at me." I felt like I was interrupting now. They were definitely trying to come to some sort of consensus. After what seemed like an absolute age, the two main characters seemed to be reaching a conclusion. "Please, tell me what's going on. Can you help me out here? I don't have the first clue what has happened to me or what you could possibly want from me."

"Want! Why must you humans insist on being so cynical? No other dominant species is as distrustful as yours. We work in all of the created worlds and are yet to come across any who judge others as you do. We want

nothing! Be still son.”

"Okay, okay, keep your hair on. Oh, you don't have hair, sorry. I was just wondering that's all. Another point I'd like to make is, bollocks to the whole son thing, okay mate.”

"BE STILL.”

Okay well at least a reaction. Now I was getting a little pissed, I thought maybe I could channel my negative energy to force an agenda. Shit! Who was I trying to kid. I don't have an agenda. Where the hell could I go, or what could I do anyhow. I didn't even know whether I was still in the world I knew, or if I'd been spirited off into the night, by a gang of aliens, marauding across the cosmos, looking for depressive loners no one would miss. I was utterly helpless. As I attempted to move, the weirdest feeling washed over me. I somehow knew that no matter what plans I struggled to concoct in order to regain control of my situation, my brain was infinitely more inferior to the wisdom I was now being presented with. I wondered if I could come to terms with an indefinite amount of time in this place. I hated being restrained, losing my ability to be proactive. In the past, which was starting to feel like an awfully long time ago, I hadn't ever been accused of passivity. So! I sit here for all eternity do I?

ETERNITY! O-M-G! That must be it.

Shit, now panic starts to set in and I thought, there you go again, jumping to all kinds of irrational conclusions. As I had no actual connection to a body, I consequently had no chemical reaction to rely on. No adrenalin rush, therefore, I couldn't use it; channel it to get the hell out of there. The constant feeling of vulnerability was starting to freak me out and I began to feel dismayed, like I might implode. They obviously sensed it as they seemed to turn their attention back to me. **"Relax your not in any danger and you're not in hell son."**

"Thank you." I was seriously grateful for some information. "Please, please explain. It doesn't feel much like I expected heaven to be either."

"Tell us. What do you know of the place you call heaven son? I was suddenly gripped by a feeling of indignant disapproval at the endless rhetoric. And, I, being me, reacted!

"Please, again, for Christ's sake, where am I?"

"What do you know of The Christ my son?" I thought at least this was progress, he's getting personal now. Friendly tones, apparently, I'm now *his* son, I figured I'd get further if I tried to build on any goodwill that was coming my way. And so, I attempted to answer his question.

"Not much really," I responded, trying to sound as courteous as possible. "I've always believed. I have… really, I have. A sorry example of a Christian sometimes, I know and I'm sorry…" Now I was seeking their approval or at least some sort of assurance that I was safe in their hands. Buried in my insecurity, I continued. "I understand and have even studied the New Testament. I wondered why I was I giving them my spiritual CV? Maybe it had something to do with the fact that I'd spent a good deal of the time in my hazy new world, waiting for a trap door to open and expecting to descend down into Satan's backyard at any moment. But, now they had assured me this wasn't hell, so why wasn't I feeling better about my visit to the home of the ghostly quartet. Maybe they needed to keep me calm, so they could more easily carry out gruesome experiments on me! How could I be sure I could trust them? Not that I had a choice! Once again, my mind was bouncing theories to and fro, desperately trying to form some sort of logic from an experience totally unfamiliar to me. I was becoming more and more agitated. **"BE STILL! Getting distressed won't help you."** "WELL WHAT WILL HELP ME?" God, in all the years I'd existed upon the earth, I still hadn't learned the basic principles of self-control. I had now shouted, if indeed, shouting was the word one would use for the expression of sharp indignation, within the realms of my new form of almost, telepathic communication.

I had seriously had enough and the strain of being caught in a situation I was unable to control, was starting to become apparent but at least an admission that I might be in need of help! Then there was suddenly an overwhelming feeling of peace that swept through the place we were in. It was as if, the thoughts of my new friends had released the very atmosphere we were all sharing. **"Now... Son... We have**

rested upon your fate.”
Words could never express how I felt as this
announcement came. It was just as well I was
absent of my human body, for, if I had possessed
bowels at that point, the whole universe would
have been aware of it.
I started to feel weak and managed a whimper.
“Th - Thank you. What are you going to do to
me?”
“Do to you! Nothing Son.
Why would we do anything to you?”
I guess I’d just asked another dip shit question!
“Okay, thank you. Please, what have you
decided?” The leading spiritual giant looked at
his companions, as if needing a final
confirmation of their support, before he turned
his gaze upon me.
“You will simply, be sent back. Back to your
body, back to your life. You will simply carry
on, until it is decided what your fate must be!”
This wasn’t helpful. What the hell do they mean,
carry on. Carry on doing what?
“Sorry, carry on you say,” I said, as, I tried to
suppress any feelings of sarcasm. For goodness
sake, I couldn’t even move and they were about
to send me somewhere to, carry on. Put it down
to nerves, I always resort to flippancy when I’m
nervous, but I must try and cooperate, or I might
risk being stuck here forever. I managed another
whimper. “How will I be able to carry on Sir?”
I continued, wondering why I had decided to call
him Sir **“We will simply speak it to the four**

winds and they will carry you to where you need to be. Now, try and be still my son, relax, you won't have to do anything."
He said this as if it was strange that I wouldn't have known this already. Of course, the four winds, how silly of me, of course they'll carry me! But at least he said it in those friendly tones I had heard before, so I surmised the process wouldn't be too bad. I thought I might take advantage, while he was sounding approachable and try and find out more. "Can you tell me what happened to me?" **"That indeed is a good question. We can inform you, but when you return to carry on, you will forget about this place."** Humm – I think my memory is a tad better than that, but at least they also seemed a little more helpful now. They seemed relieved now they had decided what to do with me.

"You took a wrong turning son. We simply failed and we weren't prepared to receive you. It simply wasn't your appointed time. You came to us when you ended your life."
"What the FU!!!!!!!!!!!!!"**"Please hold still, the time is near."**
"Sorry, carry on. I mean please; carry on. Did you just say I topped myself?"
"When you ended your life, it was not the correct time. We were all trusted, as those who are assigned to you, to put in motion many events, to lead you back on your intended path. We failed. We are sorry! We were too late! We were supposed to guide

your sister to you. The guidance for her was to engage you, distract you and ultimately stop you. She failed to respond! We don't know why. We are very sorry. It only happens once every thousand years or so and we are likely to be punished for our failure. We were caught a little by surprise. We were led to believe that you just would not leave Tommy, so, I suppose we were a little slow to react. "He continued after what appeared to be a very thoughtful pause....

"You have come to a place of waiting, the Place of Decisions; most are here for much longer. However, this was our mistake. So, we will allow you to carry on now. "Okay. This is surreal. I am pretty sure I have angelic beings almost begging my forgiveness, because they failed to stop me topping myself. They didn't know what to do with me, plus, they are being bullied by other angels, or worse, their boss, for screwing up. Madness! No, I thought don't be bloody daft, this just can't be real. They don't even call themselves angels! What the hell is - 'those who have been assigned' - supposed to mean? "Okay fellas what happens now? Do I go back in a giant whirl pool, like in the movies?" I turned once again, to my old friend flippancy. **"No you aren't really going back at all. We all simply just carry on where we left off."** "Ok, that makes perfect sense" **"You simply carry on. However, we have something more to say. It's about the guilt you've been feeling. Your**

instincts serve you well. Indeed, it is true, you really must do better. Your life has become something of an embarrassment, to us and indeed, to your Angel overseers. It's very important you remember this Indeed, it is true, you really must do better. if you carry on in the manner in which you seem to have adopted as the normal way you live your life you may well be plunged into the outer darkness and of course this will mean everlasting solitude and suffering no one is able to ease, my son…and, more importantly, if this is the case, when it is indeed your appointed time! We definitely wouldn't be able to help."

* * * *

All say, "How hard it is that we have to die" - a strange complaint to come from the mouths of people who have had to live. ~Mark Twain.

Chapter 2
Charlie Becker and the Tube
The costly encounter

"Oh God; you're never going to catch that tube, Fuck!" And yet there's another one two minutes later! So why the drama queen reaction, if I miss it? I wasn't going to run down the platform, looking like a complete arse, only to get caught in the tube doors. Stumbling on, like some pathetic stressed out corporate geek, who thought that he might just miss out on his next big deal, if he missed this particular carriage on the Victoria line. On this occasion I did get on though, just! It was slightly embarrassing, as I lurched forward, forcing the small and already off balance Chinese lady to stumble into the back of a rather indignant, large women, who, apparently thought that to be the size of a fucking house was justification enough to expect the whole tube carriage to give her four times as much breathing space as everyone else.

I had been off work with depression, brought on by being to indulgent with my reflections on a marriage, which had now ended. Truth be told, that was just the catalyst for my illness to latch on to. I was a class 'A' fuck up, with little to show for my forty two years on this planet apart from a very unhealthy relationship with the bottom of copious amounts of bourbon bottles. Friday seemed a silly bloody day to be returning to work, but I wanted just a taste of the stress I had left behind before returning to work properly.

My mind kept taunting me with flashbacks and images of when I was at my worse.

They say I was found in the bath with a bottle of Jack Daniels, a rather sharp razor and a bewildered look on my face. Consequently, I was signed off and this was to be my first attempt at re-entering the world, where normal people lived! I digress! I am Charlie Becker and this particular morning was where the most important meeting that was to lead to the most significant relationship of my entire existence was to begin. I remember thinking, my God, she's lovely. Waif like, slightly pinched face, very angular, thin but very naughty looking lips. Okay, here we go again, stop it now, you jerk! Try to keep staring at the dirty crumpled copy of the 'Metro' and just bloody stop. Find something interesting to focus on in the paper and try to re-direct your thoughts. Yeah right, the chances of me being able to keep my lecherous eyes off this sexy young woman were minimal, at best.

I should have brought my kindle. I'll try turning my iPod up sitting there a vision of loveliness I remember saying to myself My God, she's lovely. Waif like, slightly pinched face, very angular, thin but very naughty looking lips. Okay, here we go again, stop it now, you jerk! Try to keep staring at the dirty crumpled copy of the 'Metro' and just bloody stop. Find something interesting to focus on in the paper and try to re direct your thoughts, yeah right. But my thoughts came back to the blonde / Ash colour hair, petite, but still, very ample baps. I nearly laughed out loud when the word baps came into my mind. I remembered the crass description of this area of the female anatomy from a camping trip for boys many years ago. She's got dimples and a slightly turned up nose. Looks like blue eyes, but might be grey, thank God its summer. Flimsy dress, yellow cotton, nice white trimming, clingy. Bloody pervert, Only fleetingly assessing myself before continuing with a more than familiar train of thought. Guilt normally kicks in, but as always, I override it quite easily and marvel at the detail and effort that I put into my perving activities . Its not even 7.30am yet! I bet its see through and if I caught it in the right light and angle when she gets up…I wonder if I could see…I found myself however, not ever wanting her to get up. I want to stare at her forever. Stop, stop, stop. You stupid, old idiot.

The motion of the tube train is making me feel sick, too much to drink again last night, ah, this has to stop. The drinking that is. More self-reflection, more analysis of a soul obviously gone wrong. I was genuinely starting to feel sick of my very existence. My God, I can see her crotch when she shifts, move, and move again and again. Oh, yes, lovely, you are lovely. I think she clocked me that time looking at her. I don't care; I'll never see her again. Move again, please move again. But yes, she must realize I just saw her white pants when she crossed her legs that time. The guilt has just started to make me feel even more ill than I did already. Why, therefore, do I continue with my obsessions? I head north on the Victoria line toward Warren Street station and I'm at Victoria already. Good; lots of people got off here and I managed to grab the seat almost opposite this absolute dream I'll soon leave her and never see her again as long as I live. Lucky girl. Wait a minute, she's making a move. No, she just looks like she wants too, but that's probably my fault, making her feel uncomfortable. You freak. Oh, that thought makes me feel even more nauseous. We trundle along and I actually notice that there are other people on the tube. Not that I really care. My eyes are darting between the vision of beauty in front of me and the miserable, depressing looking crew trudging toward their daily fate. Now it's me that needs to get off soon. My feet have been trampled on, my bag nearly torn from my shoulder, even though I'm sitting down and I need a gas mask. I've been sneezed and coughed at, as well as having to suffer the god-awful body odour from the woman next to me. I had even overcome the desire to stab the person on the other side of me in the neck, just on the basis that she was in fact sitting next to me. Jeeze, be as fat as you want mate, but just don't sit next to me on the tube, or anywhere else for that matter. You take most of my seat, definitely all of the arm rest and not a little of my personal breathing space. Now, I must leave her. I take my last lingering look, I feel so ashamed. My God, I even craned my neck to see up her dress again. I had sampled a taste and now, I wanted more, much more. Yes, she's getting off too. An instant process of making plans, ignited in my mind and I worked through the gears quickly starting to look for ways in which I could catch her eye and maybe start a conversation. She caught her sandal in the ribbed floor of the carriage as she jumped up from her seat. She leaped up as if she had been bitten on her rear end. God, I would like to bite her. She let out a little squeak, as if she had really hurt herself and immediately I felt like I wanted to make sure she was okay. Suddenly I felt ridiculously protective. It was blatantly obvious to me that these well-meaning instincts were incongruous to all the other inclinations I had wanted to indulge in, up to that point. What a pathetic jerk I really was. I wanted to nail her from Brixton all the way to Warren Street and now, here I was ready to offer first aid, to what my mind had already imagined was a fatal wound to her foot! She was now standing opposite me, slightly more to the right nearer the doors. Therefore, it was easy for me to get up and look like I was allowing her to go in front of me, just so that I could get a better look at her rear end I gave her a moronic little grin. Ahh, I thought, I must look like a right prick.

As I moved and she stepped ahead, she looked me straight in the eyes and shouted straight into my face; "YOU FUCKING DIRTY OLD PERVERT."

I could feel my face reddening; bizarrely it was the *old* bit that hurt! However, she was gone and - with the crowd all fighting to get up to the ticket hall two whole minutes earlier than everyone else - would, never be seen again. No one cared and most onlookers probably had personalities that were so cauterized by the general branding life brought to them and along with the anticipation of their shit day ahead, even if my being berated had looked hilarious, they would have been too comatose to notice, or have the energy to care. I trudged up to the top of the escalators, defeated, dejected and most definitely rejected. I reached for my Oyster card and heard…."Hey" I ignored it, as it could have been aimed at anyone and to be honest I wasn't in the mood to be chatty to anyone, especially, if it was a colleague bumping into me and wanting to walk into the office together. I value my solitude as I stroll slowly into my day. I vow everyday to ignore anyone who claims to know me.

"Hey you"… "HEY, shit mate stop will ya." She came toward me grinning. Quite brave for someone who had just called me, a fucking dirty old pervert!

"Hello."

She didn't quite know how to start! I wasn't about to go out of my way to make her feel comfortable."Hello, what can I do for you?" I responded, determined not to be caught out being, un-cool or off guard. She had already won round one.

26

"I'm Lisa." "That's nice," I continued, quite nonchalant. There was no way I was going to make myself appear vulnerable to someone who was capable of shouting at me on the tube. Everyone knows there's an un-written rule, that no one even talks, never minds shouts on the tube. I wasn't about to give her any personal information either, not even my name.

"Look, I'm sorry okay. I shouldn't have reacted so badly and you look like a decent guy," she offered, while also probing for the answer. Was I a nice guy? She probably wouldn't have come to any such conclusion, if she could see inside my head. "Look I just didn't want to go without saying sorry is all." She started to look hurt that I wasn't saying much in response. I decided to join in. True to normal form, I did this recklessly, with absolutely no thought of the consequences.

"Prove it." "What mate?"

"Prove it. Have a drink with me with me later, today, after work." Where this confidence came from was a mystery to me. It certainly wasn't a normal feature that early in the morning, especially stone cold sober. I think my attempt to go on the offensive must have been a result of the embarrassment, I thought I had left behind on the train carriage. I still felt humiliated and angry with her and was not particularly looking to impress. After all, I didn't think I had much to lose, if she thought I was a bit of a git anyway. She giggled and clearly looked flattered, even though it was obvious, I was at least twenty years older than she was. "Ok." She shot her response back at me almost aggressively. I think it was her now that was trying to regain some control. I generally find, continuing to look cool while you're in shock is quite difficult. Especially if at the same time you're trying to wrestle with the thoughts in your head to organize a liaison that, only five minutes ago, would have been an impossible proposition. In addition, it was now still only 7.45am, I was seriously hung over and my faculties were barely even firing on one cylinder. After more pathetic attempts to keep my hormones contained, while at the same time trying to keep my dignity intact, I managed to arrange a liaison later that day, at Victoria train station. We exchanged mobile numbers and as I walked away, I was convinced there was more chance of next weeks tube strike being called off than Lisa turning up later that day for a date with me. "Hey," she said, as she was turning to leave, "were you really looking up my dress?" "Yeah, absolutely." I felt an alien sense of excitement, as I started to slope through my working day. Gradually feeling better, slowly starting to find meaning to life again. As it happens, the work I was doing actually gave me a lot of satisfaction. There I was, Charlie Becker, philanthropic by nature, trying to make a difference in the world, trying at the same time to build my own shattered existence. I'd taken quite a time coming to terms with my failed marriage, but at least our union had created my beautiful son, Tommy; whom I adored, but, hardly ever saw. My ambitions have gradually been tempered over the years, now restricted to just trying to survive in this mad world. My job was more of a mission to me than a means to pay the rent and had often been a welcome distraction from the distressing events in my personal life. This particular day was already proving to be a little more exhilarating than normal, as my thoughts constantly drifted back to the mysterious girl on the train.

I could always test another theory. Did I really have her real number, or, a fake one? If it were bogus, I would soon know if I called it. If she'd actually given me her correct contact details, I flattered myself with the thought that she would have at least been thinking of following through for at least a brief moment. Alternatively, she could also tell me to bugger off, having come to her senses, at least I wouldn't waste my time tonight. Waste my time, ah, I thought, what else would I be doing? Maybe I'll text later, but for now I'll just enjoy the moment. H.E.L.P was an organization that literally did help. Helping - Ex, Offenders - in London - Prosper…A Charity and to be quite honest, not a bad gig. My work is the only part of me, Tommy apart, I am remotely proud of. Its hard work, but at least it did actually do some good. Since the, err, incident in the bath with a bottle of Jack Daniels, a razor blade and a very severe hangover last month, I had been even more inexplicably driven to make some significant difference in the world.

Somehow, I knew the work I did in the third sector was not going to be the be all and end all, but a start nevertheless. The problem with doing *good* things was that often the main beneficiary was the one carrying them out. The need to be needed was so prevalent in this industry; it was often sickening to watch the self-congratulating way in which many of my colleagues literally, performed their duties. I manage a team of workers who specialize with working with young offenders.

My team is like a family to me; we've evolved together over the last five years and can almost second guess one another.

Chloe was a key member of the team. She fresh faced, eager, always looking for more and more work. She was a graduate of business studies and extremely intelligent. Nobody in the team really wanted to hurt her feelings by pointing out that her relentless over exuberance was bloody irritating, especially, first thing in the morning. The rest of the crew all had their individual roles to play out and in the main were all in the organisation for all the right reasons. Then of course, a year or so ago, I had taken on Mickey. He was an ex-client that I had carefully nurtured and literally had to force through the employment process, by bypassing the stuffy bureaucracy bound arseholes on the top floor. He had insisted when he came to us that we kept everything he told us confidential. Obviously, if he'd told us he had murdered all the people he'd met at the bus queue that morning, we would probably have had to let on. Mickey however, wanted to keep, even the finer details of his life quiet. His behaviour bordered on manic paranoia, every time his personal life was brought up. It could be quite irritating that we couldn't even make small talk about the most routine stuff, like, where he lived and what his family was like. I remember one of the team had been nearly skewered through the eye ball, with Mickey's plastic biro, when she had openly disclosed his postcode, while she was up-dating the electronic staff files for me. The indiscrete offender on this occasion had always had a habit of starting to talk out loud while she was tapping away on her keyboard and as she didn't know she was doing it. This was a constant source of amusement to the rest of us. What was more disconcerting was that Mickey had remained just as cagey with his work colleagues once he'd become a staff member, as when he was a client. Mickey had worked hard as a client and was eager to become a volunteer once his support had come to an end. When the time had arrived for me to face the fact that I couldn't justify not paying him anymore, I had hoped he would have chilled out a little. Alas, Mickey had an interesting past and he had always seemed edgy, even scared if anyone in the office mentioned any subject that was remotely related to his life outside of work. I was the only one who was aware of his offences and although they weren't exactly worthy of Capital punishment, they had over the years been becoming more anti-social, increasingly worse and the intervention of H.E.L.P had probably prevented him serving a very long stretch, at Her Majesty's pleasure. I was glad to have him, despite the occasional cloak and dagger conduct. He had rapidly grown in both confidence and ability and was a massive asset to the team.

Catch London's young people before it really was too late, was the master plan and god knows the probation services were not going to help the cause. My day was trundling along quite nicely, but of course, I couldn't get her out of my mind. So when one o'clock arrived, I slipped out. Bugger, it was throwing it down. June in London can replicate October or November quite easily within a very short period of time. As I started to feel rain run down the inside of my collar, I was irritated by the fact that, if you don't like the weather in England, all you have to do is wait for about twenty minutes. Groping around my pockets for my mobile I headed for Regents Park. I made for the most convenient tree; despite the fact I thought I'd just caught sight of a bolt of lightning. I wondered why the hell I was taking all this trouble to escape work, run out into the rain, just to send a text. I guess I was secretly hoping Lisa might text back and ask to speak to me or just randomly call when she got the message. I caught myself feeling small and ashamed at my insecurity. My text read **Hi Lisa just making sure it is not a fake number only joking -** *I wasn't* **- Charlie.** Nothing came back. I stood around for about five, maybe ten minutes, which felt a lot longer. The downpour was getting worse! I made a mad dash for it. I then went through a process of trying to convince myself I couldn't care less. I returned to my desk, soaking and all of a sudden extremely hungry. I wasn't about to go out again, my feet had started to squelch and the only umbrella I could borrow would have been one I had spied near a radiator, belonging to a lady in the admin team. All of the other's in the building seem to be carrying out their natural function, as it was lunch time. This particular model was a nice little pink number with purple blobs on it. I declined her gracious offer. To my relief, I noticed that Chloe had brought some home made cake in, God knows why. There are so many birthdays, engagements and women in the office finding out that they're pregnant, I lose count. Any excuse to bring in a cake and celebrate despite the fact that my stomach was still feeling a little tender from the previous night's indulgencies; I partook of the sweet delight gratefully. Well that's that then, I brooded. It was three thirty and still no reply. I certainly wasn't going to make any more effort. Bugger her, I childishly fretted, silly little bitch. I was well aware that my bitterness came from a place strictly reserved for times of rejection such as this. My pride had been dented and now a cloud of humiliation had settled over me.

Four - thirty pm….Five… eye darting to the clock on the far wall of the office about every half hour or so. **Ting….Ting….Ting….**

Hey Charlie cool CU where we said at 6 Lisa x

Okay, your not sixteen anymore. And yet my heart started accelerating at such a rate I thought my colleagues around me would notice and I would have to go for a walk, or, hide in the loo for a minute or two. I suppressed my elation and the fact that I was ready to shout whoop, whoop, yes my son….. The last hour of the day dragged as if it were an entire afternoon. I made sure I changed into the clean shirt I always keep at work for meetings with people I might need to impress. A quick spray of the cologne I also kept in my desk drawer for odour emergencies and I was set.

* * * *

"Hi ya, how's it going?" With a slight swagger and a casual nod of the head, I tried to look as confident as I could, as I approached her. I felt like a nervous adolescent, a rabbit caught in the headlights of an oncoming situation I had so many mixed emotions about. She responded by tilting her head to one side and flashing me a wide grin. The confident young woman was definitely flirting with her eyes and fascinatingly to me, appeared to be one of those rare people who, when they smiled, seemed to lure you into a mysterious world where self-control had been banned. I quickly became enticed, but was also intimidated by her obvious air of self-assurance I was relieved she appeared to have decided to enter into the date wholeheartedly. There was no hint of shyness from Lisa and yet, there was I, forty-five years old, starting to realize she was the one more likely to handle the situation with poise, composed and secure in her own skin. I decided to feign control. "Come on, let's get a drink, there's a bar over there by the photo booths." Again, she just gave me a saucy little grin. She was disarming me with her silence and the seductive little wiggles, as she brushed passed me, giving me a magnificent view of her from behind. She knew she had the complete package and it looked like she was enjoying showing it off. I began the comical process of trying to wrestle a conversation out of her. She might have been relishing the rousing sensations of the tease, but I was starting to think I wasn't going to make it. "Had a good day?" My voice was pitched far too high, due to the dryness in my throat. I was sure Lisa was highly amused by my awkwardness. Reaching the bar, we managed to find a couple of chairs near the door. I thought if things got any more uncomfortable, at least I could make a quick getaway when she went to the loo. "Yeah, I guess, not bad." She'd changed her clothes from this morning. Tonight it was tight jeans and knee length leather boots that took her height above mine. I wondered if that was a tactical move to disarm me further. She wore a cream top that cut off to show more than enough of her midriff. Her navel was pierced at least once and god she was even sexier than this morning.

Her face had a youthful freshness to it and just looking at her made me want to smile. I sensed feelings again that, all day had been relentlessly trying to bombard my consciousness. I seemed to be constantly getting caught between the desire to become her dominating sexual predator and at the same time thinking I should be bloody ashamed of myself and should have been more interested in what I would have been thinking about this whole situation, had I been her father. This young woman didn't need to spend money on Estee Lauder products to enhance her features. She held herself confidently and I noticed that most of the clothes she was wearing boasted designer labels. There was a spoiled brat element to her demeanour and her voice, despite the fact I wasn't hearing too much of it yet, sounded like it had been cultivated in a distinctly middle class background. Lisa's cultured tones were the only feature, on show at least, that was remotely sophisticated. Lisa was no chav, but elegance wasn't the look this temptress was aiming at tonight. It was also apparent; the confident girl about town look had been mastered. However, this particular evening, to my utter shame, it was the dirty little slut image I was looking to provoke and exploit. She was more attractive than I had remembered and even better than the vision, I had fantasies over her all day. I thought I'd better not make my drooling as obvious as I had this morning. I didn't really fancy the prospect of getting the same treatment as earlier, however, tonight, Lisa seemed to be welcoming any advances I might be dreaming up in my over active imagination. ."So, how old are you Lisa?" I blurted out, knowing it was too early in the conversation and my clumsy approach would be, quite rightly, interpreted as my anxiety bubbling to the surface. She just sat back in the chrome bar chair and laughed at me! Fair enough, I thought. As time passed painfully by and I was starting to think that the whole idea of being with this gorgeous young creature was ludicrous, I began to look for a way out. I think she sensed she was losing me and suddenly became increasingly more animated, obviously thinking the evening was worth saving. To my complete surprise, she started to work really hard to keep the conversation going and although it was on subjects cantered mainly on her shallow but strangely cute interests, it became bearable. She was quite opinionated about how she viewed the world in general and although I doubted her ability to stand for parliament, she was certainly managing to be a lot more erudite than I was. For some reason, I was barely able to string two words together. I couldn't work out whether it was due to shock, as I was still trying to fathom why this sex goddess had agreed to meet me. It was more likely just a simple case of me not being able to concentrate, now that I was in close proximity to the closest thing to female physical perfection I had ever seen. By the time I was on my third Jack and coke and the Polish waitress brought Lisa's second Disaronno and cranberry, my female companion began to develop verbal dysentery. "And why the hell did you agree to meet me?" I bleated. She came back with a response that suggested she had somehow been here before! "Well, yeah you are older I suppose, but you are still kind of trendy. You don't look like your average oldie, she giggled. And don't worry, I'm no jail bait."

God, I had never thought she was that bloody young. Did she really think I would have pursued her if….My thoughts trailed off as she continued to blind me with her beauty.

She was twenty-two, but could easily have been younger. She carefully avoided any subject that might have led to her revealing what she did for a living. She explained she lived with her mate in a two bed flat, but again, she was reluctant to share any details about where her flat was situated, or the name of her friend. I didn't really blame her being cautious, after all, I wasn't giving much away either. I certainly wasn't planning to tell her where I worked, just in case the evening turned into a fatal attraction scenario. She revelled she wanted to either work at Battersea Dog and Cats home or be a world famous dancer. When I remarked that I didn't know any world famous dancers, she looked at me as though I had just crawled out from under a stone. What on earth was I doing, trying to pretend I had the first clue about anything related to the topics she broached? What was I trying to prove? The rather one sided small talk continued, until I began to feel like a small kayak in the rapids being swept along by a particularly strong current, heading for the beautiful but fatal waterfall drop. Then out of the blue she turned to me with her head tilted slightly to one side and with the cheekiest of smiles. Her eyelids then went slightly lazy and after running her tongue over her top lip she said…"Fuck this, let's go back to your place and shag each others brains out." Then she burst into fits of giggles and got up as if to leave. I think she knew I probably wasn't going to walk away at this stage. We left and caught the next train out of Victoria to my flat in SW16   * * * *

Well that was nice, very nice indeed. Vivid memories of her undressing, teasing me with her young body flashed into my mind. I savoured each one. It had been awhile and I was going to enjoy it. God, does no one under the age of thirty know what a condom is? She didn't even seem to think it was relevant. No wonder the stats for STD's are through the roof. Now I'm sounding like an old fuddy duddy in my own pleasure memories. Why on earth couldn't I just enjoy the moment? Then it dawned on me, that even though I could still smell her, I was alone. Instinct immediately informed me something was wrong. My mind whirled around grasping for rational thought, while my body was still trying to wake itself up. I concluded that if she was no longer in my flat, it must have meant she simply needed to be somewhere else very early. I glanced over at the radio controlled alarm clock. It was only six thirty! It was Saturday morning and it seemed unlikely that she would have to be away that early. Unless of course, she was, in fact racked with guilt, or worse, disgust, when she'd realized our liaison was less than savoury. I left my bed like lightening. It felt strange when I realized I didn't have the customary hang-over. It was due to my caution not to impede my performance the night before. After four JD and cokes at Victoria station, I'd stopped drinking in case it affected my sexual performance. Four singles was nothing, especially with the amount of adrenalin that was coursing through my body when we'd headed for my flat. Besides, Lisa had a body that could have raised the dead.

Shit - shit - shit - shit, I felt like a complete dick. I should have bloody known it was too good to be true. I paced around my flat castigating myself as a complete arse, a prize moron, a stupid old fool who couldn't control his stupid self. Why would I ever think she liked me for myself?

Car keys…gone…CAR!!!...gone. I leaned out of my window, only to see a freshly vacated space, in my designated white lined rectangle in the car park. Wallet…including two major credit cards…gone, gone, gone. She'd been so cool and collected; she'd even showered and used my new bottle of bloody shampoo. This, I knew because she had left the top off, for the whole damn lot to gently seep onto the tiled floor from the edge of the bath. I had never felt such a complete idiot, totally humiliated I began viciously berating myself in the vein hope; it might make me feel a bit better. It didn't.

.   *   *   *   *

No one can confidently say that he will still be living tomorrow. ~Euripides

Chapter 3
DJ &The BEA Boy's

Cancelling the cards was easy, but I hated forms
and the insurance documents that arrived were an
horrendous prospect to me. What was even more
traumatic was the fact that I had to call the police
days after their initial visit to report stuff I had
consequently found missing. "Yes Mr. Becker,
that's why we ask people to have a good look
round before submitting a list of stolen articles,."
I was seriously close to screaming, "piss off you
patronizing little git. I pay your salary and on top
of everything else, you only sound about twelve
years old." I had at least realized, this approach
would have sounded as ridicules as it actually
was. I resisted and bit down on my lip, trying to
regain enough composure to be able to continue
talking to the arrogant little shit. I certainly
hadn't imagined the Metropolitan Police would
put anything pressing on hold, to go searching for
my personal effects, but I was pretty sure, it
wouldn't help to piss them off either. I'd already
had to sit down red faced that afternoon and
embarrassingly explain how Lisa and I had ended
up grinding away like a couple of horny chimps.
Yes, the afternoon! They hadn't exactly
responded quickly, or in a manner that caused me
to have any hope that I would see any of my
belongings again. I had explained all I knew
about Lisa, which was next to nothing and how
we came to meet. I imagined the hilarity that

would be had back at the station, as the *boys* in blue settled down to their coffee and doughnuts, each of them wondering whether to be jealous of my exploits, or feel sorry for the sad bastard. I didn't even know her surname, or that her real name was in fact Lisa. I gave the investigating officers the mobile number she'd given me and once I'd suffered the humiliation of being interviewed by a copper who couldn't resist smirking and pulling judgmental expressions, they finally left. I wearily sloped into the bedroom, ripped off the bed sheets and bundled them into the washing machine. While still bemoaning my fate, I reached into the bedside drawer to check and yes, low and behold, she had lifted my passport too!

* * * *

The varying degrees of dark shadows, lurking in the hearts of every man and woman on earth, could well be represented in the group that continued to congregate for reasons that were often lost, even on them.

They were not exactly a gang in the traditional sense anymore. They had inevitably had to move on. They were now, supposedly, all grown up! Individually they all did their own thing most of the time, mainly only coming together socially. Now, they were an aging group of extortionists, pimps and thieves. They also had among them, those, who, if caught, could have cleared up most of the Mets unsolved murder cases in South London. The semi retired groups were all ex members of the feared BEA boys of Brixton. A gang definitely appealing to younger displaced individuals based near Brixton's Electric Avenue, hence BEA. The desire to hunt in packs had not completely dissipated and so, they often congregated together, still convinced safety in numbers and the security it provided was the best MO. Dwayne's place was the most popular venue to meet up. It had a certain garish style about it, the extravagant décor that appealed to individuals who had been starved of all material comforts, until they had discovered how to take by force and violence. The gaff was also very comfortable and large enough to accommodate the whole crew, if that was what was required. Ostentatious in the extreme, the house was completely surrounded by CCTV cameras and very well protected behind meters of black iron bars. Anyway, as Dwayne – better known as DJ - was the leader of this dubious little rat pack, he was used to people congregating around him. "She's bin moanin again DJ?"

"Yeah, Lisa, again, that little bitch, she don't know when she's well off." DJ, answered, with a weariness that was tinged with no little irritation. He had been there before and over the years Lisa's relentless desire to break free had been seriously pissing him off. The risk of all she knew about the group becoming general knowledge on the street was too great and it weighed heavily upon the gangster, as he now had much to lose. DJ had rescued the young girl, from a Father who couldn't keep his hands off her. Her Mother had died prematurely, stricken by a particularly aggressive form of bowel Cancer. Lisa only had a few precious memories of her mum to draw on, but her lecherous Father had given her a lifetime of material to fuel her many nightmares. DJ and the lads just happened to be in the wrong place at the right time, as the drunken bastard came home, mid burglary, with the intention of taking out more of his psychotic frustrations out on his kids. The Royal Borough of Kensington and Chelsea wasn't an easy area to hit, but was invariably lucrative and universally Considered among the criminal fraternity to be well worth the risk DJ had clothed the *missing person*, fed and *kept* her from the age of twelve, nurturing the girl, until she eventually became a woman, in the vein hope he would one day win her loyalty in return. The brother came as part of the package deal but was only really taken because he had seen everything. He was captured a little more reluctantly than his big sister. However, despite the fact he had bitten DJ on the hand and had to be carried kicking and screaming from the luxury apartment, he was seized nevertheless. The local paper had eventually revealed that the Police had once again taken the path of least resistance, consequently place the Father in the frame as prime suspect. They managed to make quite a convincing case, despite the fact that they had to eventually admit defeat and release Thomas Jacob Baker. His life was effectively over in any case, which many would have considered poetic justice, after the press had managed to dredge up every accusation, insinuation and even bit of pure speculation found against him over the years. Despite the fact the Police were convinced of his guilt, even with their dubious methods of enquiry, they'd found themselves lacking certain essential elements to the investigation, such as, the bodies of dead children. All they were left with after two and a half years of spending the tax payers hard earned, was, another file stamped – Murder - DC Flanagan - unsolved February 1995 – to cram into the archive room.

Over the proceeding years, DJ had protected Lisa utterly, sometimes, even from his own voracious posse of renegades. "Ungrateful little whore!"

"Maybe it's time to let her bounce man." Max had tried to defend Lisa's case before and always with the same result.

"She owes me! She'll owe me till the day I rot Maxie boy, and besides you haven't given wot I have given over the years, so keep it shut, right."

"Okay buddy, relax, but I'm always havin to listen to it again, an again is all."

"She bin blabbin, she'll bring em down on us some day, I swear, maybe its time for another little reminder who's in charge round here." DJ reached inside the combat pocket on his thigh and pulled out a mobile. His predatory instincts were starting to bubble and he wasn't about to let anyone go anywhere, not while they were still valuable to him, especially one as precious, as little Lisa Baker. One very brief call saw Lisa winding her way through the busy south London streets in her new car. It hadn't taken Pixie Pink long to bang on a couple of fake plates. One of the few benefits of her association with DJ and the crew was that the small matter of bunging a couple of plates on a stolen motor would not be a problem for long. There would be many willing recipients of past favours and more significantly, future courtesies queuing up to help out. She was surprised at the quality of her new ride, as from what she had gleaned of Charlie and his life, she wouldn't have thought he could afford such a sleek beamer. Upon arrival DJ wasted no time.

"Sit down and fuckin listen to me."

"Okay cool it man, what the fuck." She started to

feel her heart beat just that little bit faster. She'd
seen DJ in action many times before. Although
he hadn't ever laid a hand on her, there were
plenty of victims to refer to, as grim reminders of
his particular form of psychosis.

"Okay, listen, you bin blabbin again, an, I had a
belly full of havin this same old shit through wit
you girl." "Bu…"

"Shut it, this time I talk, you fuckin listen and
you do as you is fuckin told, that's it, that's the
deal. You owe me, you will carry on payin, and
you will stop riskin us all by running your stupid
mouth off out there." He pointed to the smoked
brown window. "Out there, where a million
wankers would kill to get to us. We can't even
risk em knowin where we hang." He suddenly
shot up and for the first time in the fourteen
years, apart from the short spell she'd done
incarcerated in a young offenders unit for
continually being picked up for shoplifting on
Oxford Street, he'd been grooming Lisa, he
looked like he really wanted to hurt her in ten
years and in one swift movement, from chair to
victim, grabbed Lisa, wrapping one hand around
her throat. "I'm gettin older, I'm gettin meaner.
I don't give shit okay, I will fuckin end you. You
never happy. The more I give, the more you get,
an' the more you wanna fuckin take. I let you
keep the motor from the last gig and all I hear is
you fuckin moaning again." He was in full
swing, ranting furiously, she could smell his
rancid breath and his spittle started to pepper her

face. The muscle bound gangster became wild eyed and Lisa was wise enough to let him vent. Eventually, after he hadn't said anything for, what she believed was an acceptable pause, she responded, conscious she was walking on very thin ice."Okay, okay, please let me go."

"That's it bitch, that's it, you never, and I mean never goin anywhere, so you say it now and make it good. I wanna be convinced, or I swear, I squeeze now and its over."

"Okay, you're hurtin me."

"The next thing that comes out of that prissy little mouth of yours, better convince me your gonna stop with the attitude babe, I swear to God."

"Okay, okay, I'm sorry. Please DJ it's me, your Lisa, your little lise. I'll stop, honest, please your hurtin me, I'll stop, I promise."

DJ let her go as quickly as he had pounced and was back in his chair looking as serene as can be in a moment. Lisa's relief then allowed the tears to fall; she couldn't sob, as she knew well enough that would irritate the bully even more. Her tears were gentle, falling softly away, from the saddest eyes in South London.

Max or Maxie to those closest to him, looked to the ground. Even with his hate filled heart, which had been steadily hardened over the years from the violence that surrounded him, he was saddened. His attempt to get DJ to extend some slack to Lisa had failed miserably. All he'd achieved was to draw more attention to Lisa's plight, instead of persuading DJ it was time to let his little bird fly. Wiping dried saliva goo from the sides of his mouth, DJ continued issuing his directives. "You'll prove it, is what you'll do. For the next few weeks, until I reckon your right wit me, you work harder than Eva. I'm gonna keep you so fuckin busy, you won't ave time to do any bleatin." Lisa knew it was pointless to argue. Those who were associated to their infamous chief had learned long ago, that it was a very precarious endeavour to be challenging this massive ego. The only hope of winning any ground over DJ was to carefully manoeuvre around him, letting him believe he was in perfect control at all times. The testosterone had been pumping and DJ had obviously set his mind on flexing his leader of the pack muscle.

"You contact Willy at the Escort Agency tomorrow and tell him you want three gigs this week and three more next week okay. I don't wanna hear you've failed me babe, now, get out, and don't say shit, just move out, now." She turned toward the door, her heart pounding and her palms sweaty. She knew that any sign of rebellion would result in a greater punishment. He had never asked her to book so many appointments in such a short time and the anger within Lisa was reaching critical levels. The more pressure DJ applied, the more determined she became to, somehow break out. Helplessness swept over her and in anticipation of what lay ahead, she felt dirty right down to the core of her soul.

Lisa did, however, manage to give Max a glance of appreciation as she left. She knew he was fighting her corner and also knew she needed all the allies she could find.

LISA   CARLA

Lisa knew she could rely on a healthy income from unsuspecting, usually older males, revelling in the attention and invariably feeling flattered. Despite the fact that the scenario was wholly sordid and devoid of any genuine affection, they still queued up to spend any amount of time with the blonde sex goddess. She felt nothing but utter contempt for their naivety not to mention their clammy, alcohol ridden attempts at sexual prowess. She was yet to meet one she had the slightest amount of respect for. Lisa had known no other adult life, but from an early age, she had twigged that there could be another option. It would take a lot of endeavour and even more guts to break free from the iron grip of DJ and his crew. Lisa's flat mate and best friend Carla had shown the way. Carla had also begun her adult life in turmoil, being forced to join the same Escort agency as Lisa. However, times had changed dramatically for Lisa's sidekick since those squalid early teenage days and witnessing her friend's dramatic reinvention of herself, made Lisa equally resolute her day was coming. The disreputable and highly successful Escort agency that doubled as a massage parlour was managed by one of London's leading sleaze merchants going by the name of Willy Adebayo. Willy was a former BEA boy and a dedicated entrepreneur in the sex, porn, human humiliation industry. The agency was, although Willy would never admit it, ultimately controlled by DJ and the boys. 'Seventh heaven', was regarded by the Police and local religious leaders, as a particularly seedy little establishment, mainly because it had an ever growing reputation for catering to the more creative weirdo. Carla had finally managed to completely extricate herself from the world of vice. It had been a gradual, carefully planned getaway, over many months and she had eventually saved enough money to start her own business venture. Working from the flat shared with Lisa, it was a nice legit operation and for the first time in her life, she was able to control her own destiny. Virgin Enterprises, It wasn't and the business was never going to provide Carla with her own private Island, but it had grown steadily over the first year and definitely going in the right direction. Who would have thought that designing hand making and eventually selling cheer leader team outfits in South London, would be so successful. Carla had been right on the money when she'd predicted the popularity of the sport in the UK and even shrewder when she'd recognized the lack of companies currently designing and providing the team kits. Carla hadn't ever adopted the attitude that the world had owed her a living, but she did need help and she knew where to go to get it. Lisa was in deeper, much further into the gang's inner circle, much further in the shit, which was starting to look like it would never shift. Lisa was also aware, that DJ had a point. She did actually owe him. Her

father had abused her young and frail frame.
God knows where she would have ended up, if
DJ hadn't robbed the apartment that night. She
yearned to see her brother Mickey again, but was
in full agreement he had to flee when it became
apparent DJ wasn't about to give him the same
close protection she enjoyed. When the
Pederast's had started to notice how beautiful he
was becoming, she was as desperate for him to
escape as he was himself. But why, why hadn't
he come back to save her?

Yes, Dwayne had been there for her for a long
time, rescuing her from a degrading, base life that
she barely survived. He had however; thrust her
straight into another dangerous and humiliating
existence. Yet in his warped mind, Lisa was still
being protected. Although it was often difficult
to decipher the form this protection took, DJ was
confident his prize asset was perfectly safe, as
long as it was him, who was controlling the
levels of abuse she was exposed to. The ever
increasing problem Lisa was presented with was
that the more she paid back, the more he had to
use against her, to keep her captive. Like a
princess in a tower. She had been rescued and
preserved at the cost of her dignity and worse of
all, her freedom. The commodity, we covert
above all things had been denied her from a very
young age and she was determined she would
never become resigned to her fate.

She pressed the button on her iPhone that was programmed for one purpose only and it immediately dialled through to 'Seventh Heaven` Lisa's heart sank deeper with every digit.

"Hey, is Willy there?"

"Nah; who's this." "Lisa - Lisa Baker."

"Hey Lisa, Willy will sure be pleased you've checked in again, where you bin babe?

"Norma, that you? I was let off the leash somewhat, but it's back on now, firmly gripped about my throat again, hi.""So, you wanna work, you wanna date?""No, but give me one anyway Norm' and fix me up two more for the weekend okay.""Well, well, you are back in town arn't ya honey" - There was a pause - "Expect a call around midnight babe.""Yeah right, no problem Norm', take it easy. I'll check in Sunday and we'll divvy up the spoils.""Okay honey, I won't be here Sunday, but like I say, Willy, will be wrapped your back.""Oh great I'll look forward to seeing him later then. What a treat!" "Ha, he's not that bad.""Yeah, they said that about Tony Blair. Look what he managed to do to Iraq. Norma laughed. "It's good to have you back babe." "Well Norm, as long as you're a whore with imagination, I guess there's always room for you in Willy's heart."Tragic as it was, Lisa couldn't help giggling with her old friend.

"Don't worry babe, I'll get you a caller who might be as warped as fuck, but I won't give you one who's gonna be dangerous. Don't worry sweetie, I'll get you a regular, one we know, he might be freaky, yeah, but he'll be safe, okay Hun?""Thanks Norm, you're a lifesaver …Literally, she thought, as she thanked Norma again and flicked off her iPhone.

* * * *

Carla sat on the sofa looking at her friend feeling awful. She knew what the night held for Lisa. Small, vulnerable, sweet, lovely little Lisa. As she contemplated the evening she knew was in store for her friend, she was wracked with guilt. Carla had been there herself and was painfully aware how much more degraded and defiled Lisa would be feeling about three hours from now. Three hours if she was lucky, three hours if he didn't decide to splash out another twelve hundred notes to keep her trapped within his repugnant imagination for the entire night. The phone rang… "Shit, here we go," Lisa groaned, looking over at her friend for moral support. The midnight chimes, certainly weren't the indicator that this particular Cinderella could scuttle back home, in the hope her Prince would come running. Lisa would have welcomed the chance to take on a couple of ugly sisters, compared to what she was about to walk into.

"Love you babe" Carla offered.

"Love you too, don't worry, I'll be Okay."

Lisa picked up the vibrating mobile she reserved for her nocturnal activities.

"Hi, is that Candy?" The voice clearly hailed from the USA.

"Yeah baby, Candy here sugar, can I help you tonight?" "I sure guess so honey, that is, if you're petite, blonde and like role play?"

"Why yes Hun, I sound like your kinda date. Where are you tonight, sweetheart?"

57

"Grafton Hotel - Tottenham Court Road, you know it?""Yeah babe, it'll take me about an hour, Okay?""I'll be waiting - room 301 - Ask for 301 Mr. Grande – I'm well known here honey, so they'll look after you at the desk. Oh and don't expect to be away before dawn baby doll." "It's your dollar lover boy; I'll see you in an hour then?" "Sure sweet cake, as long as you're feeling adventurous." "Adventure just happens to be my middle name big boy, see you in an hour."

* * * *

Millions long for immortality who do not know what to do with themselves on a rainy Sunday afternoon. ~Susan Ertz, Anger in the Sky

Chapter 4
Brother Mickey

"Oh God, here we go." Lisa couldn't help the verbal exclamation escaping her, as she entered the hotel foyer. "Yes madam.""Room 301 - Mr. Grande is expecting me."

"Certainly, go straight up, third floor, turn left and it's about seven doors along the corridor. Yes, he told us you would be arriving. He's definitely expecting you."

Lisa resented the tone used by the receptionist, but decided to let it go. She had bigger fish to fry. "I'm sure he is – Thanks."

Suffering the indignity of judgemental scowls from the high heeled receptionist, who looked as if, had she smiled, her whole face would slide off, due to a make up landslide, she continued on her quest. The cold flagstone flooring in the foyer was a perfect reflection of the cold contempt Lisa felt toward her date and certainly mirrored the ever growing chill in her heart. The lifts were directly in front of her and as she passed the arrowed signs directing guests to various suites and dining areas, she knew a wholly contemptible and humiliating fate awaited her at the other side of the lift doors.

Lisa made her way up to Grande's room, hating DJ, hating Grande and all of his kind, hating her mum for dying when she was only six years old; hating the life she had been forced to live, hating her father for not protecting her as he should have. Most of all, she loathed herself and what she now had to do, to remain safe, to remain grateful. She knocked on the door and found that it was already open. Sighing heavily and with a resigned acceptance, that despite how she felt, she now had to enter into the evenings role play. "Hi, Candy service, the man of the house in?" "No mummy, but Sammy's here. Sammy's been waiting for mummy to come home. Sammy wants to play with mummy." She didn't think her heart could sink any lower. Grande was in all right. He was sitting in the corner of the smart and tastefully decorated Hotel room. The room was dark and as Lisa's eyes adjusted, she started to make out what awaited her. He was stripped bare, apart from a very large towel that he had fashioned into a make shift nappy. The baby effect had been exaggerated by the fact that he had shaved his entire, massively overweight body of all traces of hair. He had pinned the nappy neatly around his huge girth and equipped with pacifier and toys, he was ready to play. Lisa's heart sank further, as she realized Grande was surrounded with the kind of toys that would have been easily acquired from one of the many sex shops in Soho, which quite conveniently was only a stone's throw from the Hotel. Lisa couldn't help musing nervously at the possible outcome, if this type of play thing was introduced to Grande's seriously warped imagination. With goose bumps starting to cover her whole body, despite the centrally heated room being quite warm, Lisa decided to get into

60

character quickly. She knew it might be her only chance of getting out of there before sunrise and even more critical, before she sustained any injuries. "Hello my little Sammy. I think you've been a very naughty boy and not left mummy's money out. Now, you know the rules don't you Sammy. Mummy must get paid, if Sammy wants his bottom smacked." A short, thick index finger pointed up to the side dresser, where two thousand pounds lay in a neat pile and Grande flashed a sinister little smile. Coupled with the malevolent look in his beady, fat little eyes, with what she knew of his intentions, Lisa thought she might hurl. As she cast a closer eye on the *toys* strewn out on the floor, her heart missed a beat. She had been with some whack jobs in her time, but she could see some of these toys could easily hurt her! She thought tonight, she might not just get away with what was left of her dignity becoming scarred. At that moment, Lisa knew, she had never felt so lonely in all her life. She was also aware she couldn't afford for Mr. Grande to call up Willy complaining he wasn't given the service he had paid for. DJ would get to hear of it within the hour. Six appointments in two weeks would soon escalate into twenty in the following month and so on, until she had learned her lesson. She had been there before and she wasn't about to return to those dark days. Finances out of the way, the evening's entertainment could now begin.

* * * *

61

I found myself reflecting upon my life. God Charlie mate, why do you have to continually have to put yourself in these god awful situations? I often did this and over the years, with the ever growing material, it had become like a hobby for the deeply depressed. The Becker marriage had ended quite abruptly although, as a couple we hadn't been close for years, living more like brother and sister, than two healthy individuals who still desired one another. Caroline had suddenly announced her utter boredom with all that constituted our union and despite her strong Christian ethics, had decided to reject me and the vows she'd taken and move in with Colin. Colin was a nice safe bet, he would look after our son, no worries and more significantly, would provide financially. He was a hedge fund manager for a large corporate organization that wasn't going to go bust anytime soon and I was convinced Caroline had been presented with an offer; even I wouldn't have discouraged her from taking; she couldn't refuse. Colin would also indulge Carrie with all the lovely nice things our own turbulent life had denied her of. What's more, I didn't really blame her – much. No, it was much easier to blame myself, This way, I could wallow in self pity, take to the bottle and adopt an attitude of, bollocks to the world and everyone in it. Truth be told, I wasn't a great husband, but I wasn't a bad Father and leaving Tommy was the hardest thing I'd ever had to do. There was just one small problem with this ever evolving and incredibly negative attitude, I had adopted. The truth was, I actually did want to do some good in the world and since the incident in the bath, the desire to make a difference and to help those less fortunate than myself grew and grew like an angelic type of cancer latching itself to my soul. This overwhelming desire to save the world just refused to go into remission no matter how much alcohol I poured on top of it. It had been hard sometimes to figure out who those less fortunate than me were, as my own thoughts and circumstances were often found to be in so much torment. But, find them I would and when I did, they would be helped whether they wanted it or not! I was utterly alone in the world apart from the fact, my son, although still only eight years old, did seem to register a deep understanding that I was a significant person in his life. No matter how much Caroline had tried to replace me and introduce a new *Daddy* very early on, after our split, Tommy had remained loyal. My own Father was dead, well no, he wasn't actually dead, but, he was to me. I often joked that when he did finally croak, I would need to turn up at the funeral, just to reassure myself he was, in fact, dead. Mum, was also still alive, along with my elder sister. It must be said that since the incident in the bath, I had began to feel inexplicably closer to them all and not just them, I seemed to be generally well disposed toward the human race on mass. Why this was, I didn't know, but I can definitely say that my attitude too many significant relationships and events throughout my life had significantly changed since that night. I hadn't seen much of my family for what was approaching two years now and I missed them even if I refused to admit it. I had remembered my sister Phoebe making a token effort when I was freshly divorced to entertain the notion she was concerned about me. It had never really materialized into anything other than a few fleeting words on the telephone. Even her well meaning words, which were probably motivated by genuine good intentions, became more and more remote and insincere with time. I vaguely remember that on the night of the incident, out of the blue, Phoebe had called to say she was going to come round to the flat. I was to say the very least, worse for wear, but from what I can remember of the brief telephone conversation, she regretted not seeing me and *really* - she often put lots of emphasis on the word really - She *really* wanted to get closer to me and *really* missed me etc…I still can't bring myself to call it, my suicide attempt and even thinking of it makes me feel humiliated. It wasn't the fact that I'd tried to commit suicide, no, it was the fact I'd bloody failed. I mean, what kind of pathetic loser can't even end it all.

The whole sorry event had however, cleared my head and certainly served to change a lot of my perceptions. I now find that I'm drinking less, well, a little less. I've got a clear plan of redemption and yes, I do realize that the plan will probably be a complete failure along with the rest of my life to date. But at least now, for the first time in a long time, I feel like I've got some forward momentum. I certainly feel a lot lighter, less burdened. So, let's hear it for near death experiences!

* * * *

Lisa had finished with her sweaty client by two thirty am. Not bad at all, she thought, as she made her way home. She had to shuffle about on the car seat to get comfortable, but as much as she could tell, did not think there was any permanent damage to her under-carriage. Just a few minor abrasions and it could have been a lot worse. The fact that Willy's customer was already half pissed when she had arrived had helped and had certainly aided Lisa in bringing the bazaar session to a premature end. She got home in half the time it took her to get to the Hotel earlier in the evening. Maybe it was due to her determination to shower and the lack of traffic to hold her up at that time of the morning. In any event she didn't mind how, as long as she continued to put distance between herself and Mr. Grande. When she burst into the flat she literally flew into the shower and started to scrub. There wasn't a single inch of flesh that didn't come in for the after appointment ritual she performed on herself, each time DJ sent her out. Bless her, Lisa whispered to herself, when she realized Carla had changed the bed sheets in anticipation of how her friend would be feeling when she got home. Lisa crashed headlong onto crisp, clean, fresh smelling cotton and slept almost instantaneously, in the vein hope that she would wake without the ability to remember the night before. Two more appointments this week, three more next week! What the hell was Dwayne thinking? The thought of it nearly sent her into a depressive spin, but she was stronger than that. If she held her resolve, she knew she'd eventually get away. One extremely large glass of pinot was all she needed and even before she'd managed to down half of it, dropping the glass on the floor, she crashed into forgetful drifted off to sleep. Finally, the end of the second week arrived and all Lisa could think was, I hope he's going to leave me alone for awhile. She hoped he felt like he had regained control. Lisa's mobile started to vibrate and it was him! "Hi babe." she purred into the device, thinking maybe the seductive, submissive approach was the way to play it at the moment. She wanted to catch DJ off balance just in case her tormentor was still brooding. Inside she was burning with hatred, but she kept her voice buoyant so that DJ didn't guess he'd really got to her."So, lise, you feelin a bit cooled off now, a bit more fuckin grateful? A bit more like keeping your stupid little mouth shut about wanderin off?" She wondered why DJ hadn't learned a wider vocabulary, in his thirty eight years on the earth.

"Any chance you could leave me alone for a bit DJ. I need time to recover from those skanky morons you tossed me too."

"You'll get time away, as always babe, *if* you stop talkin bout gettin away bitch. You can never go, you know too much, an I need you round, so get used to it, enjoy your spoils and stop moanin. I need you to tell me you are gonna be cool okay, an make it convincing."

"Okay man, okay, I'll stop okay, just give me a break okay."

"I'll break your pretty neck, it you start again, now make sure you see Willy today. Today, you hear me bitch." With that he was gone…………..60% of her earnings to Willy, plus she had to swallow any expenses incurred. All he had to do was sit on his skinny little arse pretending he was Mr. big conducting some kind of sick whore orchestra. She made sure she got over to Willy's place early She wanted the chore with the slimy bastard out of the way, as quickly as possible, so she could get on with her life. He sat on his stool with a smirk that suggested he really enjoyed his work. At least DJ had ensured he had never taken payment from her body, as was the fate of many of the girls in his sordid little stable. She left in a hurry after exchanging the usual - banter of the damned - with Willy, sneering at her, taunting her, trying to provoke her to rebel, so that DJ would punish her again.

"Hey pretty pants, come an' see your uncle Willy, soon now, you hear. There you were thinking you were too posh for us these days." Willy gave a rasping sneer and spat, just close enough to just miss Lisa's left arm. Willy so wanted to get his grubby hands on her and Lisa was well aware the threat of the nasty little sex workers stable lad going running off grassing to DJ was very real.

Willy was also well aware Lisa was his best asset and so, to ensure the revenue, and to keep sweet with DJ he made do with his other helpless fillies, to satisfy his own twisted desires, for now anyway. After all they were well capable of satisfying his own brand of creepy bedroom preferences. Lisa spilled out onto the street; it was over, at least for awhile.

* * * *

.

"Oi, good lookin.""Oh God, who's this now,"
she said out loud as if to warn whoever it was to
keep the hell out of her face. She was in no
mood to exchange pleasantries, with anyone.
"Sis."She was stunned, literally frozen to the
spot. "Mickey?" "Ello babe."
She reacted like anyone would who was stood in
the street staring at the brother she thought had
died four years ago. "My god Mickey, what
the…""Look, I need to get off the street, let's
duck in this café. Mickey had done it; he had
escaped the clutches of DJ and the others. He
had many skills and had realised quite early in
life that he could survive without the protection
of the gang. They had taught him well and there
wasn't a house he couldn't break into, a safe he
couldn't crack, a scam he couldn't pull off, or a
woman who wouldn't take him in, given half a
chance. Mickey had found life with the gang all
too claustrophobic and certainly was not going to
be told what to do and when to do it by Dwayne,
or anyone else for that matter. .What with being
molested by one off DJ's older male house
guests, Mickey had simply, left. This, he had
done, after carefully learning how to disappear in
London leaving no trail or clues behind. Lisa had
fully believed DJ had caught up with her brother
and done for Mickey and she'd never trusted
DJ's story that Mickey had just took it upon
himself to leave the gang. She'd never been able
to cope with the thought that her only brother
could leave her in the clutches of such people, for

good without so much as a word. Maybe, she had often thought, her own mind wanted to comfort itself by thinking there really was no way she could imagine her sweet, caring brother not finding a way to come back for her, if he remained alive. "You've hardly changed bro." "Well I've probably become a bit more savvy sis.""Where you stayin, oh sorry." She had seen the look on his face that simply said. "I wouldn't have got this far if I was that careless."

"Do you need anything sis?"

"Yes, to get out, like you did. Where the hell you bin?""Well, maybe we can elp ya there babe, jus' maybe."Hope flooded her body as they chatted and caught up. Lisa did find herself becoming a little irritated by the fact Mickey still wasn't prepared to give much away about his personal life, his work, girlfriends etc…But she put it down to the fact that he had not been used to being off guard, or else, how could he have hidden for so long? She still had to fight back the resentment that was welling up inside her. Why, hadn't he come back to help her sooner? Mickey was one of those boys who can be described as truly beautiful. Chiselled features without looking too lean or hungry, Mickey held himself up-right as if to tell the world he was ready for anything it had to throw at him. Dark, thick hair, slightly tousled, broad shoulders and deep piercing, brown eyes. eyes that, positively glistened with a cheeky London charm. And yet Lisa couldn't help thinking how much real substance lay behind the magical appearance, given the fact he had left her there alone, at the first sign of any real trouble.

"Oh come on." Carla had often chastised her with, as they lay awake at night sharing their inner most thoughts and fears. "You couldn't expect him to stop fuckin running babe. If you ever get out babe, don't look back. "

Mickey had worked hard to adapt his voice to whomever he happened to be trying to influence at the time, turning to middle class airs, when needed and sticking to his rough cockney, jack the lad tones, as the norm. As he had been rescued from his monstrous Father at the same time as Lisa, there was camaraderie between the two of them immediately they were reunited. This, despite Lisa's many questions and conflicting emotions. The escape hadn't been plain sailing and he had eventually been able to establish a new life. The desire to see Lisa again had finally over taken him. He stayed as long as he could and after two rank awful coffees, that tasted more like lukewarm dishwater than coffee, he kissed Lisa on the check and got up to leave. He left promising to be in touch. As he left he wondered if his weakness in needing to see Lisa again might cost him.

In his overwhelming relief to see his sister, he completely neglected to notice the figure that had joined them in the café and who was now hiding behind today's Sunday People pretending to read the latest bullshit manufactured by the weekend press.

* * * *

We understand death for the first time when he puts his hand upon one whom we love. ~Madame de Stael

Chapter 5
The Trusted Flatmate

Clara strode toward the H.E.L.P main office with a confidence she had never been able to experience or express until her recent venture into self employment. It had been hard to recover, due to a conviction, a year ago for soliciting for sex and more seriously, accessory to a kidnap, only four years ago. The latter, being the result of a little venture the BEA Boys had been involved in the eyes of the Police, there was no such thing as innocent bystander, no matter how innocent or reluctant to be involved. Life was starting to feel less ominous, as her application could now go into H.E.L.P and the struggling black girl from South London was eligible to receive support from the charity. She had spent most of her *time* in a young offenders institution and developed a keen sense during her time there that, it could be possible to escape a life of endless doom and criminal activity, if she planned her escape carefully. Despite the fact DJ had taken full advantage of Carla's access to useful contacts within the judiciary system, Carla was at least able to put some distance between herself and the gang of the damned. That is exactly what she had set out to do and with any luck she would duck below DJ's radar altogether. It was fortunate for her that she wasn't as deeply involved with the gang as Lisa and certainly not the financial asset her friend had become. She had no real ties to the boys and more importantly, nobody in the gang had an obsession and fascination with her as, DJ had with Lisa. God she thought, when was Lise, going to wake up and realize DJ was totally and utterly obsessed with her? She could only be there for her now. Carla was fast becoming a confident, young, black, female, in London. She had long realized that the only real help she could offer Lisa was to show her the way. She was breaking out of the preconceived stereotypes she had been fighting against for most of her life. Carla was tall, elegant and truly confident in her own ability to be able to overcome any barrier the world was planning to erect to prohibit her success. At this point in her life, there was nothing about to get in the way of her dreams. She approached the front desk with the confidence that would have intimidated any privileged, well educated, middle class individual, never mind the hunched, almost embarrassed looking figure she encountered today playing with their mobile phone, behind the reception desk of H.E.L.P, hoping not to be disturbed. "Hello I'm here to see Charlie, Charlie Becker." "Okay, I'll let him know you're here, take a seat."She was conscious that she might be bumping into Mickey today. God, she thought it would be weird if she did. It had been hard finding out where Mickey worked, as he was always so cagy. Then, it had been even harder being asked to keep the information to herself, especially as more time went by. She couldn't even tell Lisa he was alive, just in case it got out that he was close by. There was always the possibility DJ would start his own investigations into his whereabouts. The trick was, not to even give him a sniff. Ten minutes passed and just as she was starting to feel slightly offended at being kept waiting, I appeared.

"Hi Carla," I announced myself. "So sorry, got a bit caught up in a meeting with the Operations Manager. "No problem, Hiya."

I led her through the building to a room designed for 1-2-1 meetings. It was a small space, for the intimacy required for most of the client / worker meetings held there and were totally surrounded by glass panels. Although any conversations could be kept confidential, any clients deciding they wanted to kick off could still be kept an eye on. It was surprising the amount of frustration that could build up, certainly within some of the repeat offenders who had spent significant periods of time behind bars. I entered the room and was suddenly reminded of all the reasons why I did the job; I turned to Carla and beamed.

"So, how you doing, it's great to see you and if the reports are correct, your business is really starting to take off."

"Yes, not too shabby, I'm really pleased; I got two more really big orders only last week. There might even be something brewing with the team that cheers for Crystal Palace football team, fingers crossed, that would be big. Yeah, things are good, how are you Charlie?"

76

"Oh you know same old, same old. I get my kicks out a seeing people like you, doing good things."I exchanged a little more small talk and then decided to move on and introduce her to her new support worker. "Look Carla," I continued. "I'm convinced now that you would benefit from a more specialized and intensive programme of business support. So if it's all okay with you, I'm going to ask Michael to join us and hopefully you'll be able to plan together how the support we give will be more effective for your business going forward. You can work out what other specialist advice you might need for expansion, that kind of thing. Is that okay?"

"Absolutely, yeah, I'm thinking of growing the business, maybe looking at premises, so, it makes sense to take advantage of all the help I can get." While, she thought it might be a possibility, there was no chance Mickey was going to turn out to be Michael, surely, he couldn't have come this far, this fast. If he had, he was damn good at keeping it quiet. God, they'd been sleeping together for two months.

I left the room and was back within two minutes with the new business support worker. "Michael, this is Carla. Carla, Michael, although, he does like to be called Mickey"–"Look I'm going to leave you to it, okay, get acquainted, Mickey, I'll catch up with you later okay mate. You can run the notes by me, if you need any help. Sure you'll be okay though."

"Okay Charlie, see you later."

I left; safe in the knowledge, Carla was in good hands. Mickey had progressed rapidly after I'd taken him on just over a year ago and I was sure he was up to it.

Carla squared up to her new support worker. "Mate, He calls you mate!"

"My, my, wats up, Michael." Carla was obviously ribbing and ready for a bit of banter. "Look he's okay, and no he doesn't pull the big heavy boss man stunt, he's cool."

"Well, Michael," Carla continued. Apparently, un-moved by Mickey's growing irritation. "Are you going to grill me, now you are my official, Business Support Worker?" Ah now - BSW - your initials. Now does that stand for Mr. Bull shit worker?" God, when she teased, it really worked on Mickey. Carla had been to the H.E.L.P offices many times and as a consequence Mickey had *bumped* into her more than once. The relationship that had ensued, was, by now, passionate and much more dangerous than either of them would have imagined. Of course they had known each other way back when. But with Carla incarcerated most of the time, romance wasn't on anyone's agenda back then. Mickey had barely noticed her and if he had, he wasn't the sort to make a move. Mickey was used to girls approaching him with offers and Carla was well aware that Mickey was attracted to success and power, not, black sex workers with no future. Mickey had worked out from a very early age that any form of success, would inevitably bring along with it, greater influence over whoever else coveted the same. And so, they had met by chance and only briefly in a crowded H.E.L.P corridor, during one of Carla's earliest appointments with the charity. Carla had been instantly attracted by the way in which Mickey took control. She recalled

Mickey approaching her with, "Hey, I'm sorry for staring; it's just that you really have turned into one gorgeous lookin babe."Carla wasn't used to compliments, god, she wasn't even used to being treated neutral, so she wasn't about to question whether an employee of H.E.L.P should be acting so overtly flirtatious with her. In the past Carla had expected grief, as she had always got, from just about anyone who decided to throw a bigoted, prejudice, or worse, damn cruel cuss her way. Therefore, she responded instantly to Mickey's advances and the two of them were soon rolling around in Mickey's bed devouring each other physically, even before the realization that they didn't know the first thing about each other, would even ever dawn on them. It, in fact, still hadn't dawned two months later. They were still in that early, couldn't even possibly consider the other has any faults stage. And, man the sex was awesome.

"Look, stop pissin around babe, we'll get caught one day, and it'll be my job."

"Come on lover boy; take me here, now, on this desk.""No, you come on, it's wearin thin babe, and we need to do some work."

"You think more of your job than me, yeah, is that it lover boy?"

"Yes, I do, I think more of my job than you. That's why you've got me wrapped round your goddamn finger. Now stop pissin around and let's work okay."

"Ah, what would Charlie boy say, if he knew you swore at your vulnerable, young, female clients, uh, Mickey."

Carla was facing Mickey and almost had him pinned against the far wall, so when he gave her a gentle but assertive push, she quite enjoyed the exchange. The provocation was turning her on. However, she knew in reality, she didn't want to risk losing Mickey's full time attention altogether.

"Okay baby, let's work, on the condition; we meet tonight.""You're on."

She gave him a token kiss on the lips, which made Mickey jump and look around to make sure nobody was watching the room. After all, how would it look if he was caught snogging a client. Moreover, it was, after all, his very first assignment. What were the odds, he constantly mused, that his very first real business support role would involve the lush, Carla? The pair worked for the next hour or so, planning how Carla was going to bring about world domination through her business plan. In the safe environment they were in, all their plans seemed perfectly doable and indeed reasonable. At last however, they decided on a fairly more conservative version of a few earlier brain storm ideas and started to relax. "How we gonna help Lisa, Mickey," Carla suddenly blurted out.

"I donno, I really don't, but I know one things for damn sure babe."

"What's that then, cos, I'm lost for a way to get her outta DJ's shit man."

"Well, all I know is that we gotta try and find something soon, cos, Lisa's lookin like she's about to blow. DJ needs to see he can't keep her forever. It ain't gonna be easy. I'm really scared for my little sis." "Okay, me too, but how? Besides, you need to be serious careful, you don't want to go snoopin round, or messin with DJ, an risk him finding out you're back in London."

"Well, we all know that he only really wants Lisa for himself, won't jus' take her, cos he thinks that's not the same as her really wanting him back. He wants her to want him, we all know that. Why can't she?"

" I dunno babe, she's normally so bright."

"Yeah, but maybe, her not bein so aware, is keeping her safe. You know, if she was aware of DJ's lust, it would freak her out, she would probably do something stupid, and then he would flip big time."

"Your right, but, I am gonna meet with her again. I need to find out if there's a way around, DJ, or a way to get to him at least."

"It's a pity she can't come here, couldn't you help her, and she is an ex-offender after all."

"Look Carls, I need to keep this part of my life separate, can you understand that babe! I made good here, Charlie's bin great, given me a proper chance. I need to keep my old life out of my new one Okay, cos if it gets confused, then, I may as well go on the run again. I escaped that lot once, okay. Do you get it? Do you understand if we keep this place quiet for awhile longer?"

"Course mate," she said insolently. "You're the boss." "No, don't be like that babe."

"Only Jokin, don't worry, I feel a bit the same, don't really want to share too much of ya just yet, even with your sister. An, yeah, I do get the keeping it separate thing. I feel the same. Don't worry Hunny Bunny, we will keep our little secret haven just between us for the time being. Until we've got a clear plan anyway."

Mickey knew he was trapped. Despite all attempts to remain suave and the epitome of cool, he knew he'd fallen. There was no controlling it and although he was still a mile away from admitting it to anyone else, especially Carla, he knew he loved her, and so, he knew just as positively, he was utterly screwed because of it.

As she left Mickey, Carla felt a wave of different emotions wash over her almost simultaneously. Frustration was the most prevalent. Not being able to help Lisa was really starting to get to her, coupled with the more intense guilt for not wanting to reveal her own safety net, for fear of exposing it to DJ. This deception was proving to be a mounting pressure that she didn't think she would be able to hide from for much longer. Carla also felt panic. Scared that Lisa might find out she was seeing her long lost bro' behind her back. She even felt paranoid that Mickey's scent would be detected on her if Lisa got too close. Maybe it was time to break away from the whole scene, including Lisa, ah, more guilt. Then there was also the satisfaction that she had started to be really successful and the thrill she felt as she anticipated putting even this afternoon's business plans into effect. Basically, the whole situation was a great big massive emotionally layered chocolate sundae of an assault on her nervous system packed with cream and nuts…To top it off, It all had a huge dollop of sizzling lust plonked right on its summit. God, she was gonna nail Mickey tonight and no mistake.

* * * *

"Life has no meaning the moment you lose the illusion of being eternal"
~Jean-Paul Sartre.

Chapter 6
G.P.S & thoughts of Suicide

I took a trip not so very long ago.
I the drunkard that was me Charlie Becker;
sometimes didn't give myself time to sober up
before I clambered into my car! Today was
different; today I had Tommy with me; well, for
the journey home at least. The trip was about a
week before I took to the bath and so I was
feeling rather; well let's just say my senses were
heightened somewhat.
Trying to decide whether one wants' to make the
considerable step between feeling depressed and
actually ending it all, does tend to take it out of
one. You know what it's like! No! Okay, well
let's just say that when I was taking my son home
this time, I was absolutely certain it would be for
the last time and yes, I was feeling high,
exhilarated, a kin to an out of body experience I
suppose, as all feelings of depression dissipated
the moment I had made my plans. The moment I
had rested upon my fate, I was instantly at peace
and at the same time very excited.
But wait, I'm getting ahead of myself! Needless
to say, my senses were heightened in such a way
as to make everything around me appear almost
psychedelic.   It wasn't until the trip was over
that I realized that the whole journey, how it had
come about, how I had responded and reacted to
the diversions, the roads I eventually took etc.
was an exact analogy of my life. If only I could

understand why my journey had taken this random form! I feel almost predestined to continue in the same way. I wish I could learn the lessons it highlighted and find a way to turn onto another road, another course. Find a better way, find peace, and find my salvation. Who knows, maybe one day!

I was essentially taking Tommy back home to Bournemouth, after a brief and rare day out with him, or rather; I had actually already dropped him off. I had very nearly recovered from the nauseating feelings of loss I felt each time I took him home. The epiphany began on the way to Caroline and Colin's lovely home. It was a huge relief to me that I had realized long ago that, I didn't covert their comfortable middle class life at all. The idea of a normal, two point four children kind of existence caused me to want to run blind into the hills. Maybe this was a little clue, as to why my marriage wasn't a complete success. Anyway, back to my journey...I had noticed an accident on the opposite side of the motorway. The route I would normally have to return on a little while later. How fatal, it was, it was hard to see from the other side of the busy roads. But, it looked bad, certainly at least a two lane hold up scenario. I thought, ah, I will endeavour to out smart the world and its chaos returning home victorious having taken a different route. This G.P.S is a little miracle machine and I will not sit on the motorway for hours on end, waiting for it to clear. I will be the master of my own destiny.

I turn to my saviour - SETTINGS - QUICKEST ROUTE - AVOID M WAYS – NAVIGATION - press HOME, press GO, press OK. Just over one hundred miles and I'll be home. How long can it take? I'm shocked; I'm led onto a remote dusty track of a road. Bournemouth had led me onto a detour through the sleepy and pretentious town of Verwood. Onto roads I had never previously travelled. I found myself feeling the anticipation of adventure and exploration, setting off into the bright unknown, a wonderful and totally exhilarating journey home. I didn't realize the G.P.S would even recognize the little lane I was directed too and yet why wouldn't it. Ivy Lane to be precise and so, the analogy begins. Nothing in my life that has worked out to be successful has ever been planned. The opposite had been true, the more I planned, the more I failed. I sat and wondered about how many times I had told my clients at work, that success was impossible without stringent planning. This little lane was indeed most unexpected and yet it led me into a little paradise. The sun had been strong today and as I wound my way through the New Forest, I could smell the heavy scent of the bark on the huge trees. The moss was still drying out in the shady areas and also smelled divine. It was perfect, appealing to all my senses. I was warm and the rich aroma of the Forest was engulfing me. Around another turn and my eyes met Pony's nuzzling their gangling foals. A fallow deer positively skipped across the narrow road and through the bracken and then I reached a herd of majestic heavy cattle lumbering along the road. The huge animals were totally contemptuous of the cars and cyclists passing through and not about to budge for anyone. I had set my destination, intending upon taking the path of least resistance and I hoped to get home before midnight. I had never expected the most pleasant of journeys and yet one that took me far longer than if I had stayed on the crowded Motorway, to be in store for me as I had set off. And yet, like I stated earlier, everything in my life that had worked out well and led to any feelings of satisfaction or fulfilment had been thrust upon me like it was planned, not by me, but by someone else. As if, it was carefully executed by someone trying to test or possibly surprise me. "Let's see how he might handle this. Let's see if he accepts it. He didn't want, provoke or invite this situation. Let's see if he can welcome the opportunity to be vaguely fulfilled and make the most of it, even enjoy it. Or, will he default into his usual habit of finding a way to fuck it up, utterly?" I rounded a sharp corner and immediately slowed down as the horse and rider had already heard my engine. The rider, an attractive red head, was looking anxiously over her shoulder, probably, to see if I was going to respect the country code. I slowed and she smiled and waved, making me feel like I had just won a Nobel peace prize. I thought this was a reaction totally disproportionate to the gesture at hand. I could enjoy her pleasure and gratitude; however, at the same realizing that tomorrow morning I would be ready to swear like a mad person, at the first moron who walked in front of me, blocking my path on the busy London underground stations. Here, was a bloody great horse blocking my path, when, I was just as anxious to get home, being very tired and yet, I found myself, just gazing benignly at the rider, as if I was the one holding her up. What complicated paradoxical lunatics we are. Or is it just me? I gradually weaved my way toward a greater and more familiar reality, with the uncomfortable dawning that, inevitability, the wonder and excitement that the New Forest life had evoked within me wasn't going to last. I was unable - and this had been true of all lovely moments in my life - therefore, to, fully enjoy the moment. I had past the Bramble Hill Hotel, with ninety two miles to go. I exited the forest and still the experiences were quite pleasant, but, yes, the inevitable experience of deterioration had begun. As I continued upon my unexpected detour through life I started to feel much more comfortable now in the knowledge life was starting to reflect my limited expectations. Winchester was pleasant, quaint, pretty even, but the decline had begun. The best had past; the forest was perfect, but just as it had seemed in my youth, the best was definitely over far too briefly. "Please secure your seat belts and prepare for decent. The only way hereafter, is down………..." I could hear all the voices that had invaded my head for decades and they were all warning me of decline. As I reached, Basingstoke with its traffic and complications, doubt, uncertainty about how long this 'A' road traffic would hold me up, ah, I knew I had reached about half way. Middle age! I had certainly not taken the most popular route from Bournemouth to London and therefore, why didn't I realize that I should expect to meet a plethora of barriers and frustrations? I had failed to avoid a traffic queue and the build up of traffic leading from a major diversion. As a result the fallout from the very accident I had so carefully avoided had caught up with me. Was there just no way of avoiding consequences? It was, as if I was destined, somehow, to be obliged, or forced to learn a lesson, predestined for me, upon my path through life! Now, I was becoming hot and bothered. There was a bloke cutting me up and refusing to let me into a single lane of traffic. I wanted to drag him out of his car and make him eat his ridiculously ugly wife's head scarf. No, this journey had definitely not lived up to earlier hope filled expectations. Guildford was next leading onto the Epsom Road, my back aching. My legs feel like lead and I thought for a minute I was going to eventually succumb to cramp. Deterioration of the body was totally out of my control. I remember Woody Allen, in one of his early films looking at the joggers that had passed him and as he reflected upon the lunacy, that is jogging he remarked; "all they are doing is staving off the inevitable decay of the body." This friend is the feeling of middle age.

I even took a wrong turning and grinned at the sternness of the GPS woman's voice chastising me rudely. RE-CALCULATE - TURN AROUND IF POSSIBLE – RE-CALCULATE. Why can't we re-calculate, re-assess, turnaround and pretend we hadn't fucked up in the first place, as we travel through life? Why can't we re-set our navigation? Why isn't it obvious, where we even roamed off the right path? So many consequences, loss, tempting us to regret! By the time I saw I had thirty miles to go, I just wanted to get home, get there as soon as I possibly could, while remaining cautious of the yellow hooded monsters, that also threatened my progress. I nearly swerved, as I tried to slow down quick enough to get back down to 40mph and avoid the camera monster flash – flash. I was shocked at the paradox that although I was tired of the long journey, I was also amazed how quickly it was coming to an end and how transient the magical part had been. I wondered if the elderly feel like this most of the time or just some of the time. London, the busiest, dirtiest, most crowded bad tempered place involved in my whole journey and yet I was now more at home than ever. The grim, comfortable, feelings of familiarity. I knew the paradise bit at the start wouldn't last, but wait then I realized most profoundly that, I could have also chosen to have taken a vital decision right in the centre of the most exquisite part of my adventure. I could have stopped the car and made the best part of the journey last longer at any stage, instead of relentlessly forging ahead believing I wasn't deserving, good, clever or simply lucky enough to be worthy of the best life had to offer. I could have lingered, but as with the impetuous of youth, of course it didn't occur to me at the time. I was on a journey, why would you want to stop? Home at last and it was over so quickly in the grand scheme of things and yet, at the time it was difficult, uncertain, to be honest I didn't even trust the G.P.S to actually come through and get me home. Why should I trust the unknown? Why should I trust the unseen satellite links and radio waves to lead me, to guide me through such an uncertain journey? Looking back on the experience, it had been even more vivid than in reality. The forest more beautiful, the deer, more dainty, the pony more nurturing to her foal, the cattle more impressive and the girl on the horse more attractive. The end came much quicker than expected. More significantly, I hadn't faired well from the experience, as I was reminded, by my inability to get out of the car easily. My back felt as though it had been rammed by an articulated lorry! I wonder if there was any milk in the fridge, as the futility of life kicked in once again.   ****

"Eternity is really long, especially near the end"~**Woody Allen**

Chapter 7
Regis & Lisa's escape plan

"Willy says he wants to see you."

"Ah uh, why?"

"Wouldn't say, but he assures me, it's in your best interest."

"Wat an idiot. Why the Mystery?"

"I have no idea, do you want to see him or not?"

Regis, who had been adopted by the gang, only a couple of years ago, stood before DJ.

He didn't mind that sometimes DJ treated him as little more than a sort of groupie come gopher. Regis was one of those individuals you meet in life, who you always look back on and remember as being tall and imposing, when in reality they are quite easily to be found being of moderate height and cowardly. Ruthless and yet lacking in any moral integrity whatsoever.

Here was a man who would carry out most tasks at almost any time of the day or night. This is how Regis got to know just about everyone involved in just about anything that was going down. He worked for anyone in the group of ex BEA's, who wanted a dirty deed, or a sickening chore accomplished, with minimal bother, leaving absolutely no evidence leading back to them. Regis was used to reporting to DJ and would practically do anything as long as the task adopted two main features. He was highly motivated by money. His second motive, while stimulating him and providing the enjoyment he needed in life, was actually more like an addiction. Regis was a man who needed to hurt people. The complexity of the man everyone in the group secretly feared was multi-raced and yet nobody could ever really work out which particular races his blood was extracted from. His skin was olive brown, the eyes could well have been bordering on the oriental and his iris colouration' as they appeared to be jet black. He was a monster who had no history, less friends and little interest in anyone.

After completing a few jobs, none of the aging gangsters any longer wanted to face, he had come on board with DJ's group after he just happened to be able to make the interest in certain crimes committed by one or another of them simply disappear. Somehow Regis managed to know someone, somewhere, who knew someone else, somewhere, that would have known the certain individual, who was responsible for pulling out files at the Met central office, or someone who had just happened to mention at the Police briefing that they probably needed to look into that, (whichever crime you care to name) a little more closely!

Regis knew people who knew how to get close enough to other people to make problems simply go away. A more resourceful and manipulative psychotic, it would be very difficult to find. Therefore, Regis was useful to DJ and quickly rose through the invisible ranks that still existed within the group. Regis was well travelled; he spoke three languages as well as his own and could easily have outwitted DJ, influencing the often mindless individuals who orbited DJ's sordid little world, stealing all the power and the glory for himself. But even DJ was clever enough to know that would never happen. No! Regis didn't want to be a leader of men. All Regis wanted, apart from being paid for his specialist services; was to hurt people. At present he had been doing rather a lot, by way of chasing debts for Willy Adebayo and business was very good.

"Tell im he can come over tomorrow night if he wants."Regis gave a very slight nod of acknowledgement.

Regis was a man who couldn't fail to make the skin of even the hardest heart positively crawl and DJ was no exception. Regis had no code, nor any honour, even within the group and would rape his own Granny, as long as he thought he could prove someone else did it and exact revenge. DJ hated the man, yet admired the work and his trait whereby he would make sure if he did a job, he would carry it out to perfection. After all, if you wanted someone beaten and tortured for creaming off more than the acceptable percentage from a local cocaine deal, you surely wouldn't want them to be able to have the ability to eat solid foods again as long as they lived, now would you? Regis was the only man DJ had ever known who could pull this off with the guarantee his victim wouldn't die. This of course was so important, because as everyone knows, if you need to make an example of someone, you really do need them alive and acting as a living demonstration to every other potential thief, in regard to any intentions they may have toward your money.

Regis was good. Very good and everyone, while not exactly comfortable with his presence, knew that while he was the shark in the tank, very few other predators would come swimming by.

.

* * * *

Lisa made her way thoughtfully and not a little anxiously to the H.E.L.P offices. More guilt.......She had looked for, stolen and called the number printed on the H.E.L.P business card Carla had in the desk drawer of her work desk. Why hadn't she just told Carla what she had planned? Somehow lately they were drifting; the trust was drifting with it. Lisa loved Carla, but her gut was urging her to be cautious and say nothing about Mickey's return. At least until she was sure it wouldn't leave her or Mickey more vulnerable than they were already. Lisa had to be sure. Just imagine if DJ found out, she thought. It would be the end of Mickey, if the pack went looking for him again. But Carla didn't even know him now, so it probably didn't even matter anyhow! Confused, lonely and very cautiously, Lisa managed to navigate her way through the reception Nazis, who in any organization always seem to think their screening role is somehow greater than the overall agenda of the people who pay their salary. No matter how many customer service courses the company ploughs into the average receptionists 'personal development', they seem to inevitably default to suspicion and the resulting abruptness, when faced with anyone who they decide is either inconvenient or difficult to communicate with. The reception desk seemed like a huge imposing barrier to Lisa. It was at least fifteen feet long and had spaces for at least three people to work at it. Yet, only one solitary person sat, glaring out over the PC that was positioned as to create a second, rude and very corporate barricade. A warning to all, that the people behind the lines were of a different world and if you were ever to be considered worthy to join in with their commercial secrets, you would have to choose whether you were prepared to conform or perish. Lisa thought, being a Charity it might be less imposing than she had initially feared, indeed the people milling around behind the desk, seemed very friendly and Carla had always raved about how different the people she had dealt with at the charity had been to the rest of the twats she had encountered since leaving Prison, especially at her probation offices.

But for now, to get to these people, she was amazed herself, just how difficult it was proving to move beyond the initial blockade that presented itself as; The Reception!

* * * *

I was absolutely swamped. Work was taking
over and the last thing I wanted to do right now
was organize calendars for staff that were more
than capable of doing it for themselves.
However, result; I have another victim in my
sights. Consequently, Jenny, the new temp, was
going to get the job for the rest of the foreseeable
future no matter how boring the task was. The
Temp' in question was less than confident, so it
was quite amusing watching her organizational
skills in play. She approached people like you
might creep up on a pissed off Crocodile having
a bad day. "Err, Chloe, err, I wondered, if, err,
you could see someone in reception. I see your,
err, calendar is free," she ventured forth, not yet
having served the time at H.E.L.P to realize that
Chloe actually didn't mind work, was of an
extremely mild and happy disposition and would
need no persuading whatsoever.
"No problem babe, I'm on it"
It took Chloe about ten minutes to get to Lisa and
rescue her from reception, find a meeting room
and make Lisa a coffee. Although, Lisa had been
waiting longer than this, due to the Nazi
receptionists attentions, Jenny's introduction to
the process and Chloe, having to finish off what
she had been doing before Jenny had plucked up
the courage to give her the job. At least she
didn't have to sit there alone, as, the lady sitting
with her was being really friendly. This, and a
lot more in my department was going on around
me and I was blissfully unaware of most of it and

any of my team's comings and goings. To be honest I really didn't care. As long as the results came in and the senior management was kept happy I saw no reason for micro management? "So, its Lisa, is it, Lisa Barker?" "Baker!" "Oh, I am sorry Lisa; could you please fill out our profiling form? Are you okay, reading and writing? We don't like to assume to much and I'm happy to help if you need me too."
"I can do it."
"Cool, I'll just go and photo copy your ID, thanks for remembering it."
"K." Lisa had struggled to find the ID needed, but had scraped together enough to convince Chloe that she lived, at least, at the address she was staying with Carla. She planned to use the fact that H.E.L.P had assisted Carla to further convince them that she was worth supporting. This was a valid argument, as; her best friend and room mate had proved to be a monumental success for them and their stakeholders. The meeting took about an hour and despite herself and her determination to avoid trusting anyone ever again, Lisa found herself warming to Chloe and her sunny disposition. The two of them had thrashed out many ideas in terms of what Lisa might need support with. Her options were limited, but they could at least look at further education, training, voluntary work, or, even a proper job. Although, she was going to have to be damn lucky to land paid employment at the first attempt. Even as the two girls were talking,

Lisa was starting to formulate a clear plan and none of it included hanging around London for long. It could be put in motion almost immediately, at least in her head. How hard would it be to escape, change identity, find herself far away and just vanish? She wondered if H.E.L.P would organize relocation packages. She was pretty sure she wouldn't have been the first ex-offender to ask the question.

"Okay, Lisa, I think at least we've a way forward. It might be a good idea for you to go away and have a think and we'll meet up again when you're ready. You can call me when you feel its time."

"Yeah, that's great, thanks."

"And don't forget the leaflet, just in case you need help with housing, benefit claims, or, well, anything really."

Little did Chloe know, Lisa could earn more money in a single evening than Chloe would see in a month. "Okay, thanks, see you then."

"Great, super, I'll see you out then. Lovely to meet you Lisa."

The second cup of Chloe's coffee had taken effect and so, Lisa announced the need for a convenient little room and Chloe duly obliged, explaining that there was a loo near the reception. She had assured her she could take her time, which, had made Lisa wonder why she might need permission to take as long as it took to have a pee? She then Informed Lisa the front door was just opposite, so she would leave her and let her see her own way out. Lisa managed to avoid too much hassle at reception and realised it was far easier to escape from organisations than it was to access them. The Nazi type, who had eventually let her through the barrier, must have been on a break. As she was just reaching for her packet of Mayfair cigarettes, she vaguely thought…No, it couldn't be, and Carla had told her she was off to buy materials and stock today and that her supplier was nowhere near the H.E.L.P. Office. This had come up when Lisa had suggested they go to the offices together. Lisa had at the time, felt that Carla was trying to, put her off, but she had put it down to being over sensitive, as Carla would never lie to her. Ha, Carla would never, ever think she would get down there alone. But Lisa had grown increasingly desperate over the last few months and feared for her sanity if she didn't make some positive plans soon. Help would be accepted gratefully, as long as she could get the hell away from the torment orchestrated by DJ.

A high pitched squeal came from a corridor just leading from the left of the receptionists, gun-tower. She gingerly edged her way toward the noise that sounded like someone extraordinarily like Carla, until she reached one of the rows of meeting rooms. Unfortunately, the rooms had walls of glass and were completely see through, so, it would be a challenge to get to the room that was now captivating her attention, undetected. She nearly jumped out of her skin when someone came leaping out of another room directly in front of her, startling her and she contemplated turning around and escaping before one of Chloe's colleagues found her mooching around the building. As she approached the room she thought Carla's voice emanated from, she released a sigh of relief, as both people in the room had their backs to her and the corridor. She would at least be able to make out if it was Carla. Man, that girl would get a piece of her mind if she was in there and blatantly trying to keep H.E.L.P. to herself.

Lisa could think of no earthly reason why that would be the case, but the closer she got, the more convinced she was. She edged, slowly, closer to the couple, only to discover, to her astonishment, they were actually a couple and they seemed to be in an embrace. The guy was hidden behind what was now obviously that lying little cows body, sprawled all over him. Lisa started to feel indignant, as she wouldn't have thought H.E.L.P encouraged that kind of intimate support to their clients. Then, just as she was trying to work out why she was finding this situation both amusing and irritating at the same time, the realisation that the woman kissing the H.E.L.P worker was in fact Carla. She burned with anger immediately upon her discovery and wouldn't even have been able to articulate why she didn't rush into the room and rip her roommates head off. Lisa's highly offended thoughts raged with anger! That bloody little bitch, why wouldn't she want me to be helped as well? When you are alone and desperate, looking for anyone in the entire world that you think might be worthy of your trust, you simply cannot accept betrayal. She thought Carla knew this and although this wasn't the worse sin in the world, Carla would have understood the code they lived by. She of all people would have known that it wouldn't have been the fact she'd turned up at H.E.L.P when she said she was somewhere else, it was the lie. They simply didn't lie to each other, they left that to all the other bastards that would try and put them down and treat them like scum, just because they had done time. But now! What else was Carla hiding?

She was now almost square on to the two of them and although Carla was playing the little tramp, he seemed to be resisting somewhat. So, yes, the guy with Carla must have worked for H.E.L.P and he was anxious about being caught.

Lisa spared one more look toward her treacherous friend before heading back to plan how she was now going to confront the insult. With that look, she nearly let out a scream that would have definitely given her position away. Mortified and just before she felt that she might lose her self-control altogether, she buried her face into her arm, trying frantically to muffle squeals that threatened to expose her advantage of anonymity.

Lisa's heart had nearly stopped! Mickey had pushed Carla lightly away from him, just enough to expose his features to her fully. A million questions flooded her head as she dived away from view and started to jog toward reception and the front sliding doors. She moved as fast as she could without drawing any attention to herself, although, her obvious discomfort would be hard to disguise as she fled. It was difficult to move in the right direction, feeling so nauseous, her emotions numbed. How long had they known each other? Why was Carla deceiving her, by not letting her be relieved in the knowledge her own brother was okay and not really lost forever? After all Carla must have been seeing Mickey before he had decided to reveal himself to her himself at the café. Why had Mickey contacted her recently? Why hadn't Mickey mentioned Carla when they had met up? He knew Carla knew her? Why were they cutting her out? On and on her mind was spinning until she reached the train station. When she had walked for half a mile, the humiliation and feelings of utter betrayal had totally consumed her. She was no longer numb at all! She was being utterly betrayed and the anger was now burning into her very core.

* * * *

I decided to stretch my legs. Eight and a half hours a day, at least, staring at this computer screen was starting to do my head in. I could eke a little trek around the building out if I gathered all the bits of info' everyone in the building needed from me and deliver it all in one grand expedition. Charlie mate, I thought to myself, God you're getting old God, I was getting old. My legs creaked as I got up, my back positively screamed at me to stay put and my head was throbbing and protesting that I might want to consider proper Health and safety rules in regard to the amount of time I spent beavering over my PC. "Hi Wendy." Receptionist extraordinaire No-one was getting past our Wendy, unless of course they were male, good looking and up for it! "Where's Phil, Wen?" Phil was managing the volunteer team and we had been meaning to catch up for ages.

"Hang on Charlie; I've got the wrong screen up."
"No worries, no rush.' It was a good job there was no rush!"
After a couple of huff's and one long, very drawn out puff...........Wendy managed to respond.
"Room 14."
"Thank you Wendy. Is he with anyone important? Or can I interrupt him?"
"Well, according to this, he's on his own, and he said something earlier about just needing to escape the main office area to do some real work - whatever the hell that meant."

"Once again; Wen thank you."I called her Wen
as often as I could, as I knew she hated it. Small
victories over someone who apparently seemed
to have a job description that included the
directive to make everyone else's life in the
building, as difficult as possible. I made my way
down the corridor; Chloe and her new client were
in room 13, so, I could pop in and meet her too. I
like to meet all the clients, even if I won't work
directly with them. You could bet sooner or later
some problem or another would rear its head and
at least if I had some info' on them, it would
help. I hate the term, 'Client'. It made me feel
like we were processing people, on conveyor
belts, not trying to help them. One more turn and
I was outside thirteen, oh, Chloe had popped out
and her appointment was working away at her
forms. I caught her side profile, as she was
sitting to left of the door. Then it dawned on me!
"Hang on a minute! Shit, shit, what the fu..."
Well, it was definitely her! Absolutely, no doubt
at all. Lisa was indeed Lisa Baker. I wasn't sure
if I was glad or not, that the girl who had so
dramatically ripped me off, was now seeking
help! She had failed to look up when I briefly
passed the room. If she had done she would have
clocked me for sure. But I can't help but wonder
what her reaction would be. I feel like I'm going
to have a bloody heart attack. What's she doing
here! Stupid question, now get a grip. I made
my way limply back to my office. "You okay

Charlie?" "Yeah, no problem Wen," I lied. I was so, not okay. Well, a crime was definitely committed. I should know it happened to me. My sense of duty was already conflicting dramatically with my own sense of self loathing, as the flash backs from, *that night,* came to me rapidly. I didn't care at all back then about doing the right thing, or exercising my high and mighty moral code. No, all I could think about then was getting my end away. I had been happy to defile and use a young girl, purely to gratify my animal instincts, however willing she had been. Now my thoughts raced back and forth! She has committed a bloody crime, I didn't. I caught a glimpse of myself in the reflection of the glass office door and looking at my contorted features, I thought, you bloody hypocrite.
Shit, what the hell was I going to do?

* * * *

"Wat you want Willy, an, I'll tell ya now boy, I am not in the mood for games so just spill okay." DJ wanted this meeting over quickly.

Willy was in his element. He spent a good half hour carefully explaining his skill as an undercover masked hero, albeit, the mask having been a grubby copy of the Sunday people.

He had followed Lisa last Monday morning and bingo, two birds one stone. DJ was impressed, but he would never admit it. The discovery that Mickey was back in the manor was big news. Lisa was meeting with him and therefore, the threat of him aiding her escape from his clutches was increasing by the day. DJ's eyes grew even wider; as Willy's devious little exploits were further revealed. Willy was even more proud of the trip to central London. Lisa had fled the offices of H.E.L.P her tears and distress were obvious. It was all Willy could do to stop himself approaching her, enquiring as to the nature of her turmoil, satisfying his own twisted need to explore any human pain he could find. Well, the trip had obviously not gone well, but this did little to convince DJ Lisa's escape plan wasn't well under way. Not for the first time lately, the aging gangster reached for his mobile device, in an attempt to quench Lisa's thirst for freedom. He punched in the number of his right hand man. Max, I wanna gather some of the boys together...tonight."

* * * *

"Earth to earth, ashes to ashes, dust to dust, in sure and certain hope of the resurrection into eternal life" Book of Common Prayer

Chapter 8
Taken

The blacked out windows on the transit were in themselves an illegal act. However, we were in Greater London and the boys were well aware that this little known fact was of little interest to the Met. They'd risk getting a pull, as there weren't many coppers who, once getting a glimpse of what the inhabitants of the van might involve, would really want to take them on. Regis had been tailing his quarry for a few weeks and therefore was confident of his routine movements. He would exit Vauxhall tube station at about 6.15pm and make his way, on foot, over Vauxhall Bridge, crossing the river, continuing on to Vauxhall Bridge Road, to finally turning right onto Willow Place. Arriving twenty minutes later to his one bed flat. Regis couldn't understand why Mickey walked from Vauxhall station, when both, Pimlico and Victoria underground stations were closer to his digs. Regis hadn't ever himself cramped against hundreds of sweaty traveller's armpits, on the tube and therefore he wasn't really the best person to judge. The only quiet area he would enter all the way from Central London, until he reached his modest home, was Mickey's home street. Another risk, was of course someone who knew him recognizing him if he was taken in the street. The very fact that he took the same path every week night added a risk that someone would notice abduction. The boys would have to be double careful tonight, as, the summer evening would ensure, they didn't even have the cover of night to mask their deeds.

It was relatively easy to take him, he was tired and off guard. Regis had done DJ proud volunteering to be the one who got out of the van and approached slightly behind the victim. One quick, sharp thud and he was out, falling forward gently into the arms of Max, as one who was welcoming a cuddle. The reality of what was in store was to prove less pleasant than this initial innocuous interaction suggested. It was all over very quickly and Mickey knew absolutely nothing about it. It took four hours for Mickey to wake up. When he did he was alone. Confusion filled his consciousness; he had no idea where he might be. He knew he was lying on the floor and it was cold, he guessed at concrete but he was so groggy he could well have been lying on the surface of the moon. The place was dark and all Mickey could rely on in his tortured mind was his imagination. That same mind, kept replaying a never ending loop of anxious thoughts, flitting between; what could they want and what have I done, the pain Mickey was in was excruciating. His arms had been bound behind his back, but, yanked far too far backward and therefore, the joints were screaming to be released. This predicament, in turn caused his chest muscles to be stretched, causing a burning sensation across his torso. His head hurt, but it was difficult to

decide which pain to concentrate on more, as his
body parts were all fighting for his attention like
a child having a tantrum to be noticed. Even his
gums seem to ache as his head fought against the
trauma inflicted upon it. His legs were also
bound. The lower half of his body had been
immobilized, rather than stretched. But, as it
meant his body couldn't get enough blood
circulating southward, so, it was no less
uncomfortable than his upper half. He spent a
considerable amount of time trying to distract his
mind away from the pain by attempting to solve
the mystery of who might benefit from keeping
him in this place. What he thought must have
been hours went by and he wondered if this was
it. Was no one going to come? Maybe he was
lucky if they didn't, his body was now riddled
with pins and needles, probably soon to become
more or less completely numb apart from the
throbbing in his head and ears. He wondered if
this might be an infinitely better end than the fate
he might have to face if anyone actually decided
to turn up. A few hours after he'd came to, there
was an almighty crash; the sound rang through
his ears as if someone had let off gunfire in his
face, as the heavy door opened violently and
crashed shut even louder.

"Alright - Mickey boy."

"Who's that, where am I?"

"Nah, ya see, you already approachin this wrong
matey boy, I'm gonna be askin the questions and
doin the talkin, well, for a while anyhow, okay

Mickey boy?"

"Right, okay, but I tell you this, whoever the fuck you are, if you don't make these ropes a bit looser, I'm gonna pass out."

"You might ave a point there. So, if you answer the first question I have for you now, in a manner I appreciate like; I might jus do that very thing."

"Go on. Try me."

"I intend to try you Mickey my boy. I intend to do that very thing. Now, are you gonna help me boy, or you gonna be a pain in the ass?"

Well Mickey knew this idiot wasn't American and wondered why so many non Americans had adopted the habit of continually talking about their asses. What he didn't know was that his old friend DJ had sent in Regis in to, lets say, have a little chat with Mickey. If he had have known this small fact from the outset, he would have been even more convinced he was in the kind of trouble that few escaped from. There were a few good reasons for this. Mainly, he was reminded from a now distant life, that Regis would find out as much as there was to find. If only he could figure out what it was they were after. DJ too was supremely confident Regis would wheedle out every detail Mickey knew about Lisa, how she was planning to break free and anything else DJ could learn to avert such a disaster. DJ was aware Regis would really enjoy the liaison without actually killing Mickey. Regis was a master at executing this kind of appointment and DJ was quite sure it would be over pretty soon.

Regis motioned to the door and a couple of heavies immediately entered the room looking for a fight. After Regis had given the order and with absolutely no resistance at all, Mickey's restraints were relaxed. He felt his hopes rising disproportionately, compared to the situation he found himself in. But at least this guy seemed to be up for negotiation. Maybe his superior intellect would win the day? Any misplaced feelings of relief were abruptly terminated as Mickey glanced over to the corner of the room. His eyes had become accustomed to the dim light and he was alerted at the sight of a wooden table, complete with restraints. He could just about cope with the idea of being laid out and maybe horsewhipped. As long as there wasn't going to be any sexual messing around with any of his man bits, he thought he might cope. God knows he had had enough practice resisting pain inflicted by his less than loving Father. However, a chill entered his spine and ran up and down the full length of his body, when he spied the plastic wheelie table next to the *rack* like table. An assortment of gleaming steel instruments winked back at him, as light from a single 60 watt bulb was switched on and reflected off the daunting looking collection. Any former confidence he may have held of being treated with any semblance of humanity, quickly disappeared.

"Okay Mickey boy! You worked out how difficult you are goin to make this yet?"

"What the hell have I got that you might want?
"You gotta have the wrong geezer."
"Oh come on Mickey, it don't take much! You know, DJ knows, it was you, who was the little fucker who ran away all those years ago. Now, it ain't gonna take much for Mr. DJ to want to hurt ya for the sake of it, for being such an ungrateful little wanker. So come on pretty boy, lets not fuck about." Mickey's heart sank and he immediately regretted meeting with Lisa so publically. His next words seeped out of him weakly. "Okay, wat do you want?"
"Oh come on, lets not make it too easy." Regis twitched his head toward the two henchmen and they immediately sprang into action. This time there was a little more resistance as they manhandled the bound figure. Mickey didn't relish the idea of being strapped to that thing and being at the mercy of someone who clearly embraced their work.
"That's better; you must fight a little, make it a little challenge in for me."
The nameless gorilla type, hard men, looked like twins; the obvious problem with this was that one was black as coal, the other pink and pasty looking. The second man looked as if he had never been exposed to sunlight in his entire lifetime. The similarities between the two men were mainly in the way in which they moved in perfect sync. They had the exact same reactions, expressions and malevolent sneers as one another. It was as if they had been trained

115

together in some sort of fast track training school for meatheads. If Mickey's anxiety hadn't been rising by the moment, he might have wondered, as he looked at the pair, if it were possible to do an NVQ qualification sponsored by the council; entitled, 'Brainless Brawn and Bastard Behaviour` - NVQ Level 2 - Maybe an innovative aid to the increasingly ailing job opportunities in South London? Strapped down, Mickey was now quite worried, mainly, that they might want something he didn't have or couldn't give them. Surely, as they still had Lisa in their clutches, it wasn't her they wanted handing over. Nobody knew about Carla as they had been so careful and anyway, Carla hadn't had anything to do with BEA for years now. As Regis was so obviously trying to provoke Mickey into a state of fear, as he began more mind games all he could think was; what the hell do they want? Regis movements started to be slower and Mickey could detect little smiles between those carefully choreographed taunts. He handled the instruments with careful gentility, as if preparing for a dinner party. Mickey's thoughts raced faster. Why the fuck does he has to clean every implement before he…… Mickey was getting psyched out, panic setting in now, the adrenalin free flowing. His heart started to pound and he could feel the pressure in his ears. He was stripped to the waist, his jeans removed and he nearly fainted without any pain at all when his boxer shorts were removed by Regis. Using small scissors, Regis cut at them unceremoniously realizing the vulnerability this would thrust upon his latest victim. There was what seemed like, a pause lasting some minutes before Regis spoke again. Mickey had started to shake. He started to hope against hope that the main objective of the exercise might be to just utterly freak him out. Maybe they just wanted to warn him off Lisa, persuade him that helping her wouldn't be in his best interest, that sort of thing. "Okay," Regis began. "DJ has advised me I can get medieval on ya ass, if need be. So be aware and take on board right from the get go, I'm deadly serious bout gettin wat I want. All I need to know is, why and how you bin trying to get Lisa out of DJ's circle of influence, as it were? Why did she visit you, at work?"

"What! She didn't, never."

"Okay, since we ain't got any lie detectors in the house, I'm gonna do my thing now. If that's okay wit you Mickey boy."

Regis slowly picked up a scalpel. "Did you know that as a little boy I really loved drawin Mickey?" "Look, if Lisa came to my work, I didn't know okay, honest, fuck, I'd tell ya."

Regis started at the centre of the chest and started slicing. "I'm drawing a picture Mickey. When I get to here, I'll take this nipple as a souvenir."

He tapped Mickey's right nipple, as to mock him. "Then, I'll just start to work back the other way. If we aren't gettin anywhere afta a little while, I'll start goin down. God, you won't wanna leave it that long Mickey boy."

Water started pouring from Mickey's eyes, not tears as such, just a release as the pain ripped through his chest. Regis was skilled, the cuts were deep enough to hurt like hell, but they wouldn't prove fatal, unless of course, the *procedure* went on too long. The relief when Regis paused was met with Mickey gasping for air and projectile spitting and spluttering, as he struggled for breath. He was now writhing and pleading that Regis might stop. He was barely aware he was starting to fall in and out of consciousness. "Okay, let's try again."

DJ was right and it hadn't taken long. Regis knew how to do this and he also knew when people were lying, or when he was wasting his time. When he realized he had got all he could from Mickey, he carried on cutting for a little while to satisfy his own gratification, but alas, the only trophy he could claim, was the right nipple. It galled a little that he didn't need to continue on down to Mickey's nether regions, but Mickey was getting weak and the torturer had been instructed not to become an executioner. When it was over, the muscle bound double act once again entered the room, right on cue. Mickey was only half conscious but he flinched anyhow as he saw them approaching. More agony was inflicted as the bully brothers man handled Mickey off the blood covered table and practically threw him back on to the concrete floor. To add excruciating pain, to an injury that

118

was severe enough to scar him for life, they sniggered, as he landed on the rough surface, with all his weight upon the injuries that had just been inflicted. At that point Mickey threw up, made a gruesome gurgling noise, that came from somewhere at the back of his throat and passed out.

* * * *

DJ was standing in the centre of his large conservatory area, waiting for Regis to return. "So, you mean ole bastard, watcha got for me then?""Well, yeah, he admits he met wit Lisa. He say's it was just to catch up. There again, he did admit that he would ave helped her to get away if he could. He said he didn't ave a clue how to. Unfortunately, in my opinion and considerable experience, I believe im."

"Anything else?"

"He admitted shaggin Carla, even mentioned some shit bout love after I pressed him.
He wasn't resistin me much, once he'd got all woozy on me that is."

"He said he didn't know Lisa was goin to his office an that she'd talked bout it several times, but had never bin there . That's all he knew."

"Did ya hurt him a bit for fuckin off, an leavin us in the first place? Did ya warn im what would happen if he tells anyone?" "Course man. The most useful info was that he said there is someone in the picture who you probably need to know bout. Said this geezer was much more of a threat than him. Said you need to watch im, if you wanna keep hold of Lisa."

"Did he now. Go on, spill."

"His boss is the main man, apparently. Think about it, he said, cos he was gettin really scared by now and jus wanted it all to stop. Think bout it he said, my boss, Charlie's the one you want. The guy who rescued him, gave him a job. Apparently, this Charlie, is afta saving the world.

120

He reckons he might be afta Lise an all you know infactuation. He told me how he helped that other bitch Carla out. He's ya man, not fuckin me, he kept screamin. Them lot, them fuckin do gooders."

"Charlie, Charlie who?"

"Charlie Becker. He looks after the good Samaritans who sort out offenders, at this elp place up west. Get's em jobs an shit, that sorta thing."

"Okay, is that it."

"Yeah man. He ain't bin around long enough, to know much else."

"Ok Regis, you can bounce if ya want. Off you go now, good job. Now fuck off. I need to think bout what I'm gonna do bout this Charlie boy."

"Right. Well, ya know where I am, if ya need any more *work* done."

"Oh Yeah, I know how much yo enjoy all this pain un shit. See ya later, nipple boy. You fuckin freak." DJ sat for awhile, a spliff in one hand, while he poured a brandy for the other. He never could decide what his drug of choice was, so, he just continued with both. He was far too shrewd however to do any class A, or controlled drugs. No, DJ wanted some measure of control over his depraved life. Then it hit him. Charlie, Charlie Becker. It was that geezer Lisa ripped off not long ago! DJ had seen a lot of the documents, including the passport, before they were sold on. Or, did she really rip him off, the little bitch? Maybe they had faked it, teamed up. He wouldn't put it passed her, the way she'd been behaving lately. He sat, going over all the possible scenarios, demonstrating perfectly that; a little bit of knowledge is a dangerous thing. In this case, he was starting to think it might prove very dangerous indeed. Well, for Charlie Becker anyhow! By the time his overactive imagination had worked on the subject for awhile, his paranoia had got Lisa plotting against him with this Charlie Becker. Just how many dirty little secrets had she told this interfering little wanker? Worse of all, DJ started to feel his blood pressure rising as he thought about them both planning how to whisk Lisa away forever. Away from his control, his payroll and the role she played so perfectly. More importantly, how would he live with the true object of his secret affections removed from his presence forever?

* * * *

"Every action in our lives touches on some chord that will vibrate in eternity"
~Sean O'Casey.

Chapter 9
Guardian Angels on Trial - The Assembly!

There is nobody on earth or, for that matter, upon
any other place where lesser mortals dwell, who
compare, in any way shape or form;

To THE POWER.
The spiritual realm thereafter may be mistaken as
to be just as disorganised and chaotic in places as
your normal Saturday morning [written for the
benefit of human readers] spent Christmas
shopping in any one of your shopping malls.
Whilst you may see a certain semblance of
discipline and order; in the main, the spiritual
world is a very dangerous place to be!

The Allocation:
Human beings, unlike more civilised creatures,
are allocated 4 guardians', who are referred to in
their own realm as 'Those who are assigned.'
Those assigned to Charlie Becker;
Micah (Angel of the Devine)
Rashnu (Angel of Judgement)
Dina (Angel of Learning)
Gavreel (Angel of Peace)
These creatures are supervised, disciplined and
trained by 7 more of the same species of angelic
being, generally referred to as;

'Those who are Overseers.'
Overseers who were assigned to **Charlie Becker;**
Nathanial (Leading Angel)
 Also known as the Angel of fire
Urim (Angel of Light)
Zuriel (Angel of Harmony)
Murial (Angel of Emotions)
Sofiel (Angel of Nature)
Omniel (Angel of Oneness)
Mihael (Angel of Loyalty)
 The spiritual buck, as it were generally stops
with them, as far as referring back to another
more deadly rank of spiritual mortal. [Yes
indeed, all of the above have the ability to fear
annihilation, just as you yourself probably do!].
The individuals who hold the greater power are
those who are referred to as 'Those who report to
The Power' and of course please don't ever be
tempted to forget 'Those who advise, or serve
The Power' or 'Those who carry messages on the
four winds'. Contrary to popular myth among
those who seek such comforts, the aim of the
above is not to seek the good and all that is
praiseworthy within the cohorts that they oversee
and guide. No! The sole remit and the onerous,
nay thankless task of these creatures is to ensure
that those they represent fulfil every purpose in
life they are expected and indeed destined to
complete. It just so happens that to do so,
requires a propensity on the part of the often
clueless humans to have a soul that harbours such
virtues as integrity, a keen sense of justice and an

appreciation of the highest value placed [by the Power] on their human colleagues. As with most other spiritual dynamics; when one stumbles upon those values cited above, one will inevitably find an army of beings who are dedicated toward achieving the opposite goals. The reason for this is because the choicest of spiritual assets have always eluded the opposition and having found that they themselves couldn't possibly live up to any standard other than moral cowardice or fear, positively excel in opposing the efforts of others. This is where The Darkness comes in. For the moment however, all one really need to concern oneself with is the fact that Charlie Becker's death was a dreadful mistake and someone will have to pay!

The overseers were assembled once again. The seven who today sat in judgement, regarding the human Charlie Becker they would soon themselves be required to report to those who served in the presence of The Power. They still had a little more data to collect before they would be ready for that crucial meeting and tensions were running high.

The overseers had been carefully selected over many ages and each had a special role to play in the Ultimate Realm. It was still a source of great wonder that those living on the Earth knew and cared so very little about realms, other than their own. So much speculation and theorising over the centuries seemed to have confused them even more. Rather than serving to bring any real clarity to their understanding of the wider universe, it seemed the longer The Power allowed humans to exist, the more confused they grew. They still had no real wisdom relating to relatively common occurrences such as, the fact that those living beyond the Earth were capable of commuting fairly easily between the various different realms. Those who were chosen to be overseers had extensive experience of each realm and more significantly, each planets various species. Although they had never been fully human, they understood the ways of men, far more than men had any real comprehension of themselves, their capabilities, or indeed the worlds around them. The overseers summoned the beings who were assigned to Charlie Becker and who were reasonable for their mistake "Are you ready to submit your reports?" Rashnu (Angel of Judgement) responded for his group. "We, who are assigned to Charlie Becker, are ready to submit our report." "We are sincerely hoping you conferred and are ready to submit a joint report. We stress, you need to all agree on the detail. So much now may depend upon the outcome, not only of the mistake that was made, but also, upon how you attempt to rectify this situation. Do you understand? Do you all agree in the detail of your report?" "Yes, we all agree and we all stand by our report." "Go on." Rashnu (Angel of Judgement) continued with a lengthy discourse, explaining carefully, the events leading up to the time Charlie Becker attempted suicide. He carefully explained that Charlie's state of mind was becoming increasingly unsettled over quite a few 30 day periods and that he had been starting to plan how he might end his life on earth. "We were aware of the path that The Power had decreed for Charlie. We all knew that Charlie was close to straying from that path. We confess we didn't really believe he would end his life. However, the activity around him was increased and every time we saw any danger signs, one of us stayed very close. Charlie Becker has an incredibly strong human will. He has a very determined and resolute personality type. As you know, these characters can often challenge our ability to guide them. All of us remarked at the time that we were concerned Charlie wasn't hearing all of the messages we were trying to transfer into his consciousness. We sent repeated messages, warning him of the long term eternal dangers of suicide, reminding him of the work he still had to do, reinforcing the feelings of love he holds for Tommy. We worked tirelessly to convey hope to him. We are absolutely satisfied that we did all we could to reach him, through many different interventions and almost constant attention. As the night of his death approached, barely anything was getting through and so we went to those who are assigned to his sister Phoebe."

"Did you gain their full cooperation?"

"Yes they could see our attempts were failing to reach Charlie and they had their own concerns, due to the inconsistencies Phoebe was presenting to them. They had been committed to guiding her through her marriage years and she too was proving difficult to adjust." "Go on."

"Phoebe is also a very independent being. We believe that she did in fact hear the guidance of her assigned, but, they were constantly struggling against selfish intent and good intentions. Phoebe often started to travel down a planned and acceptable route, only later to double back on to a path of her own, serving her own agenda." "Is this why you reacted so slowly to Charlie's needs?" "Yes, to our own embarrassment, we trusted that Phoebe was going to carry through her visit to Charlie." "Well, why were you not on your guard considering all you knew of her inconsistencies?" "This directive would have caused Phoebe to arrive at Charlie's residence just as he was about to carry out his plans to leave the earth.""Are you telling us, you simply weren't watching her closely enough?"

"Phoebe has a tendency to change direction so quickly. She was actually on her way to see Charlie, in her car."

"Yes, but given the danger at hand, surely one of you should have been monitoring her every step, especially, as you were aware of her inconsistencies." "We contacted those who are assigned to Phoebe and they were struggling to get through to her, just as we were frustrated in our task. We even involved others who are assigned to neighbours of Charlie.

One gentleman's day had to be disrupted, as we attempted to intervene with events that caused him to lose his keys and knock on Charlie's door. We needed someone to disrupt Charlie's train of thought. The interruption was planned so that the human in question had to check if Charlie could find the number of a locksmith.

We tried all the tactics we were able and included as many as we could in all the realms, as we sought to interrupt Charlie Becker's evening." "Continue."

"We were moving very quickly and even went to the extreme measure of contacting one of our own kind who had previously been assigned to the Earth." "You went to Earth without first coming to gain the required permissions?"

"It was simply a question of time. We simply wouldn't have been able to access the correct level of authorities and concentrate on Charlie in time to save him! I understand we have cause for reproach and we are sorry. At least two of us thought we had the experience and the ability to do this safety. "This is a comprehensive report, however, I fear it will produce more questions than answers." "We proceeded to contact one of our own on Earth, who was geographically close to the Becker's residence. We contacted Michael who resides on earth as Dr Simon Williams. He was helpful and willing to do what he could. We were worried about the time we had remaining and so we asked Michael to make his way to Charlie Becker's flat and try to keep Charlie occupied until we were all sure he was safe. We explained that Charlie was in serious danger of wandering off his intended path. He was very helpful and responded immediately Michael is operating on the earth as one of their doctors. When we were able to make contact with him, he still had about seven of their kilometres to cross before he could reach Charlie.

Please try and appreciate, we were incredibly stretched. Even so, we still managed to continue with many attempts to speak into Charlie's inner self, not to mention all of our attempts to motivate his sister to visit. I have, of course given this issue a great deal of my attention, but, alas, no, I cannot think of any other activity we could have engaged in. It seems when humans decide to close their ears to the heavens, they become as deaf as it is possible to be." "Have you considered the lives of those who see experience may have been altered, since Charlie Becker was allowed to carry on?"

"Yes, of course, but obviously we can only take responsibility for the life of Charlie. We have been in contact with those who are assigned to humans Charlie has interacted with. There is a particular situation we are working on with the spirits who are assigned to a human called Lisa Baker. We cannot possibly understand at this time, to what degree Charlie has changed his own path, so it is almost impossible to determine how others have been disturbed. It won't be until we start to realise how radically Charlie has changed his outlook to life that we will even begin to understand how others may be being diverted from the path that has been predestined for them. Until we learn more, we believe it is far too early to add this information to our report."

"As your overseers we are well aware of the Lisa Baker issue". We are monitoring the situation closely, as this female, seems to be yet another headstrong subject, who may prove to be difficult to get through to. There have been a number of complaints raised with those who serve The Power, from a number of other teams. Some are saying that their humans are starting to act unpredictably, but more significantly, that they are acting out character with their normal behaviour. I do hope you all realise the gravity of this situation!" Yes we do and we are doing all we can to cooperate with all the teams who are in contact with us." As well as a sombre reminder of the realities of life as a spiritual messenger, serving in these capricious times, Nathanial was the only overseer who had ever experienced any period of time serving in the Ultimate Realm.
 He was, therefore, fully aware of the terrible events that could be unleashed if the Power decided punishment was required in the heavenly realms.

"You must realise that this situation is not going to be without certain consequences. The Power has one objective and one objective only. He will do all that is necessary to ensure the fulfilment of these wretched Human's and their destiny, no matter, it seems; how inconvenient or dangerous for the rest of us! Look; we have known for a while now that it looks pretty certain that The Power has grandiose plans for this race, so; remember, remember before all things, The Power appears to value this race above all others and although Charlie Becker is many things, he is also; very Human".

.

****

Scientists are peeping toms at the keyhole of eternity. ~Arthur Koestler

Chapter 10
Betrayal & a Beating

Lisa sat in the empty flat and none of the anger had subsided. If anything her rage had only increased as she sat and brooded upon her betrayal. She hadn't seen Carla now for a few days and even wondered if she had herself been spied at the H.E.L.P offices and Carla was strategically staying well out of the way. Initially, she had thought that some relief might come her way when she finally took the opportunity to scream and shout at her friend. But as she sat, she realized she would probably never be able to trust her flat mate again. There simply couldn't be an acceptable explanation, for Carla to talk her out of going to the charity offices together and be secretly meeting the brother she hadn't seen for six years. She was fidgety to the point of distraction, twirling her cigarettes endlessly and moving around on the sofa as though she was dealing with a particularly bad dose of thrush. Determined to end all concept of fingernails for evermore, she had successfully gnashed them down until she had produced nothing more than bloody stumps. It was becoming apparent she was also now incapable of making any trip away from her place of brooding that didn't involve visiting the bathroom or searching for another cigarette packet. Lisa, despite all the crap and abuse DJ and his cronies had heaped upon her for year upon year, had never felt so paralyzed by anger and confusion; she thought she would either go mad or burst with the pain she felt. She realized she cared, she realized she loved these people and so, how much harder it was to be betrayed by them. She knew it was time to fly, time to make a statement that she was no longer willing to be a victim. It had just been possible to cope with the concept of being trapped while she had allies, but now, alone, the rules were beginning to change rapidly. Carla, of all people, she thought she could trust. Mickey! It didn't make any sense to her at all, why he would bother to contact her and offer to help after so long, only to turn out to be another person destined to let her down. Why would he promise to help and then be a part of the reason Carla had tried to dissuade her from visiting the charity. It was finally all too much. Her two greatest allies were not trustworthy and Carla's deception had destroyed all the faith she had left in human nature. She was more determined than ever to escape, more determined than ever to look after number one. Where the hell had Carla got to, she didn't even have the satisfaction of being able to rip her eyes out!

* * * *

Friday at last! At least they come around as quickly as Monday mornings. I'll have to think about this dilemma quite soberly, so no; don't pick up a bottle on the way home. I have got to at least decide what I'm going to do. I make my way slowly out of London. I learned long ago, that it's unproductive to rush around and expect to be able to move quickly through the crowds. I still find myself getting frustrated and end up hating the world and everyone in it. I'm slightly tempted to push a tourist down the escalator, when, despite the constant reminders over the loud speaker, to keep to the right, if standing and walk down the left side, she just stood there looking gormless! She had no awareness at all, even though it was bloody obvious everyone else was doing something different. Rather than the preferred option of stabbing her violently in the neck, I settled with just reaching her on the escalator and then startling the living crap out of her, by shouting -EXCUSE ME - in her ear as I barged by. Why do I have to be such a horrible, disagreeable wanker? I had started off my journey almost smug in the knowledge that I was perfectly calm and had handled the events of the last few days with surprising tranquillity. As well as the normal stresses of the week, I had dealt quite well with the shock of seeing Lisa on Monday. I had, after all, done nothing illegal, I hadn't broken any codes of working practice, as, Lisa hadn't been a client on that fateful evening

of, well, I was going to say Love, but, love had
very little to do with most of the things we did
that night. No, I had handled it all very well.
However as soon as even the slightest pressure
was applied, i.e. someone blocking my way on
the escalator, it was immediately obvious, I was
still in recovery. Maybe, I will get that bottle,
weak bastard. Okay, so, my dilemma was easy, I
could go to the Police and do my duty to society,
slightly reducing the risk of some other poor
unsuspecting old idiot getting burned. This
scenario obviously leaves me wide open to the
humiliation of everyone at work potentially
discovering by grubby little secret, but that's
unlikely, as I doubt Lisa would still want to work
with us when she discovers the reality of the
moral calibre of the staff. This kind of thing
doesn't exactly breed trust and openness between
client and worker! When I get home I will sit,
and I won't move until I have decided whether to
take the Police option or, risk humiliation in a
different guise. After all, I could simply present
myself to Lisa and promise to butt out while she
works with Chloe, giving her further assurances
that our little secret would remain confidential.
This option would be brokered in the vein hope
that maybe, just maybe, Lisa could be prized
away from a life of crime. Of course I ran the
risk of the Police catching up with Lisa
independently. Then there could be the
uncomfortable issue of, why the hell didn't I file
a report, stating I was working with someone I'd

reported to them a few weeks earlier. I wasn't even sure that didn't constitute some kind of crime, probably something like withholding vital evidence. Even worse, there was the very real possibility that some smarmy young PC would be staring back at me from an interrogation room in a few weeks, blaming me for a string of crimes Lisa had subsequently committed. This would all be possible because I had decided to play the naïve, caring, social worker type, charity worker who did more damage than good with their misguided care, concern and advice. Plus, where the hell had Mickey pissed off too? I had spent a good deal of my time between stumbling upon Lisa and Chloe, wondering where the hell Mickey had got to. Who just disappears from work without a word? I was pretty sure I was going to give him a bollocking for not letting me know he was off work because he was sick. I was struggling between, when to notify HR and telling them he had just disappeared and genuinely caring whether he was okay or not. He'd been very reliable before, his work record was good; he didn't usually take the piss. Maybe I would pop round to his flat later to satisfy myself he was at least alive.

Bottle in hand, I approached my communal car park, which only reminded me of the lack of a car sitting in my designated space, anger again bubbling up to the surface. That bloody BMW was the only item of any material value I had managed to salvage from eleven years of marriage. I kicked an empty Stella that had been tossed out of the communal garbage area by last nights furry nocturnal visitors. God, there were more foxes round here than rats, and the rats were starting to just look at us all, like we were the invaders. I felt like a trespasser as I approached the bin area assigned to them, the squirrels and the flies. I passed my communal garden and entered my communal front door and looked through the communal post pigeon holes. Excellent, another letter in the long line of misery, issued forth from Caroline's solicitors. What the fuck does she want now? The cars gone! Panic seized me, as I reached the front door to my flat, which I'd noticed was already open. I rushed back down stairs, as I'd remembered there was a spade near to the communal salt bin everyone used to dig their cars out when it snowed. Cautiously, I crept up to the door and with my usual lack of discretion, I let rip. "Who the fuck's in there?" My high pitched, anxious voice wasn't sounding at its most intimidating.

"Me bro' I'm in here."

."Okay, well who the fuck are you?"

"Sorry to bust in, but I figured it was high time we had a little chat."

"You needed a fucking chat! You've broken my fucking door." Somehow, I thought I would sound more aggressive if I swore a lot.

"Sorry man, come on, lets talk bout Lisa."

I was stunned, who the hell was this, talking to

me about Lisa?

The bastard had fooled me by using my curiosity against my better judgment. I walked in; flexing the grip on my small and probably ineffective spade. I turned into the living room and was surprised to see just one man standing in my flat. I had assumed there would be more, but looking at him, I guessed he could look after himself. I wouldn't have thought he was sweating about needing any buddies to protect him from the likes of me. I did feel slightly pissed off that he assumed he could walk into my flat and violate my personal space,

Wreak my door and risk my wrath without any help whatsoever. Then it hit me, literally. The realization that this intruder wasn't actually alone, hit me at the very same time the bastard behind the door hit me. I just had the time to make a half turn, when he clubbed me. As I turned, he caught me awkwardly, a dull thud, on the side of the neck, causing me to hit the deck like a sack of spuds, bang, I was down, crunch, a kick to my rib cage, crack, shit that must have been a break. I passed out briefly and rallied to the realization I was being man handled onto a chair. I didn't know whether to concentrate more on the fact I couldn't breathe, the pain, or what other delights these uninvited guests had in store for my evening's entertainment. I started to exaggerate the pain by wincing dramatically, so they might assume I probably couldn't take any more.

"Mate, chill man, we ain't even hittin on ya bad
yet, relax man, we jus wanna chat."
"Okay, what do you want?"
"Are you fuckin my little Lisa?"
Okay, good, straight to the point. At this rate I
could be in casualty by nine! "What." I
whimpered. He couldn't be her Father, he was
the wrong colour.
"No sadly, I'm not fucking anyone, not regularly
anyway." This at least raised the semblance of a
smile across his hard as nails looking
countenance. The main man nodded toward his
mate and I was immediately grabbed by both
arms. As they were wrenched behind me I nearly
passed out, as I struggled to breathe. My
assailant didn't even notice and just pulled until I
was red in the face, breathless and completely
vulnerable to whatever these two big bastards
eventually wanted to do to me. Now I was half
sitting, half elevated in the air, arms stretched
behind me, in bloody agony, breathless and now
being stood over by this big tosser who had
decided I was forming some kind of unsavoury
relationship with what could well have been his
misses.
"Look this cud be real easy my friend."
"Oh good, cos I was thinking you weren't my
new neighbor, round here to borrow a cup full of
sugar." The grip on my arms tightened and to
make a shitty situation even worse, the main
man's face was about a centimetre away from
mine and his breath smelt like crap.

"Stand him up."

I noticed their careful lack of the use of names, although, I couldn't understand why they were quite happy for me to see their faces. I was thinking that I'd probably seen too many films, when it struck me, they were probably going to kill me anyway, therefore, it wouldn't really matter how much I'd clocked their pretty little knurled up features.

I was pulled upward, the boss man rising with me, so that our eyes were always at the same height. However, by the time we were standing, he had had to stop his rise and remain crouched and bent in front of me, due to the fact he was at least 6' 2". I topped out at 5' 7" so it was a significant crouch. Just when I thought I couldn't take anymore pain, feeling my cracked rib burning into my chest cavity, the man standing in front of me suddenly turned very nasty. The first punch was aimed straight at my midriff. I reached forward with my whole body and tried to twist in the vein hope of altering his trajectory, to have less of an impact on my gut. I was obviously just proving my inexperience around the ignoble art of street fighting. The resulting effect was far worse than if I had just taken the blow. My arms had now become more wrenched; my rib cage now felt like it would actually explode, propelling shattered bones out of my back. The twist I had just attempted had caused the blow to be nearer the cracked rib than it would have been if I had just kept still and accepted my beating. I now found myself looking for the first opportunity to throw up. As I was hit, the main guy's ugly assistant released my arms and I slumped to the floor. The second blow, very nearly caused me to lose consciousness. It was a kick to the head and it sent my head back in a whiplash movement. I found myself listening out for another crack, as I fully expected to hear my neck break. I wanted myself to be angry and use all the adrenalin I could muster to either get out of the flat altogether, or, better still, in my wildest superhero fantasy's, turn the table on my aggressor and win the day. The reality was, I could now taste the bitter iron tang of blood in my mouth and I was dizzy, desperately trying to hold on to consciousness. The superhero option was looking less and less likely. These boys had obviously done this kind of thing before; I however, had definitely not had anything like this done to me before.

Once they were satisfied I wasn't capable of any kind of recovery that would threaten their dominance of me, they relaxed again and both sat down. I rolled around on the floor awhile, again, trying to give the impression of, leave me the fuck alone now. But even that was too bloody painful, so, after taking on the appearance of a landed carp for a few moments, I just lay still and tried not to whimper.

"I gonna say this once, cos, I don't wanna ave the trouble of commin back to finish the job."

I wanted this whole ordeal to end and so I motioned him to talk, as to indicate my compliance and unconditional surrender. The quicker route available for me to access the bottle of Jack Daniels anaesthesia was the route I was definitely committed to taking.

"You my friend, are gonna keep away from Lisa, okay, this is not someink I'm prepare to negotiate, or discuss and I certainly ain't gonna talk bout joint custody, so, you gonna convince me, in the next twenny seconds, you gonna stay away from my woman, boy."

"Well sure, I'm not going to say anything else am I. You've caught me at a slight actual bodily harm type scenario."Again with the inappropriate bravado I told myself in my head to; shut the fuck up Becker!

"Okay, boy, but you really do not eva wanna see me again, so be aware."

They looked like it was time to leave and the main man rose, sneered at me, and then, spat on me, just in case I wasn't feeling vulnerable enough. He then declared, with unnecessary repartition, that he wouldn't expect to ever hear of me communicating with Lisa again, as he really didn't want the bother of another visit. Oh yes and he got another kick to my groin in, just as a little leaving present. He seemed to enjoy that one more than the rest, probably because it made my face turn purple. As they left, the man in attendance, leaned over and very gently picked up the bottle of Jack from the corner of the room

143

and said, "Cheers bro." Bastard!
When I had stopped feeling sick, violated and not
to mention very sorry for myself, I quickly
surmised that Lisa had whipped my wallet, along
with my identity and address, round to her boss
on the fateful evening. It seemed that night of
pleasure was proving increasingly impossible to
forget. The stolen wallet scenario was the only
explanation I could come up with that made any
sense out of the fact my address was now
apparently known by South London's
underworld. Little did I know there were other
people involved in this dangerous little escapade
to consider and moreover, be aware of! Then,
the anger, not to mention considerable pain
started to really kick in. I limped pathetically
round the corner to the local Shop smart all night
convenience store, to acquire another bottle of
Jack's finest medicine. Who the fuck did they
think they were, walking in here, throwing their
weight around. God, my body had never hurt as
badly and in so many different places, ever
before!

* * * *

"After we lost our son, we started to decorate the
house a lot more. We wanted him to see it from
heaven"
~Mike Gutierrez.

Chapter 11
DJ Tightens his Grip

Mickey had been more or less left on a concrete floor in DJ'S basement until the wounds had at least stopped weeping. The basement was huge and exactly what you might expect from a house boasting four garages, an indoor swimming pool and a games room. On the rare occasions when the pain had subsided and the relentless itching had taken over, there were moments he had used to observe his surroundings. The instances when DJ's minions had flooded the room with light to bring their morsels of food and water were very helpful in the pursuit to discover if there was any vague chance of escape. Mickey had wondered why the basement seemed to have been sectioned off. He was tied and the top his left arm had been numb now for what must have been about twenty four hours. He didn't think he had any major injuries, but his right knee hurt like hell when he attempted to apply any weight to it. He could remember being thrown onto the ground from the table and smashing his knee on the concrete. It was difficult to gauge the damage, due to his lack of movement. All he could think about was the pain and the uncertainty of not knowing what else these fuck wits had in store was starting to seriously distress him. Mickey wasn't exactly the anxious type, but he'd suffered greatly during his short life, not least at the hands of his loathsome father and he often thought that his mind might be the faculty to cave in, way before they could break his body. This particular situation was unfamiliar to him, as, even his bully of a Father had been fairly predictable with his sadistic games and various punishments. The worst of the suffering was the thirst; his captors had no idea how much water a body needed on a daily basis just to be able to function properly. The heat wave the nation had been enjoying over the last few weeks or so just meant that for Mickey, he was lying on a hard, rough, concrete floor, hurting, worrying and sweating profusely, to the point that, he thought he would eventually pass out forever and his ordeal would be over. The last visit from the zoo keepers who had been assigned to feed him had brought a new occurrence. When they had left the sandwich and glass of lukewarm water, they changed their usual routine, by visiting what seemed to be at least two other rooms in the basement area. A chill that was vastly exaggerated by the fact that he wasn't exactly feeling at his best ran through his soul, with the thought that these animals may well have been keeping other prisoners down there, in adjacent rooms to him. All of the sectioned off rooms must have been sound proofed if this was the case, as he never heard a sound, at least until his feeding captors had moved from room to room more recently. He had been convinced he had heard other voices and whimpers over the last couple of days, when the doors had briefly been opened. Mickey had been out cold, or feverish, for the majority of the time he had spent in the depths of DJ's house. He was well aware that some of the ghostly noises that had disturbed him could well have been mere echoes from the wailing in his own tortured head. Today however, as far as he could tell day and night apart, was slightly different with the first visit of the day. After they had left his food, his visitors went straight out again and came back with three objects, before continuing on with their rounds. They didn't say a word to him and he had only ever got any reaction at all on the occasion he had dared to ask for more water. This request was met with a short sharp smack from the back of a very large hand across his face. Consequently I hadn't asked for anything else. He also wasn't about to give them the satisfaction of asking them what the mirror, the chair and the table lamp were for. They had plugged the table lamp into an extension lead and positioned the chair just within sitting distance, allowing for the length of the ropes that bound him. The mirror was leaned against a supporting post in the basement, ensuring the light of the lamp was adequately positioned to aid his view. Well at least he could use the mirror to inspect his wounds. The only mystery was that this was obviously what they wanted. He remembered the boasts of the one they called Regis, he drew pictures did he! More fear swept over Mickey, it must have been a proper work of art for them to want to show it off to him. Curiosity finally took a sharp grip on a prisoner, who had been fretting for days whether his once princely frame had been mutilated beyond repair. With the little strength he could muster Mickey started to drag himself over to the chair. He felt light headed but he knew this wasn't going to take long, as, he was already stripped down to a new pair of boxer shorts, he assumed they had applied to him while he had been unconscious. At least the heat and resulting dehydration was marginally better than if they had thrown me down here in the freezing cold weather, he thought, as he heaved himself on to the chair. He blinked and wiped the sweat from his eyes so that he could focus and then, with horror, witnessed what had been inflicted upon the perfectly formed physique that up until that point had been without blemish. He knew in an instant, his body had been ruined forever. He also knew that something at that very same moment in time, snapped in his psyche that would also prove to be irreparable.

He stared for what must have been five minutes before he could believe what Regis had done to him. The right nipple area was now just a bloody lump and from what he could make out, his entire torso had been segmented into six box shapes. There were strange shapes that, due to the lack of healing, really could have been anything in each box, apart from the very last box, which he could just make out. The final box just had a tiny question mark placed above what essentially was a blank square. It looked like a child's comic that had been drawn by a psychopath. It was impossible to make out the gruesome story being told by the boxes because he was dirty and caked in dried blood. Mickey had the distinct impression that the question mark in the last box indicated the end of the story was yet to be decided. What was blatantly obvious however was that the effects would be permanent. He had remembered an intense stinging, that had turned into a burning sensation every few minutes during the ordeal. This sensation had been constant in between moments of losing consciousness and Mickey had also remembered seeing a blue, green mixture mingling with his blood as it dripped to the floor. The bastard had crudely poured and rubbed ink into his wounds. It was the cartoon from hell and was so coarse and irregular; it could never have been described as a tattoo. There was more. Nausea gripped him again as he looked further down toward his lower abdomen. Just below the cartoon like boxes, the word JUDAS had been carved into his skin, written as a comment on those who choose a life outside of the BEA boys. For the first time since he was a small boy, Mickey sat and wept.

* * * *

One night of lust and my life was starting to go down a little path of its own and if there was one thing that really galled me, it was not being in control. I'd been left with the same dilemma I'd been forced to ponder even before my visitors had caused my head to ring with pain and even more confusion. I let the choices run through my tired brain once again. I could butt out, by allowing Chloe to do her thing and help the girl into some kind of positive life choice. Lisa need never know I was anything other than one of her ex victims, fast becoming just a distant memory. But surely I had a greater responsibility toward society? As I thought it through, I realized there was a significant part of my consciousness that was screaming at me and fighting every good intention to aid Lisa into a better future. This part of me ached for revenge, moralizing over and over, considering the countless others who might be saved the indignity I had suffered at the hands of this reckless and immoral young person. I caught my pompous expression in the bathroom mirror, as I paced my flat, as if searching every corner for the answers I was seeking. You hypocritical fool, you hypocritical *old* fool. If you hadn't been so eager to unleash your hormones with gay abandon on someone young enough to be your daughter, you wouldn't be sitting here nursing a cracked rib and an even more splintered ego.

By the time I'd completed a dodgy makeshift repair on my door frame, watched a good couple of hours of crap late night TV, finished off the JD and brooded solemnly for what I considered to be an acceptable time, I knew. I knew what I had become convinced of, was the only course of action I could ever live with, for good or ill.

* * * *

"K, Mickey, it's time we let you loose."
It had been a week since Regis had so sadistically demonstrated his artistic prowess upon Mickey's perfect young flesh. The agony was now mainly etched into Mickey's psyche, as the physical pain and irritation had largely subsided.
"You worked out wat Regis drew yet?"
As the blood had dried and started to fall away from his flesh, Mickey had indeed worked it out. The grisly story etched into Mickey's frame was a representation of a cleverly fashioned hunting scene. To be more precise, the pictures depicted a cartoon caricature of a big tiger like cat, chasing a rather small and pathetic looking animal that probably looked more like a deer, than anything else. DJ and Regis often remembered sitting transfixed as small boys in front of the TV devouring the imagery of the big cat chases over the Serengeti and marvelling over the power and magnificence of these majestic animals. They would both sit open mouthed in wonder, watching how the very pinnacle of the food chain could totally govern over their environment. As they grew, these images formed the basis of the only tangible aspiration these lads had ever possessed in the harsh world they'd been abruptly thrust into. They knew from a very early age, that their only real desire was to utterly dominate the world about them. The giant cats they scrutinized so carefully would chase endlessly, relentlessly and the images always ended in violence. The crudely slashed boxes

were hardly up to the standard of a master artist, but Mickey could still make out the conclusion of the chase, the final leap into the air, as the cat, in the last but one frame pounced to end its prey. "Yeah, I worked it out."

"Gud, an so you'll know the last box is a work in progress right. If we don't have time to fuck about with our paintin box next time son, I'll jus, put a bullet through the last box, if need be, ok." Mickey didn't answer as he was trying to work out if it were at all possible to launch himself at DJ's throat and keep ripping at it until he could be certain DJ had reached hell. Alas, he had no more energy than to let out a shallow and resigned acknowledgement of DJ's threat.

"Oh an don't try and get any of that shit removed. It jus ain't gonna appen boy, the ink is Regis special concoction and it's gone in deep. He learned bout it on a trip to India in the eighties, burns stain into the skin, far more potent, an deeper, than tattoo ink, so, leave it be unless you wanna die of fuckin shock. Now, I gonna tell you how the little deer can stay breathin. How the last box can see little Bamby escape the big nasty pussy." DJ threw his head back and laughed a deep satisfying, raucous cackle. "Your gonna do two things for me boy." "Two?" "You, my small and bloodied little deer, are gonna make sure Lisa stops all thought of leaving our way of life. Your job is to keep her focus." Mickey's voice was weak and he had nothing left in the tank. He felt delirious and

153

wondered if he'd contracted blood poisoning.
All he could think was to get out of the basement
and his mind was slowly starting to get away
from him as it tried to escape the reality it was
faced with.

"How the hell?"

"Not my problem, my little Mickey boy. But, I
do ya a deal ok. If I don't hear of any more talk
of my property runnin away, in say three, four
months, I might give ya somthin wat you want."

"I just want to get outa here, please, honest come
on; I can't fuckin take much more."

"I'll tell ya wen you had enough." Once again,
DJ couldn't contain himself and a hellish cackle
echoed through the basement.

Mickey finally blacked out from the sheer effort
involved in having to concentrate, as DJ
continued baiting him.

Tweedle ugly mug and Tweedle thug, the two
keepers of the desperate, entered the basement, as
if by intuition they had realized it was time for
them to make an appearance. They didn't enter
the darkness alone. As Mickey slowly came too,
he squinted and tried to focus against the light,
allowed in at the doorway. The silhouette in the
doorway between the two hulks was
unmistakable. Mickey practically screeched;
hope draining away from him as rapidly as he
knew he was losing his grip on his mental
faculties. He wondered what more they could do
to him. "Carla, my God, Carla, baby, what the?"

"Hey man, she bin keepin you company most of

da time you bin here. Jus next door, but don't worry, we keeping this one safe. We gonna keep her safe, *if* you look after Lisa. Like I say, I wanna be content; you will convince our sweet little Lisa that flight ain't no option."

Carla looked weak and just stood looking pleadingly at Mickey. She began welling up with tears, but she had no energy to cry.

"Okay, okay, I'll convince Lisa okay."

"Yeah we thought you'd say that. You gotta choice boy, your sister, or your lover, choose lover and you two get to live, cos you know we'll find you. We ain't letting you get away again Mickey boy and she ain't goin nowhere till I'm happy. Choose to help sister escape me, an well, before we do for your woman, I'll let Regis loose on you. He don't like pictures he can't finish."

In his anxiety, Mickey had forgotten DJ mentioned he wanted two jobs completing on his behalf. DJ started to walk toward the door, stopped and looked back at Mickey. He paused as if trying to decide whether Mickey was going to come through. Then he announced; you gonna also make sure Mr. Charlie Becker, gets sacked from that pussy fuckin job he's got. Put him off seein Lisa, make his life miserable, fuckin kill the little bastard if needed. This charity thing down west is too good at what it does, an it needs weakenin. Make sure he's gone, an soon, I need to finish the bastard off, I'm pretty sure beatins ain't gonna deter a do gooder like im, might even make im' more determined. Losin his job be a

different deal for this mother, an it might jus put im off, putting his beak in business he shouldn't." Mickey was too dazed to argue, wonder anymore at the madness, or complain. Carla had been dragged away from him, in fits of screeching and tears to her underground cell. In a last flurry of bravado DJ turned to his two muscle bound puppets, waved one arm toward the broken young man, and said;
"Get that shit outa ere."

* * * *

"May you get to heaven a half hour before the devil knows your dead"
~Irish Book of Blessings.

Chapter 12
Evil comes for Help

Where the hell do they come from? And why do they all gravitate toward us? I'd just managed to get to work, after, having to practically wrestle an emergency appointment from the local GP's receptionist. God, I thought, where do they breed these heartless bitches? It was all she could do to raise her head from the computer monitor. She was staring at it, as if it contained all the answers, to all the mysteries, ever created by the universe. I needed my chest strapped up and some bloody good pain killers, as, I'd only managed about an hour's sleep. It was touch and go, they wanted to send me to St George's hospital, but I'd convinced them I was capable of getting there myself if I developed any breathing problems. I didn't bother to tell the incredibly ugly nurse, I was already struggling to breath and had hardly slept. I wondered if the bulging growth on her left cheek was a mole or a wart. As she brutishly manhandled my arm to take my blood pressure, I wondered if there had ever been a time in her lifetime when she'd dressed up like a princess, or whether she had any children. I couldn't imagine any circumstance whereby, anyone would ever want to make love to her.

Being at work was a relief and the perfect distraction from the whole Lisa issue. When I was just getting to the point of maybe thinking there was normality to be found in the world, I had to meet with this tosser. H.E.L.P. often attracted organizations that wanted to be associated with it. We had a strong brand name, as; after all we were the best specialist workers with ex-offenders in London. The downside was that on occasion, they came in their droves to work in partnership with us. The challenge was to separate those who could genuinely add value to what we did and those idiots who just needed an extra injection into their own coffers, via our good name.

"Hello Mr. King, is it?"

"Well, Reverend King actually, but you can call me Jed." "Well Jed, I saw your emails to our personnel department, you were quite persistent. I agreed to see you, but I'm afraid I can't see too much overlap between our organizations and as you should already know, we can't be seen to align ourselves with one particular religion over all the others. Tell me about AT-ONE-MENT, is it?""Well Mr. Becker." "Call me Charlie. A young apprentice interrupted at this point with our coffees and already I was concerned about my gut feeling to Jed. All I could think, as I clocked his phony smile and his phony cheap suit, was, oh god, this is going to drag on and on and then, after I've sat and listened to his endless phony waffle,

I'm still going to have to fob him off.

"Well Charlie, we at Atonement believe in second chances. We work with a mix of different clients, referred to us from all sorts of agencies and we certainly are not, despite your inference, associated with main stream Christianity." He went on......... "We are increasingly working with more and more ex-offenders as they struggle to readjust to life outside of an institution."

"Yes, I see, however, you are a reverend, so just what is the connection to religion?"

"Well, we sort of disconnected from main stream Church a long time ago, as the elders and I decided to seek a purer truth."

"Umm, go on."

"We are a community; we are a haven for those who need comfort, support, and religious instruction."

"Oh, tell me more about the religious instruction and with respect Jed, I'm still struggling to understand where you think H.E.L.P. might fit in and why you've travelled all the way from Brighton to talk to me about what you do. Sorry, but I'm just being honest and would hate to think I'm wasting your time."

"Well, we thought you might want to consider referring your younger clients to us, you know, those who need a little more pointing in the right direction. You probably have quite a few who, you just don't know what to do with, surely?"

"We are quite careful who our referral partners are Mr. King, err, Jed and to be honest and please, if I'm wrong about this, please forgive me, but it sounds like you, well, it sounds like you're almost recruiting. We concentrate in helping ex-offenders find jobs, work experience placements, self employment opportunities even

159

voluntary work. We help our client's access rehab facilities and carry out very specialist mental health and substance misuse treatments. On top of all that we support and help our clients access long term accommodation opportunities. Now Jed, are you or your organization involved with any of these services?" My chest was starting to hurt! I thought my cracked rib was going to poke out!

It usually takes me a little longer to offend people, but Jed was already starting to adopt an expression indicating either offence, or constipation. Little strained beads of sweat appeared on his furrowed brow as he desperately tried to convince me that my organization should be randomly handing over a proportion of our caseload to him on the basis they will live in a community very near to Brighton and receive his special brand of spiritual guidance. To top it off, he thought it would be a great idea to focus on the young ones. I was starting to be proper freaked out by this creature! I'd also realized by now that Atonement was some sort of sect or cult and in my book, Mr. Jed King was the worst kind of predator. I always like to let people feel they've had there say. This is so that when I finally show them the door they know I've taken the time to fully hear them and completely understand all the reasons why I have utterly rejected them. I let Jed carry on while I nodded and smiled an insincere smile every now and then. However, nearing the end of his exhaustive discourse on the merits of communal living, with spiritual guidance, he said something that I knew I would have to follow up on. "You know Charlie; we really are committed to our people." Our people? With every passing word, he confirmed my suspicions of him and his kind. "Well," he continued… "We have, as you know, been in contact with you now for awhile and having not heard anything, my personal assistant Camille happened to be in London about a week ago. She took the opportunity to drop by and see if she could see you herself and maybe set a meeting up. Now, the point I'm making is this," I was glad there was a point, as I was starting to count the number of pin stripes on his suit jacket, I was so irritated and disinterested in this horrible little man's agenda, I feared it wouldn't be long before I would be compelled to show my true feelings."The point I am making, is that even after a very short time in your reception area, Camille started talking to a delightful young lady. Can't say I remember her name now but Camille will surely know. Anyway, that's not the point; the point is that this young lady was very open indeed to what Camille had to say about our community, took literature and has indeed been in contact with us very recently. Now, Mr. Becker, does this not clearly show that there are young people out there with no hope, who would just grab at the opportunity we offer. First family some of them would have ever had, I'm sure of it. Now, what do you think Charlie? Can we work together Mr. Becker?"

Mr. King really didn't want to know what I thought of that and I spared him from it. Long experience had taught me to be beyond reproach no matter how provoked I was by the many people who crossed my path in the course of the day. I made a few repeat affirmations that we didn't work with groups who represent whatever religious stance they decided to take. I remained calm and was able to finally lead him back to the reception area, ending our meeting as quickly as I could. I did however, make sure I saw him leave the building with my own eyes, fearful of him running around the establishment recruiting young virgins, ripe for kidnap and sacrifice back home at his weird and wonderful cult, in sunny Brighton. When he had gone, I crept back to reception and asked when someone introducing themselves as Camille from a group called Atonement had previously been in."Hi Charlie." Fantastic another was on reception *-filling in -* She was friendly and would go out of her way to investigate for me. The down side was that she wasn't over bright, so, there would be about five minutes of fifing about and a lot of…"Oh God, yeah, no, hang on that was Monday, hang on, err, yeah, I'm sure it was then, oh no probably not, hang on a min'…That sort of thing! But, I was sure she would come through for me eventually. She did. "Tuesday the forth, there it is. Ms. Camille Parks – Atonement – No parking space required." "Thanks; does it say what time?"

"She didn't have an appointment, but we made her sign in and out - in 11.15am - out 11.50am."
"Bless ya, thanks again .""That's okay Charlie anytime."Alarm bells were ringing all over my head, as I was seriously concerned " one or more of our clients had been given the Atonement treatment. A lot of the people we worked with were extremely vulnerable and scared to death of the prospect of having to adjust to independent life. I was pretty sure there were quite a few of them who might fall for the whole community, love one another routine. The next thing they would know, would be that they would find themselves drafted into a mass wedding and then, on honeymoon with a carefully selected herd of barnyard animals. I fucking hate cults!

Another poignant question rolling around my head, was, "Has no one heard from Mickey at all yet?" I must find time to go round his flat, try and find out what's going on with him.

Then, it hit me! Nooooo, surely not, how could I have missed that, he never mentioned a sister, Mickey Baker - Lisa Baker – no - and anyway, same surname could be a coincidence. In the meantime, something more pressing was on my . agenda.

* * * *

"Chloe, when's your next appointment with Lisa Baker?""Haven't heard from her Charlie, she probably isn't ready yet, you know how it goes."
"What number have you got for her Chlo?"
"Chloe sent over a post it note with Lisa's mobile number on it and of course it was different from the one I had once used in my ridicules dalliance with Ms. Baker."
"Chloe, give her a call will you. I know we don't usually chase people, but, she looked vulnerable. Just give her a, how you doin type of call, would you, just to check in."
"Sure Charlie, you old softy."
If people didn't stop referring to me as old soon, I was going to do some damage!
I suddenly had a vivid flashback to when Lisa was pealing her flimsy underwear away from her tight little body. I wondered what Chloe would think, if she were privy to the secret, private, video rewind button in my head. I accessed my outlook calendar and went straight to Chloe's shared diary. I instinctively knew what I was going to see and bingo; there it was - Meeting Rm.28 Lisa Baker / Chloe Arnold – 11.30am – Smack bang in the middle of, Tuesday 4 July 2011. I knew that the extra fifteen minutes she had been in the building, plus, the time Chloe might have been late picking Lisa up from reception, was plenty of time for one of those zealous parasites to do their thing. Lisa hasn't contacted Chloe and mad Mr. King had said the targeted young person had been in touch with the

loony group since Camille the evangelist had done her worst. What's more, we had, not only one Baker missing, but two. I was becoming more and more convinced there was a connection. It did cross my mind, the guilt I was feeling about positively devouring Lisa's body with a desert spoon, plus, visits from Johnny gangland resulting in my broken ribs, might have been heightening my paranoia. But Mickey had disappeared and Lisa had more than likely been engaged in a conversation with a zealous religious nut. Paranoid or not, I thought there was enough here, to at least warrant a little more scrutiny.

* * * *

Lisa was all packed. There wouldn't be much to carry and there certainly wouldn't be any trace of her intentions left behind. For once she praised the fact that working for DJ had generated so much ready cash and possessions, she'd never had any need for bank accounts or hire purchase. Cash had always been converted into goods, as swiftly as she was now planning to convert her life from slavery into freedom. Even the rent documents were in Carla's name. Brighton was far enough and if the nice lady she'd meet was reliable, she could disappear forever if she wanted too. The wrap on the door sounded desperate and the sight that met her as she looked through the tiny peephole looked equally fraught. "Mickey". She let him in due to the distressed look he had about him, despite her feelings of anger, abandonment and betrayal.

"What's up babe?"

"You look like shit Mickey, what's happening?"

"Had a fight with a combine harvester babe, look, I just wanted to make sure you were okay that's all. Miss my sis don't I and don't want to lose her again, is all."

"Oh Mickey, it's a pity this took six years." She was only half joking.

After enquiring if he was in trouble and surprisingly finding herself feeling slightly maternal, rushing around making coffee and making sure he had an ash tray, Lisa decided to test the relationship a little.

"So Mickey, mate, you seeing anyone?"

"No!" He shot back far too quickly.

"Oh, what about anyone you used to know, you know, from the old life, you caught up with anyone else yet?" "Why the third degree babe, all I'm worried about is you stickin around babe, like I said, I need my old sis, must be getting sentimental in me old age."

"Come on Mickey, tell me. If we're gonna get to know one another we gotta be honest, yeah?"

"No, babe, I'm not seein anyone, an, nah, I'm not seein anyone from the old days, Lisa's anger was lurking just below the surface and she was amazed someone such as Mickey, who was so streetwise, wouldn't have guessed by now, she didn't believe a word! Okay babe."

"Okay Mickey, just one more, where you workin, come on, what you doin and don't tell me you're a spaceman or 007's stuntman, what you doin, really, you know, for a job?"

"I work for a delivery firm in London, that's it, that's me, just moved back from the North, disappeared there for awhile, until I was satisfied no one but you in London would remember me, yeah just delivery, got a truck an everythin."

Lisa's rage finally started to bubble and rise to the surface. She had spent her whole life taking shit from someone or another. There was no way she was going to take it from a brother who had just mysteriously turned up and now seemed to be talking a load of double talk and bullshit.

"You lyin bastard Mickey. Why do you need to lie to me? I saw you, you, you fuckin twat.

What were you doin at the charity offices? Delivering fucking packages? From what I could see, you were gettin a big fat package, from that bitch; I used to call my mate. And, what were you doing snoggin Carla anyway? Hey and how long have you been fuckin her? Why you just suddenly turn up in the first place? Why, why, why Mickey?" She hadn't finished!"And, why did Carla feel the need to keep it from me, even though she knew I would want to know my lyin, fuckin, good for nothing, leave his sister to the fuckin wolf pack, brother was still alive after all this time? Come on Mickey, why all the mystery and why are you turning up today all beaten up and lookin like you haven't eaten for a freakin month? Why all the bullshit mystery, come on, tell me."

"Look Lise, you need to understand a few things."Then Mickey noticed the rucksack perched on the end of Lisa's sofa and turned so pale, it caused Lisa to stare at him, as if waiting for further explanation. Why would a rucksack on a bed make him look like he was going to throw up? "Lisa, you can't leave."

"Oh yeah Mickey, oh yes I can. I can leave and I am leaving AND........." Lisa was now shouting in Mickey's face, but running out of words. She was just about to announce that she was actually not only thinking of leaving but she was on her way for good, when, Mickey's last couple of weeks finally caught up with him. He was becoming desperate and the ordeal he had been through at the hands of Regis made him lose his cool. He was also still extremely weak and had chosen to visit Lisa, far too early in his convalescence. Mickey pulled out the small hand pistol and even as he did, he realized the last thing Lisa was going to respond to was more threats and abuse, but now he was committed. "Lisa please you can't leave, you don't understand." "No, I don't." and with one shift movement, Lisa grabbed the rucksack, swung it over her head and smashed Mickey across the head with it. She was pretty sure she knew the difference between a hit man and someone who was just scared and not really capable of holding a gun straight, never mind shooting. She'd met enough scared and violent men and women in her time, to be sure of the distinction between the two. It was still a risk to hit out, but Lisa had been desperate to get away for a very long time. The strength she yielded with that swipe at her hapless brother, represented years of frustration and pain. With it, she was up and gone, leaving her brother desperately grappling to clear the haze that had just dramatically entered his head. Nevertheless, he was no less determined to catch up with her, no matter how fast she moved or, how far she thought she could get.

* * * *

"Religion is for people who don't want to go to Hell. Spirituality is for people who have already been there "Unknown.

169

Chapter 13
Three telephone Calls

Mickey fell out of the flat and stumbled clumsily down three flights of stairs. He was still trying to gain his equilibrium and the wounds all over his torso were still weeping. He was aware his shirt was starting to show a brown gooey discharge. There was a stubborn, if not painless, determination to catch up with Lisa, who was moving surprisingly quickly through the streets of Balham. She wasn't completely sure exactly how she was going to get to Brighton, as this emergency exit out of London had been somewhat unexpected. She was as mad as hell with her momentum being helped along by the serge of adrenalin that had increased by the realization her brother had just pulled a gun on her. Mickey wasn't exactly sure what he was going to do once he had caught up with his sister, but he was sure that DJ and his kennel full of animals wouldn't be overly impressed if he did her any harm. Somehow he had to think of a way to corner Lisa and then try and convince her to return home. Surely, when she found out he and Carla were trying to figure out a way to get her free from DJ she would calm down and help him come up with a plan to get Carla free. He was feeling ever more desperate and torn. How could he let them continue to hurt and torment Carla? Surely, he continued with his attempts at rational thought, if Lisa knew her best friend was being held ransom on her behalf, she would reconsider her flight, at the very least until Carla had escaped the clutches of the gang from Hades. Even as he took up his pursuit, Mickey was trying to work out how on earth he was going to be able to preserve both Lisa and Carla from the ravages of this vicious bunch of control freaks. He was running out of inspiration. It still hurt him to run, even he had underestimated the damage Regis had done to his body and he winced as he jogged through the streets. He was naturally fit and quite fast on his feet, but tears began to escape from him once again as his body cried out in protest as he sprinted toward Balham tube station. Where could his sister be going? Why now? God, if only he hadn't been tempted to return to London.

Lisa was heading straight for the underground station. The plan, which she had concocted in the last two minutes, was to make her way to Victoria station and there she would be able to catch her train to freedom. She had about a mile to navigate and she had already seen Mickey starting to catch her up. She figured that if she could reach a busily populated area she would at least be able to put him of by screaming if he got to close. What Lisa couldn't work out was, why, was her long lost brother trying to hurt her. As she reached the cross road, she knew she would have to get over successfully, if it was going to be possible to reach a train before Mickey caught her and the traffic lights were against her. Onlookers couldn't believe their eyes as she launched herself into the busy road and some of them would have put her recklessness down to either the desperate actions of a drug user, who wasn't really aware there were cars in the road, or just another young person trying to escape the law. However, Lisa's pursuer wasn't the law and he was gaining fast. As a taxi driver narrowly missed her and an indignant cyclist shouted abuse at her apparent disregard for his very existence, she had got across the busy road and was aiming for the tunnels.

By the time Mickey had reached the road, the lights were on his side, he was straight across and the pain he felt was dulled a little by the fact his sister appeared to be within yards of his reach. If I can just talk to her, she must understand, she must realize that, life wasn't just all about her and what she wanted. People were going to get hurt and worse! They needed to plan together. That wouldn't happen if she disappeared, god if she couldn't be found, DJ would unleash hell on him and Carla and he would eventually catch up with Lisa anyway. His head was spinning with a thousand thoughts a second; making it up as he went, going through every conceivable scenario he could, trying to somehow manufacture the wisdom enabling him to conceive a plan that would result in a happy ending. He was willing to hand Charlie over, bloody kill him if need be, he was desperate and if he could come out of this with Carla and Lisa intact and free, he would be content. As content as he could imagine that was, as his plans were running parallel with thoughts that Carla may well find his naked body repulsive to her now and he was pretty sure it would take a minor miracle for Lisa to ever Trust him again. He landed on the platform just as Lisa disappeared from sight. Blast, if I could just talk to her!

Mickey's eyes darted around in front of him, he was fairly sure he'd seen his sister going on the platform heading North bound on the Northern line. He assumed his little sister might head off to one of the mainline overland stations out of London. Unless of course she was going to trick him, double back, play silly buggers, just to lose him, then head off alone in the opposite direction. He took a minute to think and found himself edging closer to the yellow line, separating fragile human skin and bone from oncoming iron and steel. The same yellow line that the mad sounding announcers - who you can never really understand - try to convince everyone in loud tones, not to get to close to. PLEASE STAND WELL BACK BEHIND THE YELLOW LINE…..God, did people really need to be tempted away from an on-coming train, couldn't they work out for themselves that to stand perilously close to an on-coming underground train was a bad idea?

Just as these random thoughts started to blaze across Mickey's ever disoriented mind, another announcement rang out, to….PLEASE ALLOW PASSANGERS TO EXIT THE TRAIN BEFORE BOARDING … MIND THE GAP. Lisa was directly behind him. He started to swing round to face her, but he was vulnerably placed. Mickey was now in a position whereby one strategically placed shove and he would fall easily in front of the approaching train. Lisa had found something sharp, and for all he knew it could well have been a knife. Whatever it was, it was now pressed firmly into the small of his back. The only thing now separating Mickey from causing yet another equally irritating announcement from the overhead tannoy, stating there had been a fatality on the line, was the fact that the same blood running through his veins also streamed through his sister's. "If you don't let me go Mickey, I swear to god, I am desperate enough, okay, DO NOT TEST ME." She was now shouting directly in his ear, over his shoulder, as the noise of the approaching carriage started to drown her out.

"For god sake Lise, Carla is in deep trouble, she needs your help!" "Well, bro, she's got you now, that was crystal clear the other day and I'm now goin to find a way to look after number one mate." With that she swivelled on her heels and with all the energy she could muster, she pushed Mickey away from the door of the carriage. She then quickly jumped in. At the same time she made sure her brother felt a sharp stab in the back, as if to warn him she meant business. Before he could even curse the fact that he'd been out thought and even out muscled by his sister, she was gone and all he could do was watch his blood that was now mingled with sweat, start to drip onto the station floor. His wounds had once again been reopened.

* * * *

In the space of one small part, of one seemingly inoffensive afternoon, I was once again reminded; by three phone calls, occurring in quick succession, that life was; impossible to control, unpredictable and most painfully of all, relentlessly unfair. Our new temp' Jenny put the first call through.

"Hello, H.E.L.P. main offices, Charlie Becker, how can I help?" "Hi Charlie."

"Mickey." I really didn't know whether to bawl him out, or treat him to an invite him to a barbecue involving a fatted calf. I decided to err on the side of the fact that he could be either in trouble or really ill. For all I knew he could have been languishing in hospital for the last four days. "What's been going on Mickey, are you okay?" At that point, I did start to feel incredibly guilty, I hadn't reported him missing, or got around to visit his flat. The relief washed over me, he was alive and sounded okay.

"Look Charlie, I'm really sorry, and will explain, honest, but it is complicated."

My instinct took over and his emphasis on the words, *it is*, made me assume his absence might be due to a set of circumstances, or a personal matter. "Okay Mickey, but as long as you are okay, you need to keep me informed though, I can't support you if I don't know what's going on, why did you disappear mate?"

"I know, I'm sorry, really."

"Mickey…." I paused, as I was trying to work out if it were wise to venture down the path I was about to take. "Has this got anything to do with Lisa?"

Good, Mickey thought, Charlie has made the connection. That would make the next bit a lot easier. "Yeah Charlie, so, you know she's my sister, well, the truth is, she turned up at my place the other day sayin she needed my help, yeah, now she's done a bunk, an I think she might be in big trouble. Has she been in to see anyone there?"

"Well not for awhile mate, did she say anything about where she might have gone?"

"No, Charlie, tell ya the God's honest, I'm really worried."

"Look Mickey, I shouldn't be telling you this, I don't think it would be a great idea, if you went running around the country and getting into more trouble, but I do have a theory about where she could be. I don't want either of you on my conscience okay, so if I tell you where I think she might have headed, you have to promise to meet up with me, so we can look for her together okay."

"No problem, Charlie, always the Father figure, I'm so relieved, well done, thank you, where's she at Charlie?"

"Look it's just a theory and we could both be wasting a lot of time, but I think Lisa met someone here at the offices, who persuaded her to leave London."

"What, a bloke you mean?"

"Worse mate, a religious nut case, a cult Mickey,

you know, the type that's into recruiting."

"What." I went on to tell him, what I thought I knew. Furthermore, I retrieved the business type card, Rev. Jed left with me, which luckily had an abundance of information in gold gilded writing strewn across it. The one thing about organizations dedicated to recruitment, the promotional material is always informative, as well as elaborate. The postcard sized glossy hand out offered, an address, phone number and nauseating picture of the good reverend smiling inanely. The open admission of where we could track them down on the south coast, made me momentarily doubt my judgment. Why would an organization with anything to hide, openly advertise their whereabouts?

Once I had Mickey swear he would meet me on the way down to the coast, I decided to trust him, relayed the address we were going to investigate and then organized a good meeting place I knew on route. The little chef on the A27 had often come in handy, whenever Caroline I had occasion to visit her parents in Hove, near Brighton. I came off the phone and immediately realized I should have asked him for a mobile number. I relaxed when I remembered Mickey had always been reliable at work. Well apart from the latest episode of vanishing into thin air that is! We would meet Sunday. It was Friday afternoon; I would at least be able to spend Saturday recovering from a bitch of a week.

Mickey threw out a huge sigh of relief. The first break that had come his way in this whole sorry episode. At least if he could deliver Charlie to be sacrificed, DJ might appreciate his dedication to extricating Lisa from the do good brigade. He would then move on to Brighton, rescue Lisa from the religious nut jobs and life would start to look a little brighter for him and Carla. It wasn't easy trying to plan Charlie's destruction, in fact it had just cost him £500 for starters, but the immoral little slut, who needed the cash, had been more than willing to take the dirty money for a very dirty deed. Mickey was sure if his first blow didn't prove at least disabling, he was determined that his plan B would be fatal finish Charlie off.

* * * *

I had literally just decided enough was enough and I would pathetically retreat home; licking my wounds, grab, yet more liquid escapism on the way and recover sufficiently tomorrow, to be able to go Lisa hunting on Sunday, when extension 1818 flashed up on my phone screen. GLORIA ROSARIO - CEO Oh God, what the hell does she want? The CEO for pities sake, it's Friday afternoon! Please let me go home, I thought, as I took the call. Oh God, what the hell does she want? "Hi Gloria. "She came back sounding serious. I put it down to the fact; she must have been feeling similarly to me about her week.

"Charlie, sorry, but I need to see you before you go home, can you come up."

I sat there open mouthed and said absolutely nothing for a whole ten minutes. It felt like about half an hour, but that's how long it had taken Gloria to propel me into shock and almost complete hysteria. I managed to control myself, but this was serious. There had been a serious complaint against me. Gloria had taken a call just over two hours ago and had spent most of the afternoon in the HR department taking advice. I had always thought Gloria wasn't to be trusted, but would she really see this as her opportunity to finally nail me? I just kept saying it over and over, a complaint, a serious complaint of a sexual nature, by one of my clients who had met with me last week! Anger, confusion,
pain and an imminent feeling of doom and

despair were all vying for prominence.
pain and an imminent feeling of doom and despair were all vying for prominence. Rational thought tried to get through the little cracks in my thought process, but I knew that many an accusation, correctly aimed or not, often led to permanent damage and suspicion, especially, within jobs that involved working with vulnerable young people.

Gloria talked to me as though she was reading from a carefully prepared script, an android, mouthing HR jargon about having to be seen to take it serious, even if it wasn't true, suspension with full pay, investigations, consultations and access to the charities helpline if I needed it. I was beyond angry.

"Who the hell would make this up?"

"I'm sorry; I can't talk about the details, as there will be a full investigation."

The person involved had apparently been quite explicit, in an elaborate description of what I had done to them; therefore, it would all take awhile to properly look into. I was sure Gloria was quite selective in the bits she could and couldn't tell me. This was a perfect opportunity to completely freak me out, or at least watch me squirm. Either that or she just saw it as a perfect opportunity, as my supervisor, to finally assert some power over me. But surely to God, she couldn't be that cruel?

* * * *

I had left the building convinced that I hadn't felt this low, even on the night I tried to top myself, so….what might happen tonight? I was certainly in no fit state to go running around the country saving another lost soul in the form of Lisa Baker. Yet, this urge to rescue someone else, anyone, was relentless, an obsession that was driven by an innate belief that my own salvation was intrinsically linked.

I had completely forgotten my mobile had been on silent all day and quickly checked it. Maybe I'd got a call from God telling me it was all going to be okay! Seven missed calls from Caroline, "shit! Fuck! Bollocks! Fucking people! Fucking world's going fucking mad! Wank! Bloody life!"…………………….This childlike reaction went on for awhile, as I usually found that an infantile response was often quite comforting. I had satisfied myself that I couldn't take anymore grief today and that I had a straight option between dancing madly, Basil Faulty style, remonstrating in the street outside the offices alone. Or, my most favoured fantasy option when I felt so mad and frustrated, I didn't know what to do with myself; grabbing the nearest tourist, ripping their intestines out and then dancing around on the mess. I was seriously wound up, but still had enough about me to realize that no matter how I feeling, after I was sure Tommy would never live down the headlines, should I have chosen the latter remedy to release my tension.

"Charlie, I've been trying to reach you all afternoon."

"What's up Carrie, is Tommy okay?"

"No Charlie, He's in the hospital, I'm there now, I kept coming out to call you, where the hell…..." Caroline's voice was cracking as she tried to explain. "They rushed him in at noon, they're doing tests at Poole General, they, think it might be meningitis, and I've got to go." If God had decided in his infinite wisdom, that, I must endure this day as some kind of punishment or ultimate test, why couldn't he have just had me kidnapped by aliens, tortured and released after excessive anal probing? No, of course, that would have been far less traumatic, than the stark and cruel realities that life constantly seems to feel the need to fling at me!

.

* * * *

.A religion without the element of mystery would not be a religion at all. ~Edwin Lewis.

Chapter 14
Maxie' Choice

Max, or Maxie to those over the years who had
ventured close to the giant gangster, had known
DJ all his life. They had grown up with the
violence, sharing the responsibility as well as the
spoils of criminal activity shoulder to shoulder
for nearly thirty years.

Max had been as angry as any of the boys back in
the day. However, the meaner, the more bitter
DJ had become over the years, had only served as
a constant reminder to Max, that despite the shit
that had been ritually thrown at them by society
when they were younger, almost forcing them to
take the initiative, life didn't have to be like this
forever. The only time Max had fallen out with
DJ was two years ago, when Regis came on
board. Never had DJ's right hand man felt so
strongly about recruitment. Regis wasn't a man
who was about to take on a cause, or stand with
his brothers. No, as far as Max was concerned
Regis was a self-serving psycho. Regis was a
danger to them all!

DJ was still a gangster, mainly because he was a
mean bastard. Maxie was still a gangster,
because he simply knew no other life, or so he
thought! Carla had realized her business was
probably lost by now. It didn't take many
unanswered calls and lost orders for word to get
around that she was unreliable and typical of a
young person who, although at one point might

have been determined to reach for her dreams, would never be able to sustain the long term commitment needed to change her life for good. The persistent critical accusations levelled at her by society, mocking her to revert to type, echoed in her ears. Max was the only member of the group who had shown any signs of weariness at the long years of oppression inflicted by the regime, so dominated by DJ's commitment to tyranny and the repression of others. Carla had desperately tried to appeal to him whenever she managed glimpse a glimpse of the huge man at the other side of her prison door! However, she was hidden deep in the dank basement, helpless, unable to communicate to any one very well and so why should even Max take any real notice of an insignificant such as her; never mind, contemplate helping her. For now at least, it looked like she was there to stay.

* * * *

The pool table with blue baize and American cowboy style silver chrome surround, stood in the middle of DJ's games room. Max had arrived for a rare night of uncomplicated, beer, moving onto brandy, pool and meaningless chat about absolutely nothing at all. Well, that was the plan. An hour passed before a word was exchanged between the two, who, being so huge in build, comically made the pool cues look more like tooth picks. DJ seemed just as distracted as Max, who had been growing more restless by the week. Tensions in the group were rising and like a aging rock band arguing over which direction to take their music in, there had a been a feeling recently, that they were all getting just a bit to old for this intense shit. Playing pool and even getting pissed, or stoned, or both, was no longer taking the edge off minor distractions, such as, prisoners being held in the dungeon below. It seemed easier when they were young and desperate, society raging against them, they were hitting back then and it made much more sense than what they were engaged in these days. The Brixton riots in the eighties were now a distant memory and the gang was no longer poor, needing to lead the way, looting and pillaging to survive and assert some authority in the world. Now they were older, richer and almost becoming the people they had started out hating so much. There was an uneasy feeling that not all in the group were as fully committed to the cause as they once were. It had been largely unspoken and hanging heavy in the air for a while now. Something was about to give and when you were dealing with men as hard as these, when it did, you could be sure there would be violent shockwaves.

"So, Maxie, talk to me, you don't seem to be lovin your work like you once did."

"Man, I probably got daughters runnin around South London the same age as Carla."

"You gettin soft on me Maxie boy? It's a means to an end; you know that, you know she'll get out soon. Wen she and her boyfren get their priorities right, you know that, right."

"Yeah, DJ, but just wat is the priority man, I'm not sure I know anymore."

"Lisa, you know it's Lisa.""Exactly, Look DJ, don't take this bad man, but everything we do these days jus seems to be about Lisa, so wats really goin on bro?"

"Where the fuck is this comin from then Max." Max knew that the shift from Maxie to Max was significant, but, someone had to do the pushing, Max was closest to the boss and most of the crew were getting increasingly irritated that all group activity seemed to revolve exclusively around DJ's wants and needs.

"Look DJ we gotta be straight wit each other man, its no good you goin off fuckin crack, jus cos we talkin okay, Christ, we are jus talkin man.""Go then Max lets do that, lets have a nice chat, wats on your mind?"

"Seems like we fightin ourselves all the time,

187

cause we don't need to fight is all, jus who are
we fightin now?."

"We fightin the same bastards we always have,
you jus gettin old Maxie."

"No DJ nah, we ain't fightin nothin no more, we
runnin around like agin bully boys holdin young
girls ransom wen we don't even need anythin
from her."

"Wat, course we do, you lost the plot man."

"Nah DJ, you need her, you need Lisa, that wat
this all about, that wat everythin is all bout these
days. We ain't fighin to survive, to kick back at
the bastards who weren't givin us jobs or treatin
us like we scum, nah, we jus throwin our weight
about cos we can, cos we get away with it. cos
this people's Police are fuckin useless.   An wat
the fuck is it about Lisa anyhow, why we don't
jus let the little bitch go man, I jus don't get why
she so crucial to you man."

 DJ thought about exploding, in fact, he was quite
surprised himself when he suddenly felt so calm.
Like the lion who has already caught the prey,
gripped his windpipe, knew it wasn't going to
escape. Knowing he could just kick back licking
himself and his prey, in the same knowledge and
confidence that nobody was going anywhere
without his say so and he was in perfect control.
DJ had never been in any danger of being
accused of being the sensitive type. Repressed
anger was his forte, years of hardening the
conscience and the knowledge he had gained
through experience, namely, that opening up to

anyone, was very likely to lead to the information divulged being held against you. Therefore, he wasn't going to admit, even to Max, how he really felt about Lisa Baker. Max was however, his closest associate and on this occasion the gang leader had assessed that his closest brother in arms, may well benefit from a bit of background context to all the violence. DJ started to slowly relay a story of violence, sadness, neglect and hopelessness in the vein hope it would remind Maxie, why they needed to remain as comrades in arms. He started with his Fatherless childhood on a typical South London council estate. The graphic detail of beatings, torture by cigarette burns, starvations and general neglect inflicted by a mother and a string of boyfriends that made the Sky TV adverts asking for just £3 a month to help abused children, look like an advert for a trip to Disneyland. The story unravelled to explain perfect legitimate reasons why a young black man in modern Britain might want to hit back and rebel to the point of psychopathic frenzy. When DJ had finished, all it had served to accomplish was to further convince Max that maybe it was time to end the cyclone of destruction. Max was ready for an epiphany that positively screamed, it would be a crime against heaven itself to risk anyone else becoming a victim to the string of collective tales of misery generated by the BEA Boys.

"Well Maxie boy, wat the fuck else you goin to do, you gonna go an work for fuckin Halfords you don't know anythin else but us. That's our strength, you know that, the group, where the hell else, is there for us to find sanctuary, ahh."

"You got a point, I know, but jus sayin is all, some of us are gettin a bit pissed at runnin around jus tryin to contain Lisa fuckin Baker all the time." "You wanna save Lise, just like all them other church goers ahh Maxie boy. You want her as your woman, ahh, is that it?"

"Well at least I want you to admit, you want her, DJ, why the fuck don't you jus take her, fuck her, get it outa your system like."

"BECAUSE SHE AIN'T LIKE THE REST OKAY, SHE AIN'T NO TYPICAL WHORE MAXIE." "Man your drivin yourself fuckin crazy, where's it gonna end DJ, you can't keep her foreva less you admit you fuckin want her foreva. An Christ man, you bin lettin her get fucked by every weirdo in London and you still want her?"

"That don't mean shit man, that's jus business." "That the point DJ, it ain't jus business, it's killin you, an it's takin us down wit ya."

"Fuck off." "Okay DJ maybe I do that small ting, maybe I'll jus fuck off" "You talkin like the wankers we bin fightin for years Max, you gone fuckin soft."Max was content that the conversation could have lasted a lot longer without DJ admitting he was obsessed by Lisa and his whole life was dedicated to possessing her utterly. Therefore, he decided to retreat. He looked at DJ as if he was looking at him for the last time ever, placed his cue pool uncharacteristically delicately on the table, turned and left. DJ sucked air through his teeth dismissively. The evening of pool playing and relaxing, was definitely over

* * * *

As Max was leaving he decided for the first time in twenty five years to take action independently of DJ's consent. He was careful to drive his A5 edition black Audi out of the front gates to be careful he was recognized in the close circuit TV monitors scouring the building perimeters. He was pretty sure DJ would be watching his departure and for the plan he was carefully hatching to work, he needed DJ to be convinced he had left the vicinity.

Two hours later and Max was convinced DJ would be out to the world and tonight, he was bang on, as DJ had broken a golden rule. He had tapped up one of the boys for some tabs, which would act as a most acceptable hallucinogenic and sedative to dull the reality of Max's earlier challenge. He knew the security once he had got back inside the grounds was poor at best. However, without the signature black motor drawing up to the front gates, even Maxie was still going to find it difficult to actually get in. There was just one weakness in the cameras scan and he made his way stealthily toward the lowest but most neglected part of the house wall. It was still a good six foot high and Max's days of scaling difficult barriers to gain booty were long gone. He carefully started to feel for a foothold, hoping DJ hadn't up-dated his monitor range or the intelligence and alertness of the two monkey's guards, who were charged with checking the screens inside the basement. He eventually dropped awkwardly onto the gravel at the back of the house. Ricky & Big Dave, were the hapless due responsible for watching the house tonight. "Wat the fuck, hey Ricky, lookey wat we got here." Unfortunately, Max had chosen the one night the two hapless unofficial guards had passed the monitor screens at the right time. "Dunno, you go deal wit it, if you're not back in 5, I'll come an recue ya."

"K, who eva it is, is gonna get a shock."

Dave, the pinker and definitely least intelligent of the two human bull terriers, made his way toward the back entrance of the basement. Without any knowledge of who he might be up against, he bundled his way outside intent on squishing the intruder into submission. He bulldozed his way out to the darkness and started to hunt the intruder. Max's first blow was effective, low to the kidneys and it buckled Dave's legs just enough to give Max time to adjust and aim the second blow to the back of the neck rendering the lumbering idiot instantly unconscious. My god have I really been knockin around with these brainless fuck wits for twenty five years, Max wondered as he found himself almost by the minute, distancing himself further from the ex gangs ethos and ideals. Max got into the grounds easier than he thought he would, despite the fact he had been spied. The thug had conveniently left the back door open as well, but Max knew that wherever Dave was, Ricky wouldn't be far behind. Even though the lights were off and he was groping around to find his bearings, Max

193

knew the layout of the basement like the inside of his very own hash pouch.

"Is that you Max?"

"Hey Ricky, how's it goin?"

"Wat the fuck Max?"

"I'm here for the girl." ."You reckon do ya?"

"An wat the fuck you think I suppose to do, look the other way?" "You can look where eva you fuckin wanna look fella.""You tryin to get me killed bro?"

"Look Ricky man, I'm goin to be walkin outta here in about five minutes, wit the girl, now you can either pretend you weren't here and Dave fucked up, or you can get in my way an get hurt bad! Wat's it to be bro?"Ricky lunged at Max and caught him square on the jaw bone. Max reeled and even before his head had realized the trauma that had been inflicted upon it he was spitting blood. Max was tough and even a hammer blow that would have put the average guy on the street to sleep for a week, wasn't going to nail him. He tried to remember what he was doing and where he was. His head swam madly and he had to take a moment to remember he wasn't dreaming. He defended his head against further abuse with his arms crossed diagonally in front of him. Ricky smelled early success and rushed in too soon. As he did Max side stepped slightly, just enough to throw Ricky off balance. He quickly remembered his teenage years that had revolved around a local boxing gym. Remembering the moves, he put his head down and like the heavy weight champion of the world, launched into a quick succession of jabs to Ricky's torso. Ricky's leg instinctively came up to connect sharply with Max's groin.

"Fuck, ahh, you bastard, wanker," was all Max could manage as he doubled up.

"You goin down Maxie boy, sorry an all that." Once again, over confidence gripped Ricky and he took the fatal step backward, giving Max more than enough time to plan his next move. He was now propelled forward by a gallon of adrenalin and the heady desire to kill anyone who was prepared to threaten his manhood and neglect the code of men in a street fight. The next blow would have taken out an African Rhino, to which, there was a distinct resemblance to Ricky. Max shielded his eyes as he surged forward and like a JCB driven by a maniac, pounded Ricky's diaphragm so hard he thought he would literally throw up his entire respiratory system in one retch. Ricky reeled backward, glazed over and looked like he had forgotten how to breathe. The contest was over, but Max needed to finish the job, placing his right hand on Ricky's forehead, lifting it slightly and having teed up Ricky's nose, proceeded to slam his left palm on it, flattening it utterly. He felt the small bones crackle and squish, as Ricky hit the floor like a dead man.

Max took a minute, just in case DJ had heard a ruckus and was prowling around waiting for his moment. He slipped the metal jailers key ring

from Ricky's belt and moved toward Carla's cell.
"Hey, you ready to bounce baby?"
Without a word, Carla was up and out of her
prison, within one swift movement of her long
body.
"Come on honey, let's go find your boyfriend an
Lise, any idea where she might be at?"
"Thanks Maxie, I knew you were alright, not like
them other animals."
"Yeah, well don't get carried away sweetheart,
it's a bit early in my redemption, to be nominatin
me for a heart of gold award."
"Yeah, and I do know exactly where Lisa and
Mickey are, well at least where they're headed,
those two fuckin meatheads didn't even work out
that I could hear every fuckin word through that
make shift, paper-thin, prison wall."
As Max gently lead the very frail and rapidly
thinning Carla out of the basement, while being
ever vigilant for a possible ambush from DJ,
Dave was starting to stir. Maxie leaned over him
and whispered, "if you've got any fuckin sense,
you'll stay there till mornin. Jus tell DJ I
surprised you buddy, he knows how gud I am."
Maxi was anxious to depart without delay and
knew that DJ would have been more effective in
a fight than both Dave and Ricky put together.
He realized that from that moment in time, he
would never return to the norm he had existed in,
for the entirety of his adult life and most of his
childhood. He also knew DJ wouldn't rest until
he had hunted him down.

Carla turned to Maxie as they scrambled into the Audi, parked 300 yards away from the escape route and whimpered almost inaudibly, "I think we need to rescue Lisa, for all our sake's."
"Yeah babe, I think you're right."

* * * *

There's nothing certain in a man's life except this: That he must lose it. ~Aeschylus, Agamemnon

Chapter 15
Tommy's close call

There isn't a problem, struggle, or desperate situation that can't be immediately put into perspective, than when your child's life is threatened. I arrived in the car park of Poole General hospital exactly two hours after Caroline's call. The journey would have normally taken at least three and a half from work, to the south coast. I feared that there were speed cameras along the way that might have exploded! The endless car park levels I had to ascend before I found a parking bay, provided more irritation and nervous anxiety, upon an already impossible day. There wasn't a single possession I wouldn't have given up, to start this day all over again and try to attempt a different outcome. Bloody, pay and display, oh, no, its pay after visit display, fuck, bugger, don't they realize people don't need this shit when they visit hospitals.

Sandy Bay ward entrance number six million out of seventeen billion, in this colossal small city for sick people. It took me two hours to get here, one hundred and nineteen miles and yet another half an hour just finding my son. I finally stumbled into the private room. Well at least he wasn't in with kids who were really sick. "He's really sick." Caroline's words hit me like they were news of the advent of Armageddon.

Caroline looked awful and yet still maintained an air of strength and resolve. I had always admired

Caroline, she was a good mother and I often wondered why the hell I hadn't treasured her as I should when we were together. We had grown up together in marriage, steadily but surely over the years, like a very decent, middle class, brother and sister. I suspected we had both, longed for, as I did, for a mad, sizzling, sex and adventure filled existence that I had realized since, was definitely not the norm in middle class, middle income Britain. We had consequently grown bored and although very much 'together' in the eyes of friends and relations, very lonely.

"What's the doctor said, so far?"

"Well it's definitely a meningitis scare, but, they're still testing his blood, trying to decide which strain, if it is, or, if its not, what the hell it is.""You okay?"

She looked at me in a way that suggested she wanted to say, "Course I'm not fucking okay," but said, "Yeah, thanks."

It was now eight forty pm and there was nothing much else that was going to happen until dawn. I looked at Tommy and felt like my insides were going to collapse. Beads of sweat rested on his small brow.

"Why is he so blotchy? Sorry, because he may have meningitis, sorry."

"It's okay."

A pretty young nurse entered and offered a half smile as if to empathize with our plight. In reality she couldn't have even approached within

199

a billion miles, the emotions we were enduring. Routine observations taken and with another half smile she headed for the door, offering no information as to the results of her brief visit.

"How's his temperature," I barked, as if to suggest, it would have been nice if you had offered to tell us if our son was okay, or, if his brain was being fried, as his body fought to cling on to life.

"It's a little high, but seems to be going down. I think the doctor's quite pleased."

"Great, as long as the doctors happy," I churlishly offered.

"Don't Charlie." Caroline snapped at me, as she sensed I was about to take a whole days worth of adverse angst out on a completely innocent NHS worker, who was no older than my favourite fountain pen.

"Okay, thanks." The nurse smiled weakly at me, as if to indicate, I was excused my bad manners, because my son was languishing before us all.

"Look Charlie, I need to get home at some stage and see to Colin. I've been here all day. I can be back first thing. Can you stick around tonight? It looks like Tommy's out of danger."

"No problem, I need to eat, let me pop out, ten minutes and I'll be back, stick around all night, okay?"

I was lying, I needed food yes, but more importantly, I needed to go hunting for alcohol. There was absolutely no way in hell, I was going to spend the night in hospital after the day I'd endured, looking at my sick son, without some form of self medication. I scurried out of the ward and figured I had about fifteen minutes before Caroline would recognize the old patterns of erratic behaviour that might suggest I couldn't be fully relied on. In five minutes I'd managed to sus out that there were shops toward the west wing exit of the hospital. They were likely to include a wine shop, plus, I could grab a carbohydrate crammed sausage baguette on the way back in, from the man with a van just outside the same entrance. I would be back in approximately seventeen minutes. I'd mastered the art of scheming and planning throughout my marriage to Caroline and disturbing memories, reminding me of my devious personality came flooding back. This, I didn't need after the day sent from Satan's own gift shop. The fact that I'd to keep my alcohol issue a secret from her still, after all these years, further reminded me I had lived my entire life either trying to hide something from someone, or trying to avoid responsibility of one form or another.

My responsibility toward Tommy, paradoxically, had never been in any doubt, so when I arrived back to the hot, clinically smelling room, I was ready to do my duty.

"Okay, I'll see you tomorrow."

"Okay, look, try and rest, I'm sure he'll be okay."

Who was I trying to kid?

The night was long...................................

After about two hundred years, my mobile

showed 03.16am. The bed side chair hadn't been too bad; I'd managed to sneak in a bottle and the greasy baguette had sustained me well. My world was still far from perfect as I ran through the catalogue of disastrous events of the last few weeks. One - I had woken up in the bath, freezing cold, after a failed attempt to end it all! Two – I'd met a girl, who'd fucked me in everyway possible! Three – I'd realized I was now faced with the possibility of having to work with that very same diva and four staff members who had mysteriously disappeared on me! Okay they had now turned up, but still the intrigue continued. Five – I'd been visited and beaten up by South London's Mafioso! Six – I'd been unjustly accused of a sexual assault! Resulting in, Seven -My suspension from work. The cherry on this very shitty tasting cake, apart from the fact, that I was very confused as to why I was contemplating rescuing a girl, who had shown me no respect at all, who had fucked me in everyway possible, and the real fact was that, my boy, my world, my reason to exist, was lying in hospital, apparently fighting for his life. He didn't look like he was fighting. He looked sweaty and defeated. He was however, calm, as he laid there on the huge linen pillow. The same pillow that had probably been deployed to support thousands of desperate heads and medical cases over many years. I sat in the semi darkness, listening to various children crying, moaning and coughing. The private room gave little protection from the various high pitched noises of suffering. There was a particularly annoying young girl next door, who seemed to feel the need to inflict back to back tantrums on to her harangued and desperate looking mother. I felt a slight pang of guilt, when I realized I wanted to smoother her. She was sick, I should be more patient. The little TV screen above my head had long gone blank. Why the hell didn't they tell you there was a time shut down on TV use at 10 o'clock, *before*, you scramble around like a maniac trying to find enough change to stuff in the token machine, to ensure you've got something to watch through the entire night. Sleep hadn't been an option, with the continual interruptions from the pretty nurse, the stroppy girl next door and the fact that I was petrified that if I relaxed too much, Tommy might expire. I found great comfort in the fact his breathing had become more even as the night stretched on. He wasn't as hot as he had been earlier and I started to hope that the day about to dawn, would be a better one. As I sat and stared at my son, I wondered how, if there really was a creator, how he / she could look upon such perfect, innocent, vulnerable, beauty, without needing to intervene. How could it be, that I, as a Father could feel so desperate and willing to do absolutely anything to save my son and yet have to literally beg the Father of us all, to just make my son better. The enormity of the world was suddenly apparent to me as I gazed upon such vulnerability. Were we all really at the mercy, of a universe and a universal sovereign, none of us could control? The cruel nature of the survival of the fittest and natural selection seemed more real to me in these moments, than the concept of a caring, loving, benevolent Father of spirits. Yet, I knew my soul was sending me a different message and that, some desire, some, force of destiny, unacceptable in the eyes of scientific research, propelled me on, to try, to strive, to labour toward an acceptance and the desperate search for some sort of salvation, for my own sorry soul.

The rare and welcome silence on the ward was suddenly shattered.

"Hey Dad." I nearly lost control of all bodily functions, as I heard my son come to and speak.

"Tommy, sweetheart, are you okay?"

"Yeah, I'm thirsty."

I found a plastic cup, kitchen and clean water, as if I was being asked by God himself to go on an errand to save the whole of mankind.

"Will you lift me up dad, please, I want to sit up."I placed my hand under the nape of his neck and gently eased him into a more upright position. It felt like I was trying to move an unexploded bomb, anxious as I was not to disturb any part of him that might be hurting.

"I love you dad."

"I love you too son." I knew at that moment, my boy was going to be okay.

Ting, ting, ting– the text from Caroline came through. "Will be there in 10, is he okay?"

"Yes he's awake; all is well, see u soon."
I could feel the relief from Caroline, over the airwaves even though she didn't reply.
The pretty nurse had been in four times during the night to carry out observations on my son. The doctor would apparently be alerted to the fact Tommy had woken up and didn't appear to be suffering from any form of high temperature induced brain damage. It would be about four hours before we would see this mythical creature, described to us as, 'The Doctor', but apparently, it would be worth it. The consultant was the one who would make all the decisions, as to when and if Tommy was in the clear and able to be allowed home. Caroline burst in the room and then into tears. We held each other as if realizing for the first time, the sharing of a son or daughter was an infinitely profound .union. While we waited for the Doctor, who did, after much prodding and poking at Tommy, declare the all clear and Caroline and I had time to sit, chat and share moments of intimacy, largely absent during out time together as man and wife "So, how's life treating you then Charlie? Still enjoying life at H.E.L.P?"
"Yeah, generally, you know, err, err." After a pathetic attempt to cover up the latest debacle involving my working life, I managed to change the subject. "You okay?" It struck me how little there really was to talk about, given the fact we hadn't really spoken for three years. I had never been able to work out why we'd decided to part

and yet this single conversation, although tender, reminded me, we had absolutely nothing meaningful to say to one another.

The Doctors managed to visit and diagnose the prospects of all the patients in Tommy's ward in about half an hour. Tommy's singular visit was over in a matter of minutes. We had been informed that it wasn't in fact any strain of meningitis attacking our son, as expected. What is actually was, they weren't really sure, but the doctor managed to bullshit his way through, with all sorts of jargon, convincing us, they knew what they were doing. He would need a course of powerful precautionary anti-biotic, lots of time to build up his strength and we shouldn't be surprised if his energy levels weren't where it should be, for up to anything approaching three weeks. Tommy was strong and the fever had already broken. The relief was overwhelming, although Colin had now arrived and there was no way I was going to show any weakness in front of him, despite the fact, I felt myself well up as I lingered over my goodbyes to my baby.

"I'll see you soon son, love you."

"Love you dad."

Caroline and I exchanged the acceptable amount of friendliness and affection ex's were allowed in front of their current partners and Colin, to his credit, expressed an acceptable level of discomfort. He then let himself down and tried to play the part of responsible, reliable, stand in superhero, to make up for the fact he wasn't actually Tommy's dad. "Don't worry Tommy mate, we'll soon have you on your feet again, down the park, kicking the ball about." He was a nice bloke, really he was, but that didn't stop me from whispering, "wanker," to myself, as I left the room. Caroline heard me and I was sure I saw her smirk. Small victories! One last lingering kiss to my son's forehead and I was out of their lives again for a little while at least.

I navigated my way out of the monstrously huge hospital once again and noticed a poster on the public board, that informed me that I could claim back my car parking fee at a little office in the lower ground floor, if, I first got a voucher from the ward staff. Why the hell bother charging people eight bloody pounds per six bloody hours of parking, if they were just going to reimburse them six of those bloody pounds when they left the bloody hospital? The world is bloody stupid! I was exhausted, fraught, scruffy and unshaven. I was pretty sure I must have looked like a mad monk, remonstrating up and down the corridors as I negotiated my parking voucher from a ruddy faced ward sister.

After trudging back to the car park and waiting fifteen minutes to get it signed by someone senior enough to take responsibility for signing off thirteen pounds, of NHS funds, I was seriously irritated and wondered if I would ever escape the hospital grounds. I began to believe there was a conspiracy to keep me captive within the system and that the only way out, would be to agree to have an operation. As I was meandering with a decidedly dejected countenance, through the lower basement level of the car park, I was forced to come back to reality….Is that Mickey's car? Why the hell would he be here? I walked over to what I thought was Mickey's old Vauxhall Corsa. I'd recognized it, as; I had sat in it on more than one occasion, having accepted lifts from Mickey, to and from various, wider regional work meetings following the loss of my own motor. Today however, my rented carriage would do me well as I had plans to progress straight on to Brighton after my emotional detour to Poole. I contented myself with the thought that I must have been mistaken about Mickey's car and finally extricated myself from the hospital grounds. As the rain started to fall heavily, I also tried to rid myself of thoughts, reminding me of my own personal torment of the last fourteen hours. I hoped that I'd be able to move onto Brighton without having the necessary sleep for such an adventure. The hire car smelled of chemical cleaners, but at least it was, in fact clean, fast and being paid for by work expenses, suspension or not. Bollocks to Gloria and all the jumped up HR managers, who knew fuck all about the work we actually had to carry out.

* * * *

The death of someone we know always reminds us that we are still alive - perhaps for some purpose which we ought to re-examine. ~Mignon McLaughlin.

Chapter 16
Shot!

I'd remembered how tranquil the New Forest had been on a recent trip and wondered if they had park rangers who turfed visitors out at night. I was entertaining the thought of kipping in the car tonight and there was nothing at home that needed my attention. In any event, I was depressingly reminded of my suspension from work, as I realized any weekend chores could now be completed next week. I smiled to myself, when I visualized my wonderful boss busying herself, furiously hunting down, knives sharp enough to stab me in the back with, while I was away. I'd get to the forest easily by lunchtime, feed deer, have a lovely walk, relax and scour the landscape for a convenient spot to crash. In the mean time I was knackered. Tommy's illness and my dash to Poole had left me drained. I pulled up on route into a deserted car park, attached to a pub that had recently closed down. Well at least I knew I could kip comfortably in the car.

* * * *

I was groggy and to my absolute astonishment, I had slept for six hours. I woke up cold and thought I might have been there even longer if the weather hadn't turned nasty. As always, my plans were now altered and all I could do now was think about slipping into the forest, finding food, eating food, preferably in a pub, sod feeding deer, sod walking, sod picnicking. I just needed a quiet corner to continue my slumber. I was starting to wonder whether my clothes would last another day, but there was no way I was going to race back to London, fighting all the day trippers, who would be on the way home from Bournemouth beach. The M3 would be as cluttered as my head and I just needed to crash. I ended up grabbing a sandwich that tasted like it had been made in the Victorian era, Christ, tourists would eat anything.

The New Forest wasn't how I'd remembered it. It seemed less magical in the cold and rain. The cold chill mirrored my mood. I was trapped in the car, cold, and beat from trying to fight off the continual onslaught of negative thoughts that had gradually gained momentum as my circumstances had got increasingly complex through the week. God, I thought my life was going down the toilet months ago, but it seemed like a fucking village jamboree compared to now! If I'd risked running around for decent, edible food, I would get wetter and my night would have been considerably more uncomfortable. Whether I liked it or not, that would force me home to London. I did however; manage to locate a Tesco Express, nestled in a little village on the outskirts of Lymington. This welcoming retail outlet, would stock enough alcohol to keep me warm through the fast approaching night.

I just about survived the night undetected apart from a visit from an inquisitive badger and a courageous, or very stupid hungry Fox. Upon each disturbance I had been startled out of my tiny mind, as, the as, the atmosphere in the forest had turned distinctly eerie after nightfall. I also discovered that having slept in a really bad position, as far as my spine was concerned, I might not be able to walk ever again. It was only six am and I had four hours before my rendezvous with Mickey. My first thought was to text Caroline, I was well aware it was early, but if she was up, she would reply as soon as she got it and I needed to know my boy was okay. It was still raining heavily, so again, any foraging for food would need to be carried out in the car. I would then make my way to the meeting place on the A27 and just wait. God, Mickey, if you let me down, I'll kill you! The rain was now pounding the windscreen and it looked like Mickey and I would be talking in the car, unless we darted in the little chef, if he turned up in time. I was hugely relieved however, when his car swept into the car park early. I could have sworn that was the car I'd seen in Poole? I waited for him to park and gave him a few seconds to settle. I wasn't about to get drowned waiting for him to park and organize himself. The rain was very distracting and I hadn't noticed that there were two other expensive black motors that had cruised into the car park just after Mickey. I waved furiously in the hope Mickey would see me, so that one of us could just dart into the others car. He had no idea I was there or what vehicle I was in. The rain distorted his view and I was in a car he wouldn't recognize. I got out and raced over to his Corsa. Mickey immediately looked up, released the door lock and I planted myself firmly in the front passenger seat. I noticed straight away he looked rough and my brain did a quick scan of recent events involving his sister, to try and decipher where to start the conversation. I certainly wasn't going to regress as far back as the night I had spent with her! "Well mate, where the hell have you been?" I was genuinely pleased to see him, but had really bad vibes about all the reasons he looked so badly beat up and tired.

"Well, like I said boss, it's a long story."

"Okay, look Mickey, I'm not going any place until I know what's going on, there isn't any rush to get to Brighton and I need to know what's happening. "Mickey looked agitated and resigned himself to addressing my persistent efforts toward some kind of explanation.

"Okay here we go………."

I slumped back in the car seat, as if to

demonstrate, I had all the time in the world and there was no way I was going to budge until I was up to speed. What was revealed gradually started to turn my face puce, my stomach liquid and my estimation of how the fuck I was going to come out of this situation with any kind of life that could be rebuilt, gradually reduced. Mickey was graphic and spared me no detail in regard to the lengths DJ would go to, to get what he wanted and the whole sorry mess was revealed. Mickey's torture, the capture of Carla and DJ's determination to recapture Lisa made the unexpected visitors at my flat all make sense. "What the….what do you mean you were tortured dude."

Mickey leaned slightly forward to un- button his shirt, peeled it open and turned to face me head on. I nearly threw up as he revealed the mess that used to be a chest and belly. Some sort of grotesque ripped up sequence of pictures in a crude, bluey, brown, bloody, shitty mess. If I hadn't already been convinced, Mickey went on to fully confirm, that DJ and his merry men would stop at nothing to get exactly what they wanted. They wanted Lisa and they saw me as an irritating inconvenience, they were prepared to dispense of. Apparently, I or rather my organisation was potentially getting in the way of them controlling Lisa and therefore in line for an early exit from this mortal coil. "They want you out of the way buddy. They've beaten you up. They laid out the money for me to bribe a

H.E.L.P. client to lie bout what you do with you're hands during a client and worker meeting and they will stop at fuckin nothin to do you over. If you resist much longer, I swear to god man, you will be fuckin gone Charlie. What the hell you doin trailing off with me, to look for Lisa? Didn't you get the message the other night mate? Christ, Charlie, if they can do this to my chest, what do you think they will do to you man? Do you not get it, I am only here to officially see you off man."

My anger was boiling over as I heard the sorry tail of grown up bully boys who had, in the space of a few short weeks, had already turned this young boy into a pawn of their delusions of grandeur and world domination.

"Look Mickey, it doesn't have to be this way. There has to be a way to beat these bastards and get you and Lisa out of their grip forever."

"CHARLIE FOR FUCKS SAKE, THEY WILL NOT STOP OKAY, AT NOTHIN, FUCKING BACK OFF, LOOK AROUND YOU."

"Calm down Mickey, what do you mean?" Mickey went on to carefully point out the suspiciously positioned giant black Range Rover and beautiful black Audi A7.

"That one contains a lovely geezer named Dwayne, DJ, fuckin, phyco maniac. Leader of the pack, leader of the ex gang members formally known as the BEA boys. His role is to regain his possession, namely, the lovely Lisa, my sister and in the meantime, hold my girlfriend, whom

you know very well, from all the good work we do back at the bloody office. She's a fuckin hostage, until he has assurances you are going to back down and leave him to his quarry. That big bastard over there is the lovely cuddly animal that carved me up. His name is Regis and he's one of the meanest Sadistic wankers god ever gave legs to. His job today, is to see DJ go off in that direction with me, to get Lise, while then following you all the way back into London, as they gain their reassurances you are, indeed, backing the fuck off. If you decide any other course of action, I will get screwed, Lisa and Carla will get screwed and you Charlie, well you'll just get fuckin shot
- NOW DO YOU GET IT?"
"Mickey, listen to me, do you honestly believe that if I back off, these idiots will let you and especially you're sister and Carla go!"
"CHARLIE, I GOTTA TRY! OR FUCK, I'M A DEAD MAN." "Listen to me Mickey; you can't just give in to these people. Think of Lisa, we've got to get her away from the loony cult people and this mad out of control gang. Come on, think about it."
"Charlie, I know you mean well okay." Mickey suddenly went calm as if he had decided his next course of action was inevitable. He knew from the look in my eye, I wasn't about to be put off and after working with me for over a year, he had also learned very early on, how stubborn I was. He produced the gun and I found myself faced

215

with a .choice. As the adrenalin surged through me, I made a move for the loaded pistol. I wasn't even sure if I cared if it went off or not. My motivation now was to fight bullies, injustice and any obstacle that was between me and trying to make any sense of my crazy, out of control world. The crack of the pistol made me wince more than the pain, which was surprisingly slow kicking in. I looked down at my wound and it didn't seem to register straight away, the blood leaking from my side was mine. My hands were still wrestling the weapon from Mickey's hand almost independently of my brain. My mind was trying to decide what normally happens in films at this stage, as; I had no real life experience to draw from. I got the gun, quite easily, as I think Mickey was as surprised as I was, when the gun went off. I took it and swung it around and caught Mickey so hard on the temple, all I could hear was a strange guttural noise coming from his throat. It wasn't a noise I'd heard before and it made me wonder whether Mickey was already in a bit of a bad way, to have crumpled so easily. I wheeled backward in my seat and pulled back my legs, thrusting my full weight to kick and force Mickey against his driver's door. I continued to kick his torso and was conscious how easy it would be to disable him, given the injuries he'd just shown me. When he was dazed to the point, I was pretty sure he didn't know what day it was, I leaned forward, wincing, with pain, opened his drivers door and let him slump out of the car on to the concrete below.

I noticed the two black vehicles, both fire up their engines! With a shift of my weight and a substantial loss of blood, I managed to gain driving seat positioning, hit the accelerator and aiming the car at the car park entrance, I was off. My rage had not subsided. No one was going to fucking tell me who I was and wasn't going to help. As I left the car park, the large Range Rover was the more prepared and so we nearly provided the few people sitting at the window of the little chef with some added Sunday morning entertainment, only just avoiding collision. The large vehicle missed me by inches, but I was away. The element of surprise and the fact that the Audi had to stop to collect Mickey from the ground gave me the head start I needed. I don't suppose DJ and Regis wanted the added complication of potentially having to explain Mickey's bruised and battered body, especially if he was able to get himself to a hospital. Mickey's car was nowhere as powerful as my pursuers, or my hire car, but I was confident I knew the area well enough to escape those who were now hunting me. For the next ten or so miles I caught a glimpse of at least one of my adversaries and with constant doubling back by exiting the M27 and re-entering it again a couple or so villages later, I was confident I would be able to make my way to Brighton undeterred. I was less confident I would make it however, before I bled to death. I knew instinctively, it

217

was a flesh wound and that, I wasn't in immediate danger. The bullet had hit me, like a powerful punch in the ever growing, fatty part of my right side. I had absolutely no idea how much blood I had lost or how much more I could afford to lose before I would pass out. I hadn't seen a black Audi or Range Rover for about five miles and thought it would be more prudent to seek some first aid than just keep driving until I dropped dead. I managed to find a small town and was pleased Boots the Chemist, were to be found in just about every town in the country. After managing to find an old anorak in the boot of Mickey's car and covering up the fact I was beginning to look like an RTA victim, eternally thankful that I had my wallet on me, I managed to find bandages and pads. I was hopeful, rather than confident of stemming the flow of blood from my side. A quick stop off at a quiet layby, a patch up job on my leaking side, a revision of my goals and reasons why the hell I was risking life and limb to pursue this course of search and rescue, for someone who, essentially was not even on my list of top 10 deserving cases and I was back on track. I headed toward Brighton, my mission was clear and my quest was to reach whatever it was that would eventually prove, if only to myself, that I was a decent person.

* * * *

Carla sat huddled in the passenger seat of Maxie's Audi. She hadn't been able to reach Mickey, since her release. Both her mobile and his, had previously been taken from them upon capture. Carla's plan, was to get to Brighton, find the ATONEMENT head quarters, convince Lisa she was worthy of forgiveness, hopefully, bump into Mickey, reunite them all and live happily ever after. In reality she knew that she was just thrusting herself into an unknown and complicated situation, that she had helped to create and moreover was hoping, she could help to resolve, in some small way. She glanced across at Maxie, his large face, set like granite, as he concentrated through the rain. She realized how fortunate she was that his crisis of conscience had coincided with her own plans. She'd overheard Ricky and his other brain cell, Dave, talk about DJ's rants about Charlie and how much he would like to disembowel him. Plus, the fact that if he had to go to Brighton to drag Lisa away from ATONEMENT himself he would actually do it. She hoped against hope it wouldn't come to that, or, at least if DJ was on route, she and Maxie would beat him to it.

* * * *

Death is for many of us the gate of hell; but we are inside on the way out, not outside on the way in. ~George Bernard Shaw

Chapter 17
Fairway's Haven

Lisa had arrived the previous evening and was lapping up the attention lavished upon her. Camille had been there to welcome her; she couldn't remember the last time such courtesy had been paid to her, unless of course, the pseudo lust fuelled attempts by previous clients had qualified. The house seemed enormous, but she had still struggled to find it in the sprawling countryside. She wasn't exactly familiar with East Sussex, but the map had led her more inland than she had expected, onto the South Downs. She had negotiated what seemed like endless dusty roads, eventually reaching a very long driveway, leading to 'Fairways Haven' – The home of ATONEMENT.

Not much had been expected of her when she had arrived and Lisa had been left to settle in. She'd met a few, odd, but excessively friendly individuals in the hallways and landings, but all in all was feeling very positive about escaping her traumatic existence in London. This morning she had woken up refreshed and even found the piped music that had entered her room, although intrusive, quite relaxing. She had caught only a few of the lyrics, but essentially, it was religious and something she thought she might hear in a cathedral. There had been a knock on the door, just as she was thinking about getting up and exploring further. The voice coming through over the music, was informing her someone would be along to collect her in a little while.

Camille and a rather strange looking man dressed somewhere between the styles of an Indian guru and a hippy from London in the 1960's, entered her room without invite, about ten minutes later.

"Hey, hang on, I'm not really decent."

"We try not to hide behind normal conformist ideas of decency, dictated by the world Lisa," stated the guru / hippy man.

"Yeah, right, but that doesn't mean you get to see my tits buddy, so do you wanna back off, an let me get ready please?"

Camille turned to Guru / hippy man. "Its okay Greg, Lisa is new to us, she will learn of her routine today, let's go Lisa."

"Routine? Can I have just a few minutes, please?"

"No, Lisa our group will teach you discipline and we may as well start now. You have an appointment with Tony and Tanya in five minutes. They will be acting as your induction team and are at the other side of the grounds so we need to go now, so, come along."

Lisa was starting to feel somewhat uncomfortable; however, she had been away from normal society, even during her existence in London, for so long, that for all she knew this weird kind of set up, could well have been perfectly acceptable to most people. She was literately led through the building, out into what

221

appeared to be a huge courtyard, from where it seemed possible to enter at least five other entrances to this colossal building, via various other doors and archways. Lisa noticed a vast contrast between the residents she had encountered so far. They either looked like they'd been dropping .ecstasy tablets from the moment they'd woken up, or, they were individuals who seemed really miserable, walking around in a zombie like state. She couldn't help noticing, most, were young women who were being escorted by those who were the ecstasy fuelled house dwellers. She was yet to encounter anyone who seemed remotely normal. Even Camille, who had been so lovely when she had first met her at H.E.L.P., looked somehow, affected. She looked trapped, in an other worldly, but very strict persona. Lisa had decided, the moment her dignity had been challenged, back at the room, that she would see out the day and if the mysteriously sounding appointment with Tony and Tanya didn't work out, she would make her excuses and politely move on. She would explain she'd been mistaken and off to explore other options away from London.

Lisa, Camille and Greg, who seemed to be acting like he was Camille's pet, arrived outside a room with a small but very heavy oak door. This part of the building was darker, more oppressive somehow and Lisa's resolve to leave quite early on into her experience of ATONEMENT was being confirmed moment by moment. The door creaked open as if it had been transferred straight of a 1970's Hammer Horror film. Lisa was half expecting to hear the sound of thunder and to see lightning appear through the small rectangle window, set in the stone wall to her left. However, the room seemed pleasant enough and although she wondered why the appointment was so important and even enforced, she was starting to relax, as to be fair, she knew she was prone to over-reacting and on the whole the house was wonderfully gothic, atmospheric and somehow quite sensual. Lisa had decided that just maybe, it was all going to work out and that Greg must have just been a one off weirdo in the house. She sat back and rested her head on the lush deep cushioned couch they had led her to, so that she was ready for her *induction*.

Her head however was propelled forward at a dramatic pace, as the door opened crashing dramatically against the wall it opened onto and fear gripped the girl, as adrenalin kicked in and entered her bloodstream at an alarming rate. All hope or thoughts of settling down with these eccentrics evaporated the moment she clapped eyes on the couple introduced to her as, Tony and Tanya came into view.

* * * *

Thank god for that, I thought I wasn't ever going to find this bloody place! My only challenge now, apart from the obvious one of trying to keep the blood flow at bay, was to approach the house undetected. Christ, I thought; if I had seen this scene in a film, I would have thought it was a bloody cliché. But as I arrived at the house the rain had turned into a drizzle with a mist that seemed to be rolling off the South Downs, starting to engulf the house. My view of the building was therefore obscured, I was feeling terrible as a result of being shot and I wasn't sure if it was loss of blood, shock, or mental exhaustion that was causing my head to throb as if it felt like there was a nest of rats clawing away at my brain. The driveway was well endowed with greenery, but from what I could see from the road I would need a bit of luck when I got closer up. It didn't look as though there were any other suspicious visitors with evil intent, so I hoped it would stay that way and said a little thank you heavenward that I seemed to be alone at the house was alone. I reached the edge of the shrubbery and was aware my side ached quite badly. I had no previous experience of gunshot wounds and figured a wound was a wound and as long as the bullet wasn't inside me and I wasn't losing too much blood, I thought I would be okay. I planned to get to an A & E after I had contacted Lisa I figured I would claim I ripped myself open on some barbed wire. My biggest challenge was becoming apparent, as I realized I

wasn't as .nimble as I used to be on this mission
and could have done with carrying a little less
weight, never mind having a hole in my side. I'll
edge around the walls until I find an opening,
there doesn't seem to be anyone out here and I
haven't seen any CCTV.

I eventually saw a small opening at the base of
the outside wall. It looked like it could well have
been a window that had lost its glass long ago,
which, may well have led to a basement. At least
it would get me in. I started to crawl inside the
small opening, having sprinted from the last bush
that was able to conceal me, to the red brick wall.
I was extremely careful not to disturb my
dressings, or twist excessively. I hadn't banked
on the fact that the opening of the window was a
lot further off the floor from the inside
perspective, than from the outside, so, I had to
hang and drop, aggravating my wound once
again. Shit, this better be worth the agro. I
reminded myself, Lisa may not even be here. I
was in anyhow and crept about in the dark,
groping around trying to work out how to
proceed. The door was open leading to wooden
stairs, which presumably, would lead me further
into the house. There was no sign of people. My
heart was starting to palpitate, as I suddenly
realized those who occupied the house may well
be as mad as I thought they were and here I was
trespassing on their property.

I managed to dodge out of sight of the first
people I had encountered so far, by ducking

behind a huge sofa in a room big enough to hold a football pitch. It looked like I was in what seemed to be a huge wing of the house. The house occupants I'd dodged seemed to consist of a relatively small take up of the vast space available to them and so, it was quite easy to duck and dive, pick up snippets of conversation, only serving to confirm they were all freaks. Then I heard a group in a kitchen area and the name, 'Lisa'. My ears pricked and ready to spy, I edged closer to see if it were possible they were talking about the girl, who, was starting to seriously inconvenience my normal routine. Over and over in my head I was castigating myself, searching, asking, wondering, what the hell I thought I was doing, wandering around half dead, attempting what may well become a rescue attempt on someone I hardly even knew. I know however, I was driven. I also somehow knew that the preservation of my very soul was dependant on this little mission and yet how? I hadn't got a clue.

"Yes my child, we do indeed have a new member. She will not be ready to join our house properly however, for some time. You must remember something of your own initial rebellion, teaching and enlightenment, when you first arrived with us."

"Yes Father."There were various mumbles and murmurs that suggested the required understanding and submission, then……..

"Where is she staying Father?"

226

"The normal preparation will take place, as always in the East Wing, until the time of her testing, in the big tower. Don't worry yourselves; she will come through, you all do you know."

Bingo, he even pointed and as I spied Jed through the crack in the door, I realized I wasn't to far away, as the tower, of which there was only one, was only a courtyard away. The East wing must have been the long row of grey buildings leading to the ominous looking tower. I was starting to feel slightly feint, as I hadn't eaten for hours and I had, after all, started my day off by being shot. I was determined to reach Lisa, as I would bet quite a lot on the fact, that, no one at Fairways Haven had told her she was in for a 'time of testing'. I eased my way away from my vantage point, turned and as I did, noticing someone was heading straight for me. In a shot, I darted left and found myself fortunately heading in the direction I needed to be going in. This led me down darker and dingier stone walled corridors and if I hadn't been scared and in pain it might have looked quite intriguing. The corridors led to a dimly lit even narrower, stone floor alleyway type area and I was starting to realize if it got any darker, I would need a torch to be able to continue. I was surprised how determinedly I was driving myself on; convinced I was going to find something that would incriminate the cult, significantly enough to see the Police crawling all over it, as soon as I could get news out. Only one dungeon type room lay at the end of the trail. The walls were again made of stone and there were plenty of areas that had fallen into disrepair. The difficulty was going to lie in finding out what was occurring within the dungeon; undetected. I heard a low groaning that eventually turned into a desperate whimpering yelp, type noise as I edged forward gingerly, not sure now what type of surface I was dealing with underfoot. It was definitely emanating from a human and again, I was spurred on by a desperately disturbing noise. Excellent! There was a huge round stone pillar, positioned perfectly in front of the dungeon entrance. The pillar had a shelf type ledge built into it at a perfect height for sitting. I could at last rest, as my side was now throbbing rather threateningly. I would need to spy on the inhabitants of the dungeon, at the same time and tried to work out if there was enough of a gap in the door or wall, to see in. I took a minute to rest, as I was starting to feel really drained, thinking I might black out. I looked down and lifted up my stained shirt as I sat. I was still bleeding, albeit slightly. It couldn't be good; I had been losing blood for a good part of the day, even if I had been quite proud of the patch up job I'd completed earlier, on the wound. There were times when I had often reflected upon the mass of experiences I had accumulated over the years. There wasn't too much that shocked me these days and I was often accused, at work of not caring enough, if I failed to react as if I was horrified enough, when I'd been told yet another terrible story of human suffering. I was on this occasion genuinely stunned at what I saw, as I peered through the cracks in the wall. I literally felt my breath leaving me and becoming increasingly harder to catch. It was well lit inside a large round concourse inside the room. I could see easily in and she was just hanging there mumbling and groaning. The bastards had tied up a young girl with ropes and she was obviously either pumped full of drugs or delirious with fear; or both. Totally naked and vulnerable, as, her hands were tied above her head, so that she couldn't cover up, or protect herself. She was twitching, sweaty and every now and then, I had heard her whisper, please, please, please, I don't know why.........It would then trail off into more whimpering. It took me awhile to adjust to this new situation and now I had to try and plan how I could help this poor girl. While I was getting over the shock and the annoyance that accompanied it, I was disturbed. Six or seven figures dressed like hooded hippies were coming my way. I moved like lightning, surprising myself, given my injury, into an alcove in a darker corner, just opposite the pillar. There was still a good chance I would be seen, but I was trapped, so, I crouched down and made myself as small as possible. As the cult members seemed to be moving, zombie like toward the dungeon entrance, it was obvious they were singled minded, almost trance like and wouldn't have seen me if I'd let off a firework in there with me in the tiny alcove.

The little troop of hippy weirdo's entered the dungeon and surrounded the girl. I regained my place back behind the pillar and saw her wince as tears were now rolling down her pale checks. One of the freaks stood slightly forward of the rest and stared into the girls face. He started to address her, "Emma, we all fought at first, my child. We are here to guide your soul into atonement and never ending peace on this earth". With that, Emma cried even more, as if resigned to her fate and the group of long haired monsters started to chant. They had formed a neat circle around Emma and proceeded to chant endlessly at her.

I had studied this kind of thing whilst doing my Psychology degree and knew exactly what they were up too. If an individual was subjected to humiliation and feelings of extreme vulnerability for long enough, hence the enforced nakedness, along with an imposed prisoner status, the theory was that they would eventually break. The victim would eventually be susceptible to their minds literally falling into a state of complete acceptance and slavish obedience. Once broken, or indeed during the process of their resolves being utterly shattered, an individual would be equally more and more open to accepting any information, or, indoctrination, anyone, or group, wanted to inflict upon them. The problem I was now faced with was that this ritual torture was something I couldn't walk away from and Lisa wasn't the only one who needed rescuing. Christ, there was a girl, in this building, who I had slept with, who didn't know I was here at all. If only she knew what a little adventure she was creating between her brother, the gang she'd left and the dick head that was all shot up and would soon be less than useless to her. I had to get to her quickly, if a rescue was on the cards. There was a girl strung up like a gutted pig, being forced to accept the doctrine of the damned, needing immediate attention. Not to bloody mention that potentially, there was a posse of gang members and rabid *EX* employees on route to do me as much damage as they were capable. I'd already worked out that it could be considerable, if not fatal damage and that was even before Mickey had been so graphic about the gangster's intent. Oh, and just so I didn't get too cocky about my chances of survival, I had a hole in my side that had just started to leak again. I made my way back through the narrow hallway, leading to the wider corridors, backtracking from earlier and wondered how I would identify Lisa's room. I need not have worried, as all the rooms had names on them, hallelujah, a break! I found myself praying Ms. Lisa Baker had used her real name as she booked in, as, she would have been fairly paranoid about being tracked down by the tenacious Mr. DJ. There was no Lisa Baker, but there was a crudely written LB, written on a piece of paper and blue tacked to one of the red painted doors. As I risked walking in on what might have been yet another naked young girl, I was suitably cautious. Another piece of good luck, the door was not locked. It made sense, why wouldn't they have names on doors and open access; after all I don't suppose they had many idiots with open wounds, running around the grounds trying to set their captives free.

* * * *

When I die, I want a priest, a rabbi, and a Protestant clergyman. I want to hedge my bets.
~Wilson Mizner

Chapter 18
Two Fallen Rhino's

There she was in all her stunning, but vulnerable looking glory. Dressed in a tracksuit type jumpsuit and asleep, she was more attractive than I had remembered. I sat next to her and checked out my intentions. I hoped to goodness and for the sake of my own sanity that I hadn't embarked upon this venture for the wrong motives. When I was suitably convinced that I would be determined to get her and all of the Emma's out of there, even if she had looked like the lovechild of Elephant man and a circus act hairy woman, I relaxed. Why hadn't there been any boy victims names on the doors I'd passed? Maybe this was the young virgin's wing of the house. Then I remembered Lisa and her possible tally of sexual partners and wondered if there were any virgin's left in the world under the age of 15? Stupid, old, fogey. I was feeling delirious; hypocritical and my head had started to feel like little hand grenades had been strategically set to go off inside it every ten minutes or so.

She woke with an almighty jump. I had to launch myself at her with a cushion to prevent her from screaming. It occurred to me that she would have already experienced a measure of weirdness and would be on the alert, ready for a possible attack. Even a girl, almost half my size, would have been able to do me some serious damage, given the condition I was in. I tried to be gentle, but, she was ready to attack. She was also drugged and only just starting to come to. I was grateful, as, my strength was leaving me at an alarming rate. After a few token efforts at, windmill hitting me, her arms flaying around with no discipline or direction, she stared at me over the cushion. Then she made a noise that sounded like a muffled, "YOU." "Hello again." I felt strangely embarrassed and flashed her a weak smile."Are you here to arrest me?"

Her words were slightly slurred and it sounded and looked a little amusing, as Lisa's confusion and drug induced stupor, caused her to dribble out of the side of her mouth.

"No, I thought I would try and save you, if that's okay."

"Ha, you look in a worse state than me."

"Thanks, but I have been shot today."

"DJ, right. The one who shot you?"

"Your brother."

Lisa went pale instantly "Oh god, what the hell is occurrin with that boy? I was trying to escape the bloody madness of my life and it's now even madder and following me around."

Rather than risk Lisa being even more traumatized by the complications of recent events, I tried to quickly relay as much information as I could. She found out who she had slept with on that lust filled night, who she had robbed blind, who had decided to help her after he had seen her at his workplace and been beaten up by her special friends. To top it off, I was able to confirm that her brother worked for me and yes, her best friend was knocking around with Mickey. She seemed quite able at filling in the gaps, knowing DJ the way she did and that Mickey was probably, blindly trying to clumsily do the right thing. She was reminded of the anger she felt for him and Carla. No matter what, they should have been looking out for her. They should have been thinking of her, with the same consideration they'd both tried to protect their own miserable interests. They had, after all, known the hell she was living in. Lisa was candid and quite apologetic herself as we recalled the night we met, the robbery and the way in which she had been able to shrug off the events relatively easily. We even managed to raise a laugh, albeit stifled, given the predicament that we were now in. I was pleased she didn't really think I was a dirty, old, fuckin, pervert and that she acknowledged her own measure of responsibility for that night. It had always been hard for me to get my head around the lines separating victims and those that inflicted chaos on the world. Lisa, for all her worldly experience and probably numerous robberies and other vices, was clearly a victim who needed help. By the time she had explained why it was so important for her to escape the clutches of DJ and offered heartfelt appreciation of my appearance, she had almost shrugged of the effects of the drugs in her system. She put her arm around me, kissed me lightly on the check and we shared a moment, suggesting that if we ever managed to get out of the house of hell, we were united in our solidarity against injustice.

"Look Lisa, I know a little about being let down by family and close friends and believe me, at the end of the day, you gotta try and let it go girl."

"Yeah, maybe."

"But, for now, we gotta get the fuck away from this place and get to somewhere we can report all this shit to someone." I carefully explained the trauma Emma was going through just down the corridors, as; I thought it might freak her out. I guessed correctly that finding out that the house was planning a similar fate for her, didn't go down to well. She didn't seem too surprised, as she had already sampled the delights ahead, with her earlier appointment with Tanya and Tony. We were agreed on one thing, we had to get the hell out. "Come on, we can't risk the corridors of the mad. I'm getting weaker by the minute and you are still likely to dribble down the hallway. They'll just follow the trail of spit and blood and catch us."

She smiled a beautiful smile, looked at me and said, "Thanks Charlie."

I looked tentatively out of the window; I was half expecting to find bars on. Even though the task of jumping out the window seemed eminently harder with us both feeling decidedly delicate, it looked doable. There was a ledge and from there we could try and climb down the foliage growing up the walls. I wondered why security wasn't more stringent, given the fact they were risking many young recruits fleeing in terror, but, realized that Lisa would never have made it on her own and they would have kept the new ones all well drugged up, in the early days.

"Okay, I'm gonna go first. Get on the ledge, then ease you down to me." "Okay, let's do it my hero." Surely she wasn't flirting? I lifted my tired, injured body, slowly, up and over the window sill. I hung for a moment, looked up at an anxious looking Lisa and dropped to the ledge. I then very briefly realized with some inevitability that my body had decided to throw out a much delayed protest. As I hit the ledge below me, I blacked out I had no idea how long I'd been lying there. It could have been a few minutes, or a whole day. All I did know was that I was in a lot of pain, felt like I had been hit by a bus and could see a pathway leading to the rear of the house from my new vantage point. I was tempted to panic when I saw that Lisa's face had now disappeared from above me and there were two familiar looking black cars parked about five hundred yards away at the side of the mansion. There was also a third vehicle more concealed from view. The two black cars were parked at the side of the road, the other, in a clearing just off the narrow country lane. I scrambled up to the window sill and lifted myself up high enough to see into Lisa's room. She had gone!

* * * *

Maxie turned the corner after the long journey from London, through the twisty lanes running across the South Downs, eventually reaching the same spot as the rest of the uninvited guests to the main head quarters and torture chambers that were ATONEMENT.

As he entered the majestic view that revealed the grand house, he immediately saw the two huge black BEA trademark vehicles parked just slightly to the side of the road.

"Looks like we've been beaten to it mate."

"Shit, they'll find Lisa you know. Come on Maxie boy, think of something."

"Well, if we go bundling in there, we risk bumpin inta DJ and who eva else he has dragged inta this fuckin mess."

"We can't just give up mate, surely."

"Who said anything bout givin up babe. Let's see wat pans out, this place is big man, plus, we don't even know Lisa is here. They might go in heavy like, but, they're not the brightest matches in the box, so my best guess is they storm in, storm out, havin cracked sum heads and come out empty."

"Hope you're right Maxie, mate, you're a sweetie for takin all this trouble. You got a soft spot for our Lise too have ya mate?"

Maxie decided to keep his council.

"We should hole up Carla, watch, wait, see wat occurs, that's wat I think." "K."

Maxie reversed and drove as far as he could away from the two vehicles already partly embedded in the undergrowth, being careful to not leave them to far to walk back and find a suitable stake out area. Ensconced safely in the trees and resting on branches conveniently available at seat height for observation, Max and Carla took up position.

* * * *

DJ was in no mood for negotiation and made a determined stride toward what he thought was the back door. Regis wasn't far behind and was confident that the arsenal of guns he had collected for the day's outing was neither excessive, nor, inadequate to intimidate a bunch of religious freaks holding DJ's prize captive. DJ wrapped on the door, left it about four milliseconds to gain a response, then blasted away with his handgun at the area of the door; he thought the lock should be located in. He wasted no time entering the building, seemingly demonstrating as little caution as he did awareness, of what might lie within. He was a man overflowing with testosterone and determination to find Lisa, if, there was the remote possibility she was in fact, there to be found. As the pair moved swiftly toward any signs of life within the house, the inhabitants had sensed danger and were already scurrying around trying to locate leaders who would know what to do about the termites who had invaded the ants nest. "Who the fuck's in charge, in this doss ouse?" DJ bellowed, leaving little doubt, he meant business. "I am, my dear fellow."
"Who the fuck are you?"
"My name is the Reverend Jed King sir and you sir, are trespassing on private property."
"I sir, don't give a shit. Now, this can be simple or painful, sup, to you mate. I'm lookin for Lisa,...... Lisa Baker, so if she's here mate, you need to make this real quick, as I would hate to

ave ta fuckin blow you're fuckin brains out."

"You've been misinformed sir, we know nobody of that name here."

"Well that's a fuckin surprise, so we gonna have a look okay. Jus remember, for every minute it takes us to find her, an you is lyin, I'm gonna take more shit outa you an your little fuckin flock, okay, it's totally up ta you."

"Look, you might be used to storming around where you come from, but here........." The bad reverend tailed off, as DJ smacked him firmly across the side of the head.

DJ had fallen into the trap common to those who were used to getting their way without question. He had vastly underestimated the strength and guile of their intended victims. As DJ and Regis had decided to move on and search the place, based on the fact that Mr. King wasn't prepared to help them, two armed gunmen flanked them. The house was full of drugs and one of the many advantages of substances that were applied to sedate the inhabitants was that they could easily be adapted for the use of powerful tranquilizer darts. A house with such shady secrets had to learn how to defend itself. The darts were expertly dispatched and after a couple of moments of DJ and Regis were flaying around shouting expletives and trying to throw wildly inaccurate punches, not to mention the odd ill aimed bullet. The two giants hit the floor like two African Rhino's, being poached for their horns. "I have located their cars, shall we take them out?" "Yes thank you". The Reverend turned to address yet another of his faithful followers. "Lay them near their vehicles" Now they know we are not undefended, they should think twice about returning. Take their guns. Well done brothers, good shooting. Now, come we must attend Ms. Lisa. I have decided to bring forward her testing. I cannot afford her jumping out the window again, now can I?"

.

* * * *

I had worked out that they wouldn't have left me where I was, if they had any idea I had been on the ledge. I was confident I remained undetected. I was concerned Lisa wouldn't be fairing well with these lunatics and was just as convinced I would definitely need to hunt for her again. This time, I feared I would also probably need to fight off some of the chanting masses inhabiting the grand house, second rescue time around! While I was coming too on the window ledge, I had spied a third black car arrive and hide itself away from the side of the house. I was in no doubt it was Carla, who had approached a nearer hiding place, but wasn't sure who her companion was. I'd also witnessed two hulking giants being hauled onto a truck and driven away and dumped near the black vehicles by the side of the road. I was enthralled by the *in house* entertainment, as it had taken seven religious maniacs to shift the dead weighted, beasts of men on to the truck. Lisa Baker seemed to be the key to a lot of people's destiny; I wondered how it was possible that just one individual could be such a catalyst of activity and aspiration.

* * * *

Suicide is man's way of telling God, "You can't fire me - I quit." ~Bill Maher.

Chapter 19
Who is Emma?

"Now Lisa, what's this I hear about you trying to
    jump out of your window my dear child."
"You weird fuckin bastards had better let me go.
I tell you, you'll be fuckin sorry, if you touch me
again."
Tanya continued calmly, as it became clear,
Lisa's opinion wasn't high on anybody's agenda.
"You are here child, because you chose
atonement for your existence. You simply can't
jump out of a window when things get a little
uncomfortable."
"You fuckin bitch, I swear to God, if you touch
me."Lisa was already tied, her hands above her
head. Tony stepped forward. This was the part
of the job he enjoyed the most. Tony had been a
founding member of ATONEMENT and had
seen many young bodies. The body that had
been presented earlier today however, had caused
him to look forward to the time of testing with
even more eagerness than normal.
"Hello Lisa, you remember me, we met earlier. I
did try and warn you then, that this time would
come. I didn't realize we would be seeing you
again so soon, but, as Tanya say's, you can't go
trying to escape; now you have chosen the
guidance we want to help you with. Oh and you
might like to stop struggling, those ropes will rip
into your wrists if you don't calm down my
dear."

"BASTARD." "Yes probably, however let us proceed." Tony reached for the syringe, handed it to Tanya and then .reached for the zip on Lisa's track suit top. In all the days that had passed working for DJ, Lisa had never felt as vulnerable or helpless as she did at that moment. Tanya administered the drug that would, in a few seconds cause her to be sedated enough to curb Lisa's desire of ripping her and Tony's hearts out with her bare hands. At the same time the drug would leave the mind aware of everything they wanted to teach her. They had been doing this awhile now and they had the dosage and formula down to a fine art.

"Bastard…..fuckin wank…..Bas……t.."

It wasn't long before Lisa was completely naked and hanging hopelessly from a rope that was tied to a metal ring, that was in turn attached to a chain that hung from a plate bolted to the stone ceiling. "Now Lisa, this is a process. It will take some time before we are able to start the first session, so there's no rush. We are going to leave you now, but when we return, we will bring those among us who you need to listen to okay." Leaving the victim alone, was part of the process, reminding them, there was no one around to help and that they were indeed at the complete mercy of their captors, that there was absolutely no chance of escape.

* * * *

245

Although I was weak, I'd been able to scramble into the room. The small bedside clock informed me, I'd been lying undetected on the ledge for about an hour. I reckoned that, if, they had walked in and found Lisa climbing out the window, they had been too employed wrestling her back in, to bother checking if anyone had gone out before her. As I sat there contemplating my next move, an overwhelming temptation washed over me to escape now and leave the house and its inhabitants, too its fate. After all, I would surely be doing my duty if I reported the goings on, in this mad house and I didn't know how long my body could keep going. My justification was valid enough; I wasn't going to last much longer limping around and dripping everywhere. After a few minutes, vivid ideas of what they might be doing to Lisa scorched across my brain and I was back on track.

I felt very old as I lurched up from Lisa's bed and tried to get my bearings again. I thought I would have to turn right, following the corridor out of this room, to eventually find my way back to the dungeon. What I was going to do when I got there, I had no idea. I was in no shape to be wrestling Lisa away from anyone, even if they were skinny little hippy freaks.

I edged desperately along the corridors again. This time I was more conscious that I'd been leaking and dripping all day. I would be more likely to leave a trail and felt in more ways than one, like a giant, slow moving slug. As I was pretty sure a bloody, gooey line would cause a bit of attention, I had made sure I took the opportunity in Lisa's room to clean up a bit. The good news was, I thought the blood had almost stopped leaving my body. The bad news was, I was feeling hotter and drowsier by the hour. It was imperative I got some treatment soon, or I feared the next blackout would last considerably longer than the one dropping out of the window. So, I moved as fast as I could, also aware I needed to get to Lisa quickly. I was convinced the sound I'd heard from the last room I passed was sobbing. It was a muffled, tired, whimpering sob, that was low pitched and sounded as if it came from someone who was having a bad dream. I looked at the name plate on the door, Emma Williams. I thought there was a very good chance this was the Emma I had seen strung up earlier, suffering the ritual chanting. I also knew I couldn't walk past the door without checking she was okay. The last thing I needed right now was any complications or to be discovered, but the sound coming from the small bedroom was heart wrenching. What would happen if I was heard, or worse, if she was so traumatized she screamed the bloody place down, if I went in there? Caution considered, I still couldn't ignore the desperate cries coming from her room, so I approached as though I was about to consider catching a very large venomous snake.

Again, the door opened easily, but as I entered, instead of hysterics, Emma sat up and as if she knew I wasn't one of her torturing bastards and started to plead with me to rescue her.

"SSSHHHUUUSSSHHH - shush now. Its okay," I said as if I was trying to convince myself.

"Please, I just wanna go home, please."

"Okay, listen to me Emma, I'm going to do everything I can okay, but I need your help, I need you to be quiet now okay. I promise, I'll protect you now, okay, but I'm injured and I need your help okay?"

It was manifestly obvious; Emma was terrified of staying in the room. Her eyes kept darting toward the door, each time she heard any sound at all outside, even the hint of a distant cough. She started to relax once I'd confirmed I was on her side and that the plan was to get the hell out of that godforsaken house.

"Look Emma, I know the last thing you want to be reminded of, is the place where they tied you up." I was careful not to use the word dungeon, but she started crying again anyway. "Look sweetheart, I've got a friend, who I think might be there now, so, I must go and try to get her out, before I can help you. But, I will help I promise. Will you come with me, help me get her out. Then we can scarper, honest."

Emma started to shake. I knew she wanted to tell me she could never go back there, but I sensed immediately that there was a substance about this girl. The reason the cult hadn't broken her yet, was probably down to the fact she seemed strong, sensible, intelligent. This I could tell, even though, at the moment she was sitting on her bed sobbing and dressed in a ridicules pink robe that left little to the imagination. What struck me most was Emma's capacity to recover so quickly and start thinking for us both. Within minutes she had got out of the little pink number, reached her wardrobe and was dressing herself in jeans and a woollen fleece type top. I noticed these were the only clothes she had been allowed to keep, along with some dirty trainers and even though I had seen her earlier, trust up naked; I turned my head away, as the pink robe hit the floor. The way in which she had discarded the silly piece of clothing, suggested to me it was a garment the religious crackpots had required her to wear. Within approximately five minutes Emma had transformed from a jabbering jelly of a girl, into superwoman. I had half expected her to go into a spin, or a phone booth to complete her transformation. I was so grateful, I too nearly cried. It made me realize just how weak the day had left me. I was starting to feel panicky in the knowledge, I just wanted to curl up in the foetal position and fall asleep. I was well aware; this was the body's way of warning me it was about time for me and it, to give up.

Emma knew the way back to the dungeon better than I could ever be able to remember and was also, thankfully, able to support me. My legs had started to buckle with weakness every few hundred yards, I couldn't help noticing how freakishly strong Emma was for a relatively small girl. Walking into her room was starting to seem like the best decision I'd made for awhile. I smiled as she even started to encourage me with statements that were half whispered.

"Come on Charlie, you're gonna make it, we're gonna get your friend and get out, don't worry, I'll get you to a hospital, come on babe."

"Babe?" I'd noticed at work, that younger people often referred to just about everyone as, babe. Then I realized that concentrating on such trivial nonsense for any length of time, was a sign my mind was drifting into shutdown mode.

Emma was astute in just about every way and now, taking on the leadership role with gusto. She picked up on the fact I desperately wanted to allow myself to give in to my body screaming at me to go to ground. She tried to keep the conversation going as we approached the narrower parts of the corridors.

"What's your friends name Charlie?" "Lisa." "I'd heard those bastards talking about a new girl coming in last night called Lisa. How did you meet Lisa?" "Trust me; you don't wanna hear that story." She gave me a cheeky half grin and a wink, as if she already knew! I don't think I'd ever seen an individual transformed so dramatically and so quickly, ever. As we approached the dungeon it was silent in every direction and I thought I must have got it wrong and they hadn't brought Lisa in for ritual brain washing after all. I slumped on to the ledge built into the pillar and as I did, noticed smatterings of blood I had left there earlier. Emma was feeling bold and went to investigate. Moments later and she was back. "Charlie, come on, someone's in there, is your friend, blonde, pretty and petite?" "That's her. Is she on her own?" "Yeah, they always leave you at first, but they might be back any minute, we don't know how long they've been gone." "Shit, we haven't got anything to cut her down with or cover her up with." "Wrong Charlie! Okay, the cover up thing is a good point but I've got a small sharp knife. I nicked it from dinner time last night, hoping there would be a moment I wasn't drugged up enough to use it on one of the bastards in here, but, I wasn't exactly thinking straight at the time." Something told me her thinking had been, just fine. There was a low mumble approaching and we knew we had to act fast. I was also preparing myself for the moment. They would realize Lisa had disappeared if we did manage to get her back. All hell would break out and I was struggling to think or plan ahead anymore. Emma didn't want to hear anything negative and had cut through Lisa's rope within seconds. "Charlie." "Hi Lisa, I'm kind of hoping this rescue is going to work, sorry I passed out before." "I think they would have got to us anyway Charlie. They were in the room, grabbing at me before you'd hit the ledge, so it was a good thing you were already out, else you'd be hanging here with me." She was drowsy, but intelligible. "Oh nasty, I don't look that great naked these days, but of course, you know that.""My God, I can't believe you," Lisa let out a desperate half laugh, half sigh of relief. Naked as she was, she was ecstatic to see us. More kisses followed and yet, this time they were received, as one who was trying to protect and redeem, rather than exploit. I felt so ashamed of myself, as once again, memories of that night, flashed accusingly at me."Lisa, Emma – Emma, Lisa." "Hi." "Hi, come on, let's find you something to wear girl."Emma came up trumps again and had darted into a vacated room, grabbed what looked like a suitable top and jeans and all within about seven seconds. We'd already passed some abandoned flip flops in a corridor, so, Lisa was clothed. Judging by the fact, most of the hippy boys and girls I'd seen around and had been trying to avoid all day, had been wearing flip flops and Lisa's top and jeans were obviously of hippy origin, I thought we must be in the corridor housing the cult's staff rooms. Emma, Lisa and I, all looked at each other and were tempted to giggle like kids at Lisa's obviously ridicules attire. If we hadn't been acutely aware, we were all still in deep shit, we might well have done. Lisa looked like Charlie Chaplin's hippy brother, in the huge jeans and T-Shirt that had so obviously belonged to a man.

* * * *

Life is what happens to you while you're busy making other plans.
~John Lennon

Chapter 20
The Angel Overseers on Trial
Recriminations!

It was time for those who were overseers, to report to those who, were assigned to serve The Power. Though the ages, this process had always proved messy. As with all forums that sought the truth about any situation, it soon became obvious that one individual's truth only served to shine a light upon another's guilt. It wasn't long before the manoeuvring and counter manoeuvring to gain advantage began.

The atmosphere was tense and everyone involved was already aware that events upon the earth had already developed to such a degree, that it would require, The Power, to take decisive action. The Place of Assembly had been cleared of all other activity and those who had been removed were grateful not to be involved with the discussions, about to take place. Those who are assigned to serve began to address the assembly.

"We have been sent to hear your reports and to transfer the information to The Power and those, who are advisors. It is important to remind every being here now, that we are not those who are advisors ourselves. We are independent of this process and are charged to submit a report only. We make no judgements today, in this place and have been chosen for this task, only because of our history demonstrating skills analysing and

reporting data."
Nathanial responded on behalf of the group.
"We all understand the process of reporting, but
thank you for clarifying." The angel in charge of
the proceedings looked indignant at being
interrupted by Nathanial and continued.
"Let us re-cap! Four of your subordinates who
are assigned to the subject Charlie Becker,
allowed him to return to his life, after finding that
their influence to keep him alive failed. Can we
agree on this matter?"
 Nathanial reluctantly agreed."Good! Now we
must also try to understand why they were
allowed to make this decision alone, gain access
to one of our colleagues upon the Earth, of course
I speak of Michael; seeking to gain his help in
this awful matter, again without the proper
permissions and proceed to do all of this with
what appears to be limited agreement among
them" Nathanial reacted; "We do not know that
they were not in agreement."
"But we do know that two of them were novices,
do we not?""Yes Dina and Gavreel are indeed of
novice status." "Well! We will need to establish
whether the two novices did give their
agreement, or if indeed the two more experienced
of the assigned decided to take control as it
were!"The angel who seemed to be assigned to
making the existence of Charlie Becker's
guardian's unbearably uncomfortable, continued
with his review.

"The events on the earth since the Charlie Becker disaster, have also raised many concerns in the Ultimate Realm, therefore, we will also need to discuss your plans for addressing, what you propose to do, in regard to the lives involved. Charlie Becker died before his appointed and intended time. This took him away from the path that was intended for him and into the Place of Decisions. The decision of those who are assigned to Charlie Becker was to allow him to continue, hoping he would not be diverted permanently. They were able to carry out this plan, as the body had not been harmed or discovered by other humans. The major concern is that Charlie Becker's life has indeed been altered due to what his subconscious remembers about his visit to us. Up until his sojourn into the Place of Decisions; Charlie Becker was self-serving, rarely noticed another living soul, never mind, helping any of them. He is a base man, with base selfish habits! Before his death, Charlie Becker's life was not going in a direction that would have ultimately pleased The Power. Although we have not yet attained the knowledge of what, Ultimate decision, The Power would have made concerning this human. We can all agree his life was not looking very promising. Since the subject human returned and carried on, we have seen a different character starting to emerge. He is demonstrating a desire to help his fellow human's. He has put himself in danger to help just one individual human, when previously,

255

throughout his entire lifespan; this would have seemed highly unlikely. He has also, started to reflect more upon his lifestyle in general and a more positive direction looks as if it might have been taken in regard to this man. We do not have the gift of foresight and we cannot possibly know when the exact appointed time is that Charlie Becker must leave the Earth, *officially*. We only serve and so, all we know is that those who are assigned to him had not been given notice of his imminent demise from the Earth before they allowed him to die the first time. Added to this problem, is the fact that, the notice for Earthly death, has still not been issued! Therefore, he is not to experience his Earthly death for at least six of the human thirty day periods. You see the problem! As we meet here today, Charlie Becker is extremely close to death. AGAIN!

It seems already, that because his first exit from the Earth was so badly handled, he is now so off course, his entire destiny is skewered. The Power will just not tolerate these random and accidental results. I do hope for all our sakes Charlie Becker does not attempt to leave the Earth again until he is supposed too!"

Nathanial could take no more.

"We do feel we have matters in hand concerning this, if I may……"

"Please let me continue," interjected the strong and almost aggressive tones of the angel who served." "You will have sufficient time to issue your reports. If he were to stray anymore dramatically, then, this will be the proof that, decisions he is making now, are outside of his predestined path. It is extremely unlikely The Power would accept that this sudden change is a result of his self-reflection and subsequent repentance. Charlie Becker is now way off course and we need to be convinced you have the situation under control!" Nathanial was now willing to let someone else to respond; as he was growing weary and beginning to believe that no amount of excuses would suffice now. Zuriel moved forward. "We think we can adjust him sufficiently, so that The Powers purposes are no longer being thwarted." "You think!""Yes we are quite sure.""Well you had better make up your minds about the difference between being sure and thinking. And you had better make up your minds as to whether your subordinates agreed together in their decision to send Charlie back!" "We were confident that Rashnu (Angel of Judgement) and Micah (Angel of the Devine) They were more than experienced to take responsibility. They are both very knowledgeable about such things and indeed were both Overseers themselves in previous missions.""And we might agree with you, but taking a lead is one thing and making an independent decision and refusing to comply with the laws that govern such things is another. Plus, you raise an interesting fact, in that the two you mention as having once served as overseers were demoted, were they not, for very good reason? Please answer directly. Were you, as overseers, consulted before this decision was made?" "No." "Were all four who, are assigned to Charlie Becker, fully consulted before the decision to send him back to his body was made?""No." "Let us remember, there are two issues here. The final decision, made, by those who are assigned is, a matter, for The Power and the advisors. Laws were broken and this must be conveyed in our report. We will listen to any other evidence you may have, but, can we first address the other weighty matter?

What measures have you deployed to ensure minimum damage to other intended paths? More importantly, how are you planning to keep Charlie Becker alive?"

Nathanial started to visibly wither beneath the gaze of his peers and those who were starting to look like his accusers. He knew their position was weak and the stories he had heard of others of his kind being, dealt with, as a result of similar mistakes caused him to shudder in such a manner, that the others were starting to notice his abject nervousness. Zuriel had noticed and so continued in his place.

"There is no doubt that the lives of many people are being effected by the mistake the assigned made. The instructions that are being sent out to them through their assigned are becoming harder to implement, as, the humans move further away from their path. One who is known as Max is particularly effected. His behaviour has become

inconsistent with his assigned party to keep him on his assigned path. We are at a loss to understand how, the very little contact he has had with the life of Charlie Becker, would have affected him so dramatically. However, the crisis his assigned have been experiencing seems to correspond, time wise, with our current predicament. I have made contact with all the groups who guide every human having any contact with Becker. Therefore, while I would agree surely one life off an intended path is unacceptable, we are communicating well with other groups and believe damage can be limited."
"What are you doing to keep Charlie Becker alive at the moment?" "We made application to your colleagues for the deployment of one who could be assigned to Earth. We thought a more direct approach would help us keep things in check until the present crisis was over."
"My dear fellow, your naivety astounds me. These incidents can carry repercussions into one age to another, effecting many eras and thousands of human lives after the event. You astound with your ill placed confidence."
One of the elder and definitely wiser advisers interjected. "I think it may be more productive to probe, rather than attack. We must remember Nathanial- is a well-respected servant of The Power and has served over three missions."
Nathanial was openly grateful for the acknowledgement, bowing his head in response to the kindly angel. "I think we will now take a

little time to fill in the details of what you have already reported and be on our way. I was also already aware of your application for one who could be assigned to Earth, as; I was involved with the selection process. I will be interested to hear how this intervention works out. What earth name did you give to our final choice?"

"We named her Emma Williams and we believe she will keep Charlie Becker alive."

.

* * * *

"Do not neglect to show hospitality to strangers, for thereby some have entertained angels unawares" Hebrews 13:2 – The Holy Bible

.

Chapter 21
Who is the new Maxie?

Mickey had waited patiently in the car. He hadn't exactly volunteered to go in the house with DJ and Regis, but DJ had decided the extra hand, would be more of a liability than it was worth. It had been noted that Mickey hadn't been able to keep hold of a hand gun in a simple car park skirmish, so what chance did he have walking into the unknown! He was fortunate he hadn't had to find his own way back to London after Charlie had left him languishing on the concrete in the Little Chef, car park. DJ had been first off the mark in his Land Rover, leaving Regis to swing round and scoop Mickey up and order him to –"Get in you useless punk." More abuse had followed, as Regis took off toward Brighton.

"Wat the hell man. Wat the hell was that?"

"I'm not as used to leanin on people as you lot."

"Well, Mickey boy, you better get used to it. You think DJ's gonna let you go now?" Regis managed to put his head back and let out a belly laugh, despite the fact, he had already reached 95mph and was obviously driving as though getting to Brighton quickly was imperative. Mickey knew when he was being mocked, he also knew that a failed attempt to catch up with Lisa in Balham and now another gangster gig debacle was all the confirmation he needed that, he was right to leave London the first time around and this definitely, was not the life for him."How's the healin process gettin on Mickey boy. You lookin afta my masterpiece?" The mocking continued, as they caught up behind DJ's vehicle. DJ's mobile came through on loudspeaker.

"You got the stupid little bastard?"

"Yeah DJ man, I got the little girl."

They reached the house after much searching and tensions were running high. From his vantage point on the road, Mickey had seen the events around the house unfold with astonishment. He was staring at the same side of the building that had been housing Lisa, but, had not expected to see her attempt to jump out of the window. This was marginally less surprising than watching his, ex boss, hurl himself, onto an outside window ledge. Mickey, stared ahead of himself for a few minutes, as he reflected on the fact that Charlie was now his ex boss. There was no going back now and the person, who had given him the opportunity to build a proper career, would never trust him again. He watched a motionless figure on the ledge and wondered why Charlie hadn't been able to move, following such a simple jump. He seemed to have numbed himself from the memory of only a few short hours ago, when he had shot the only person who had ever shown him any real trust.

Mickey was tempted to intervene, as his natural instincts kicked in, witnessing what must have been his sister, first appear, then screech and then disappear like a rabbit that had been dragged back inside its burrow. He had assumed, wrongly, that DJ must have now caught up with Lisa, not knowing the evil that was being dispensed inside the house, he had no idea that those inside, not out, were the ones doing the terrorising. Mickey had started watching the house with greater interest and was fully expecting to see DJ and Regis emerge with Lisa in tow. He could still see Charlie and had noticed he had come round, albeit, looking disoriented and frail. His eye was later distracted by an approaching truck. He left the car quicker than he thought he was able and scrambled into the surrounding bushes. DJ and Regis had been dumped like dead, clumsy looking, Rhino carcasses, directly behind DJ's Range Rover. As Mickey assessed his options, he made his way tentatively toward the two giant men and noticed that they were still both breathing. He decided he really only had one preferred course of action and started to feel adrenalin course through his veins as he realised what needed to be done. Mickey was now being driven by a desire so strong; it was seriously warping, what was left of a seriously damaged nervous system. He had rapidly approached the point whereby, he was capable of almost anything. The, anything he was now hatching in his mind, was, revenge. The body was heavy and despite the fact that movies had often depicted   bodies being dragged along by their feet easily, Mickey was finding out just how difficult a task is was. The bracken laden ground and the uneven path made the hauling of Regis into the bushes a backbreaking job. He was ready for the eventuality of Regis reviving and had made sure the cosh, secured from the back seat of Regis' car, was firmly tucked in his tightened belt. The boot release button on the Audi had revealed a veritable treasure trove, just waiting for someone with a suitably depraved intention. Mickey was confident he was well equipped for the plans he was formulating in his now, dilapidated mind. As he approached a small clearing, he thought he was far enough away from the road to be able to stop hauling the colossus.

* * * *

Maxie and Carla had too, positioned themselves on the entertainment side of the house. Maxie's field glasses had been particularly useful and his mind had flashed back more than once, to all the occasions over the years, he had been sent by DJ to stake out rival gang members, or the local hood who, had screwed them over, deciding, most foolishly, to have it away with a greater amount of drugs cash than had been agreed. They had watched in amazement as the inhabitants of this mysterious place had so easily dispatched DJ and Regis. Being further off road and consequently hidden from the truck driver, they had only to duck down slightly, just to make sure, if anyone had decided to scan the trees and bushes to closely, they would, at least, just see an empty car. Any brave souls who took it upon themselves to approach Maxie's car would be dealt with, as and when that problem was presented. Despite his recent rebellion from the BEA boys and his contemplation of a purer way of life, he was well prepared for this trip, knowing that, wherever Lisa Baker was, DJ wouldn't be far behind. As the two, motionless bodies had been unceremoniously dispatched behind DJ's vehicle; the two spectators were contemplating their next move.

"Okay Maxie, we've got Lisa being pulled around, inside. Charlie Becker is hangin off a fuckin window ledge! These two dumped outside! Wat the fuck?"

"Well I'm tellin ya now, if that house is capable

of spittin those two out, we need to have a plan babe." Max motioned his head toward the two heaps beside DJ's Range Rover.

"I gotta be honest wit ya Carla honey, I never thought this shit would find us outside sum religious gaff, in the middle of nowhere, with all sort of crazy goin on inside."

"Why are you here Maxie?"

"Wat you mean?""Well, you don't know Lisa that well, we have only just got to know each other, what's ocurrin with you mate?"

"Truth." "Of course, I'm a queen bullshit detector Maxie boy."Well, I don't see why you shouldn't know sum of my soul, hun, now we on the same team an all.""Come on big boy, reveal your secrets." "First off, it was becomin apparent, I was less than happy in my work, DJ's a mad dog man, but he ain't stupid. Sick of terrorizin folk, who really had nothin to do wit me. Mr Becker in there was the final straw I guess. I did a little visit to his flat, not long ago, wit DJ. Regis was suppose to go, but he was busy plannin some other shit, no one could find him. Suddenly felt like, wat the fuck man, this geezer's spendin his whole life helpin people like our Lisa. All I kept hearin was DJ rantin like a rabbit wit rabies bout how he was goin to fuck Becker over and keep Lisa foreva more. I even googled the bastard"

"Who, DJ?"

"Ha, no ya mad fool, Becker."

"What you researched Becker?" Carla had no

idea Max had a soul at all until a few days ago, now, he used a computer, what the hell was next? "No, not im, H.E.L.P. and if you gonna take the piss, I ain't tellin it sister. Anyways, looked em up didn't I. Shit man they work wit kids like Lisa, tryin to drag em out the shit and all I could see was me an DJ tryin to drag em back down into it. But, thing was, there wasn't no good reason, why anymore. To cap it off, I was in his flat, beatin the shit out of im, realizin he was the only one capable of savin the same person, I'd bin tryin to keep fuckin safe for years. Made no sense hun, no fuckin sense at all."

"But you never cared about anyone before, maybe you just gettin old Maxie boy."

"Maybe we all jus gettin old hunny, but you wrong.""About what, go on tell me, come on Maxie, wrong about what?"

"I bin pissed off for a long time Carla mate. I was ready to bounce long ago, but, if I left, she would have ad a much harda ride."

"Who Lisa? You bloody well stayed cos a Lisa?""Who else? So, I stuck around to make sure she survived.""Why? Oh my god........You and Lisa?" "Once upon a time, maybe."

"Once upon a time, what? Have you two, been a two into one, Maxie, you dog. She never told me.""It was awhile ago. When I was busy beatin up on Charlie fucker Becker, I realised, the only reason I was enjoyin it, was because he had fucked little Lise. That's when I knew, I had to get out. I realised, that how I felt bout Lisa was

267

gonna do for me, if I didn't fuckin try an kill DJ first, I would give myself away sooner or later. Fuckin confusion Carla mate; messin wit my head. I jus wanna make sure she's okay. An by the way, your not exactly in the clear regardin secrets, now are ya babe."

With that, Maxie got out of the car and walked round to Carla's window.

"I'm gonna have a scout round. You need to stay here babe. Wat eva did for DJ and Regis, ain't somethin, you need to be meetin any time soon. Sit tight hun, I'll be back soon, promise."

* * * *

"How in gods name are we going to get out of here Charlie?"

"You raise an interesting point my dear, however, I think we may well be well and truly, fucked." My pathetic attempt at humour did raise a smile, which pleased me more than it should have done, considering I was as close to expiring as when I took the bath with my mate, Jack Daniel's."Ha, I'm glad you're feeling better Charlie, but I don't aim to give this lot another bite out of my ass. Emma looks like she's ready to take them on as well. We need a plan."

"I'm not feeling bloody better, as you may have noticed, Emma is now keeping me upright. I feel like shit, yes, we need a plan and no, I don't know what that will be. Anyway, it looks like the cats out of the bag." There was a distinct change of atmosphere pervading the house. The pseudo attempt to emanate peace and calm was gradually dissipating as more and more staff members heard about the attempted escape and were emerging from their holes. We could hear rapid footsteps above us, as staff members scurried around on other levels of the building, like worker ants, who had detected a breach in the nest wall."I reckon we've got two chances of survival.""Go on Emma, we're all ears."

"Well, we could hide and wait it out. They will never know for sure whether we're still in the building or not. Then, when they're running around outside searching, we could pick our moment, aim for a gap in the ring of searching jailers and aim for the bushes on the east side of the building. The east side is our best chance. The bushes are a lot closer to the house. We then need to hope and pray, we can slip away unnoticed.""I don't want to stay in this place. I want to take my chances outside. I know I can run like fuck.""I know Lisa, but Charlie can't and I can't because without me, he's not going to make it." "Okay, sorry Charlie mate. What's plan B then? You said two chances." "Quite similar to plan A, only, we get out before they get organised and head straight for the bushes on the east side, take our chances, find a hiding place and hope we go undetected until we can sneak away."I piped up, becoming a little more comical and delirious by the moment. "I like to sneak, let's sneak.""Sush, Charlie, try and rest your mind." "Okay, but both options require a certain amount of speed." Lisa looked in my direction."I'm happy for you two to go, I really am." I really was. I could have quite easily have curled up in the corner and slept forever. Emma was quick with her reply and I could also see in Lisa's eyes that, although she would have contemplated this option, only hours ago, our newly formed bond, left the option of leaving me; untenable. There was no way she was now going to forsake me in a house full of psychopathic religious maniacs, who would be looking to vent their wrath, as soon as they realised I was responsible for two of their captives running free.

"Not an option Charlie, now come on, we'll make our way out and we'll help you."

"You'll practically have to carry me."

"Come on." Emma, had apparently, made up our minds and so the grand plan was, a quick exit, run for the bushes and hope to God we weren't found. We made our way as quickly as I could hobble, thinking that there must be a side entrance to the house at some stage. We passed a huge dining room and saw our opportunity.

"Look, those bay windows should be open and if they're not, we'll just smash the hell out. We're on the east side, I can't see anyone over there by the sheds, so we should be able to get out, use the sheds and conservatory area to shield us to the bushes, come on." Emma was driving us on and was obviously quite capable of doing all the thinking as well. It was amazing to me, that just an hour ago; she had been a quivering, sobbing wreck. What was more astonishing was that she seemed more concerned about my wellbeing than her own. She had taken over the lead role, supported me, as, my body was giving out and she hadn't allowed me to play to big a hero. It would have been so much easier to allow the two girls to scarper, leaving the slow, older man behind. Like an old Lion, who'd past his best and had been left by the pride, for the vultures. It was starting to feel like I was done for anyhow. The only plausible explanation I could think of for Emma's determination to see me all right was extreme gratitude. After all, I'd been the one who had shown her it was possible to escape the clutches of these animals. We entered the dining room and surveyed the bay windows, while trying to keep a running assessment of possible assailants. In keeping with every other door and window in this house, which I still found to be a strange paradox, the windows swung wide open. Freedom was starting to feel like it was a real possibility. We could see the sheds ahead of us, they led onto three parallel conservatory units and surely, there would be enough cover to aid us toward the thick overgrown surroundings of the house. As we approached the first shed, Camille and the reverend Jed King stepped out from behind the wooden structure and were standing immediately in front of us. Camille spoke first. "Lisa, Emma, how could you be so silly?" "Back off lady and forgive me if I don't enjoy being stripped naked and fuckin chanted at by degenerate throwbacks from the Spanish Inquisition" Lisa was mad her anger, far outweighed any fear she might have had of being dragged back inside the torture chamber. Camille, even living in the delusion, she had so embraced over the last few years, could see neither of the girls were going to be persuaded to trust her again. The reverend King decided to try his luck and he had a particularly menacing look about him. The inconvenience thrust upon his own personal agenda by the likes of Charlie Becker and Lisa Baker was just about more than

272

he could stomach. Things had been progressing rather nicely, up until very recently. He had managed to sell twenty four young girls already, to operatives from the Eastern European cartel. The price was almost doubled for each of them, if, they had arrived pre prepared, as they liked to refer to it. Girls that had been snatched from airports or European hotels, who were fresh into the business, were so much harder to control. It would be at least a year, before they were able to break the girls, ensure they were addicted and reliant on class 'A' drugs. It took these girls so much longer than the Reverend's, to get ready to work the massage parlours and whore houses open to the many tourists available as suitable punters. ATONEMENT had been the perfect front. The dip shit's who were always on the look out for yet another ideology, were easy to recruit as staff, especially in Brighton, for some strange reason. Jed had often wondered why so many vulnerable, substance addicted low life types were attracted to the one area. It had been so much easier here than previous attempts, even in what would have been considered as the most depraved areas of Scotland, or Manchester, three years ago. Even he had been astonished how long he was able to get away with the scam, based on such a flimsy theology that he had lifted from the internet within about an hours research into cult activity in Britain. In recent years, the demand for girls had tripled, due to the trend developing amongst English young men, who invariably travelled abroad for their secret stag nights. Most of the girls however, suffered a much more sinister fate, as they faced being sold off to various other organisations, or wealthy individuals around the globe that relied in human trafficking to supply the slave markets they fed or their own personal harems.

"You are aware, I'm not about to let you escape, are you?" He held a rather threatening looking sawn off shot gun. It looked like it might have the capability to take all three of them out, with one blast. Camille also packed a small semi-automatic hand gun. She'd quickly assessed that I didn't look much of a threat, standing there, dripping and grinning inanely. I was now feeling quite out of it and finding even the most threatening situation moderately amusing. The two girls still looked positively sprightly standing next to me. Therefore, Camille's Beretta 92FS was squarely aimed at Lisa's forehead.

* * * *

Purgatory

According to traditional Catholic belief, upon the impact of death, an individual will experience transportation to Purgatory. This place is designed to test and refine, in the preparation for heaven, or Hell. Catholicism will stress that it is by one's own free will that a person enters into the state of hell, rather than Heaven. **However, one question remains unanswered by this theory. When and how do we choose?**

274

Chapter 22
Predator becomes Prey.

"Sorry Regis, me ole' mate, I've got to rest awhile, you are rather heavy, ole chap."
Mickey's mind had finally crumbled. Like a brick resting on a length of plywood, you know, eventually, that if the pressure is applied for long enough, without remission, the wood gently starts to warp, bend and break. Left there for long enough the wood cracks and the brink falls with a mighty crash. Mickey had surely crashed and he was determined that Regis was going to pay the price. Not that Regis was at all an innocent, for if Mickey had spent the rest of the day tormenting him, he still wouldn't have come anywhere near the culmination of pain and despair, that Regis had dispensed, over the years. The psychopathic henchman had come round and found himself staring helplessly at a situation he was, completely unfamiliar with. The lack of control he was experiencing, would have been bugging him even more, than the prospect of what Mickey had planned.
Mickey had dragged the dead weight far enough into the wooded area to ensure the privacy he needed. The wounds once again opening up on his torso, under the strain of pulling and manoeuvring, reminded him of the anger he felt for his captive. Any restrain he may have shown, had he been, in his right mind, was no longer

going to serve as a barrier to his plan. After an effort of incredible endeavour, Mickey, had managed to prop Regis up, using the surrounding branches and a convenient overhanging tree. Once the noose was completed, Mickey tossed the rope over a high bough. He had to be quite careful now ensuring that he trained the gun he'd found in the boot of Regis' car, on its owner; as he had sensed signs that Regis was about to wake up. Mickey had found all he needed in the boot and was very grateful to Regis, for being so helpful A length of rope, a neat looking hand-gun and a lovely selection of knives, were now at his disposal. That would do very nicely. He was grateful that the task ahead would be quite painless. Well, painless for him anyhow. He had even found plenty of material and cleaning fluids, to be able to ensure he could wash himself up afterward. "Sorry if you're a little uncomfortable mate, but I must thank you, for providing me with all I needed to kill you with. Do you remember when we were together last time?""Jus get on wit it you little weasel. I doubt you got it in ya anyhow." "Oh now Regis, my good fellow, I assure you, all bad things will come to you, in good time. In fact I promise you, we will see what you're made of very soon." Mickey let out a laugh that would have chilled the soul of the hardest of characters; despite the fact, that, there was no way Regis was going to let on, Mickey was actually starting to cause his bowels to twitch."Literally, see wat you're made of buddy boy." Mickey continued, mocking the huge black man, just as he had been mocked, only a matter of barely a month previously.

"Like I said freak, get on with it."

"Ha, there you go again, me ole friend, you still think you're in charge. I'm in charge, I'm calling the shots, so shut the fuck up and jus enjoy. You gonna answer my question matey, cos we ain't startin, until you do." With that he swirled round catching Regis with a vicious slap across the cheeks. "Wat the fuck you goin on bout freak?" Regis was hard as nails, but now Mickey had found a convenient tree log, realizing his hands were not heavy enough for this gangster.

He approached the thug and without blinking, swung the piece of wood down upon Regis' shoulder. "Ha you wit the freak, very funny, yeah, very funny, I'm the freak. You bin torturin South London for nearly twenny five years and I'm the freak. I tried to escape the fuckin madness, but you wankers dragged me back in, an, I'm the freak!!!"

Mickey's face was now so close to Regis', Regis tried to lash out and bite him.

"Wow, that's not a great idea, now, answer my fuckin question, you scumbag," again, smashing the log into Regis' side.

"Wat question, wat, fuckin question?"

"Do – you – re – mem – ber – wen – we – were – to – geth – er – last – time? Didn't you hear me the first time? You really need to pay a little more attention when someone's tryin to torture

277

you Regis, you ugly great fuck."

"Yeah, course I do, get on wit it."

"Wat did you say to me?"

"Wat.""Wat did you say to me, last time we were havin a cozy little chat?" Thud, once again the log hit the body, as if Mickey was tenderizing a steak."I said lots, wat the......."""Okay me ole friend, I'll help, you're probably a bit nervous, an don't wanna spill it out, ha-ha, ha, spill it out, that's fucking funny, considering what I'm about to do to you, ha spill it out. You said to me, that DJ ad said you could get all medieval on me if you needed to. Do ya remember? Yeah, do ya remember sayin that to me Regis, you little psycho you?" Mickey aimed the next crack across Regis' thigh making his leg buckle and bringing tension to the noose around Regis neck."Yeah, wat of it." "Well, I bin doin some research ain't I, an, it appears one of the oldest forms of medieval execution, jus appens to be one that I thought would be quite fun as well." "Well, as long as you ave fun, you dick." Regis was still maintaining a certain level of gangster type, attitude, but even he was starting to seriously wonder, just how cracked Mickey had become. Mickey had taken his shirt off and was standing in front of Regis as if to show him that although he had been ripped up by the big man, he was still going to have the last word. He took the end of the rope away from the hanging bough and wrapped it around a higher horizontal branch of the tree Regis was standing under. The noose was already securely in place around Regis' exceptionally thick neck.

Mickey started to gently wind and tighten the rope, as though he was wrapping up the cord on a domestic Hoover. Each wind increased the tension on the rope and Regis' neck. Regis used his legs to lift himself as high as he could, hoping against hope the rope length would be too short for Mickey to carry out the hanging. When Mickey had Regis on his tip toes, he tied the rope securely to the tree. Regis was struggling for breath, but was able to maintain his balance, by resting his heels on the base of the tree trunk. He knew that one slip would result in his massive weight pulling down and his neck would be unable to sustain the colossal load. Sweat was now pouring off Regis' face and even with his face being so pitch black, Mickey could see that he was starting to go purple.

"Rememba, you said, you would decide ow the pictures would end, do ya Regis. Rememba, you an that tossa DJ, said, you would decide wat needed addin in the last box?"

He cracked the log against the side of Regis' head producing an instant show of blood.

Regis couldn't speak and so just gave a resigned nod, as to suggest, yes, I remember, now prove me wrong, but just get on with it.

"The fuckin pray, don't always lose. The fuckinpredator, don't always get his din dins. You didn't think it through you dumb shit. I'm gonna finish off your little picture Regis boy, ya

279

see, it's a fuckin super fuckin Zebra, you've got hold of. It's the fuckin Lion that's gonna get fucked this time." One last swing with the log, left Regis spitting out two bloodied teeth. Mickey took out a rather gruesome looking 15" Jackal hunting knife. Very calmly, he lifted Regis' shirt to reveal his gut. Regis was now closing his eyes bracing himself for the pain that was to come. His breathing had increased significantly since he'd seen the knife and his pulse had risen dramatically. Mickey showed great skill as he carried out the second process in the sequence that would result in Regis being, hung, drawn and quartered. It was a swift and decisive slice, from, one side of Regis' lower gut to the other. Immediately, Regis defecated himself, slumped and released a good deal of his intestines onto the moss covered ground below. It would take a short while for him to go into shock and he would be struggling to decide if his exposed innards where causing him the most distress, or the fact that he was choking to death rapidly now, as his full weight came down on the noose. He hung there for a few minutes, dripping dark brown blood, his face bloated and every trace of dignity a distant memory. Mickey took the knife again and with another clinical strike, cut Regis down. Regis was a little way off being dead and so, he lay, twitching, trying desperately for any breath, while at the same time fully realizing that he was finished.

Two things happened simultaneously the moment

Regis hit the ground. Two gunshots could clearly be heard coming from 'Fairways Havens' and Mickey also heard the loudest and most ear piercing scream he had ever heard in his life. Mickey turned around, he was splattered with Regis' blood, wild eyed, half naked and looked like an ancient barbarian in the forest, who had just carried out a sacrifice.

"What the fuck, Mickey!" "Carla, baby." Mickey started toward her but she was backing off and put her hands out in front to protect herself. Carla was shaking violently and trying hard not to gag and retch at the sight of Regis. She had only witnessed the few moments before Mickey had cut Regis down, but that had been more than enough. She hadn't been able to keep still in Maxie's car, had decided to step out for a cigarette and as the wind changed, she had heard distant, but very definite voices coming from the undergrowth. At first, she had been concerned the voices might be dog walkers, or residents from the cottages just to the left of the trees. She was hoping they wouldn't approach, complicating events, snooping around and asking questions about why she might be parked in trees quite near to their own residential dwellings. She'd followed the voices, but by the time she'd reached them, there was only one voice remaining. "Carla, I still need to quarter im, you know, cut im up. Will ya wait for me babe, will ya wait?" With that Carla threw up, which was quite a feat, as she hadn't eaten for eleven hours.

She gagged as saliva mixed with bile forced its way out of her throat and stomach. She turned to run and Mickey reacted quickly catching her by the left wrist and swinging her around. "Where are you goin babe? Everythins goin to be alright now. You found me; I've shown em I'm not goin to dance for em any more. We can be together now. How'd you get out hunny?" "Mickey, are you mad? Look what you've done.""But, it's one of them babe, the gang bastards." "I DON'T CARE. LOOK WHAT YOU'VE DONE." Carla wasn't thinking straight, she wasn't aware just how bent out of shape Mickey's mind had become in such a short time. The sensible thing would have been to humour the boy and try and sneak away while he was happily cutting up Regis to send to the four corners of the realm. But Carla was traumatized. The captivity, her hunger and the reality that she would be returning home to a decimated business and an uncertain future had been eating away at her subconscious all day. "It'll be okay baby, it'll be okay, when we get home, and we'll be together again." "There is no future Mickey. You think I could ever let you touch me again after this?""Baby, come on, we're meant to be together, you know it." "MICKEY, LOOK WHAT YOU HAVE FUCKING DONE. THERE IS NO, US! THERE IS NO FUTURE." Carla was still shaking uncontrollably and she could feel her heart pounding in her ears. Mickey's eyes glazed over and he stood and

282

stared at Carla for a moment. He glanced at Regis' slumped and bloody body, as if realizing for the first time what calamity he had wrought. Mickey then took on a new calmer demeanour and let out a gentle sigh. With a shake of his head and apparently in perfect control, reached down to the rear of his belt, in which the hand gun was supported. "Tell me it's gonna be alright baby." In one last vein effort to influence a girl, he had now lost forever, he pointed the gun at Carla and her shaking became more intense.

"Don't shoot me Mickey." She hadn't got the energy to become hysterical, she just stood and shock, sobbing, now, terrified, having been made completely aware of what Mickey was capable of. Mickey raised the gun and Carla screamed. Bending his arm inward, he directed the barrel into his mouth and blew the back of his head off. The bloody debris flying from Mickey's body hit the tree trunk where Regis had been hanging and his own body hit the ground with a dull thud. Carla just stood and trembled, her nervous system was rapidly sending out signals to her brain that it couldn't cope with current events and she wet herself, without even being aware of it. She would have been there for a very long time, if she hadn't felt the hand wrap itself around her mouth. "That's wat happens wen you mess wit the big boys sweetheart, now come with me." DJ towered over her and after swiftly assessing the destruction that had been wrought in the immediate vicinity, practically dragged her back to his Range Rover.

"Okay my children, move him inside, in there, where you have just come from and don't be silly, as, be in no doubt, we will shoot you."

"Then you'll have to shoot me, because it'll be a lot better than if you drag us back in there to fuck with us, you bloody perverts."

"Look, we will shoot, okay, we aren't playing games, you silly little tart, now move."

"Fuck off." I was pretending to be on the verge of a faint, hoping it would buy the girls some time, although, to be honest, I may have well have done, for all the use I was. Our situation was looking increasingly impossible, as the fanatics had the guns and I could barely walk. The cavalry also didn't appear to be on its way. Or so I thought! I decided to add a little caution into the mix, as, I sensed that Lisa looked like she was about to do something impetuous. My voice rasped and croaked, as I forced some feeble words out. "Lisa, come on, we don't really want to get shot now, do we."

"Charlie, I'm not goin back in there, okay."

"Lisa, look at me, there're, lunatics, you know that, they'll shoot us, if we resist okay. I need you to trust me."

"I do Charlie, I do, but come on, I can't go back in there." Jed sensed he was gaining an advantage and decided to capitalize if he could. "Listen to him, now my child, come on let's go back inside and we can sort all this out."

Lisa was really starting to panic. She had a point

and we had a clear no win choice to make. Returning to the house and risking captivity, or, much worse, where I was concerned, or, being shot there and then was a decision that was paralyzing! I tried to calm Lisa, once again, but, she had clearly started looking to implement the flight option, as, even she could see the fight was never going to be a fair one. It was making her panic more, the fact that I was apparently, trying to talk her into submission, just making her believe, I had given up. Emma was remaining extremely calm. I began to wonder if she was made out of electrons and circuits.

"Lisa, please, calm down." Lisa just took off, sprinting to her left, apparently looking like she was heading toward the road. She was screaming that there was no way she was going back and she would rather be shot. Camille, remained calm, but pointed her handgun at Emma, as Jed, turned to track Lisa's run. He was obviously going to shot her in the back, as; he mumbled something about there being no way he was allowing her to escape now. Time seemed to stand still. Two shots rang out. The first one took Jed's head clean off, blood leaving it in a fountain, at least six inches high. The second was no less clinical. Before Camille had time to register what had happened to Jed, she had taken the second shot to the back. I could have sworn I saw the bullet leave the other side of her body and hit the concrete. Camille hit the ground, immediately in front of us, with a rasping

gargling sound coming from her throat. I had
doubted she had felt, or even been aware of her
demise, as it was over in a second. Lisa stopped,
turned and without any concern at all that there
were two, messy looking bodies lying dead
before her, yelped in relief……………..
"MAXIE, yyyyeeeessss, MAXIE."
It was hardly a classic airport reunion, but quite
sweet in its own way, none the less.

* * * *

Islamic view of the Last Judgment
During divine judgment, it is believed that each
person's Book of Deeds, in which "every small
and great thing is recorded", will be opened.
Throughout judgment, there is an assumption that
God will administer justice, with perfect love.
However, one question remains unanswered by
this theory. How qualified are we to judge a
great, or even small good thing, in the eyes of
God, therefore, allowing us the wisdom to get on
and do them?

Chapter 23
Devil's Dyke.

I was seriously in need of attention, so I bleated a request to get the hell out of there and suggested we would report Fairways to the Police, as soon as we were well away. I was fairly sure all the evidence that would be required, proving that the Haven of demons was a dress rehearsal for hell, was lying in the car park. I didn't even know about the gruesome delights, yet to be discovered in the surrounding woodland. Once again, Emma took control. "Come on, we need to get to the car. I know exactly where we're going."
Sofiel– Overseer - had been assigned to communicate with all relevant parties involved with clearing up this terrible mess and coming up with a plan of damage limitation. She knew that her very existence was now at stake. She had known things had looked a lot worse, than anyone was prepared to admit. Even as Nathanial had tried to offer the assembly reports, with convincing arguments of risk management and rhetoric, designed to, dampen the drama, she was anticipating the worse. This proud spiritual being had to be very careful and if she was going to keep her options open and manage very carefully her communications back to the overseers. More importantly she knew she couldn't afford to get the messages that reached those who served The Darkness wrong. Charlie Becker was to be kept

alive at all costs. It had been decided that his intended path had been almost abandoned. The Power had revealed through his appointed messengers that not one of the human souls involved with Charlie's life since he had been told to carry on, would have died ordinarily in the events to follow. Things were looking increasingly bleak in the heavenly realms. All the signs being released from the Ultimate realm were suggesting the decision to send Charlie back was a poor one Sofiel - was well aware that annihilation was inevitable for one, some, or all of their kind, involved in this mess. Their kind were not regarded as anywhere near as precious to The Power as the beloved humans, so cherished through time, despite the obvious rebellion that was such an intrinsic part of their innate character. Mission after mission had proved that one human life saved from eternal darkness, was worth more than a thousand of her kind that were thought of as so dispensable. Her resentment grew and gnawed away at her as she travelled swiftly to the Place of Whispers and composed herself, for what was the most important session of her seven hundred and eighteen periods, called years by humans, so far. "May I speak with those who serve the Darkness?" The words left the Place of Whispers, on the four winds; to be sifted by messenger's who were assigned to the elements returning to Earth. The earth was the home of The Darkness, at least for the duration of this present mission and as such, communication was unpredictable and extremely unreliable. "You serve The Power........ We do not recognise you.""No, listen to me. I have served you well in a matter of great importance. I have made my pledge, hear me.""Who have you contacted upon the Earth? Who are you helping?""I have been speaking with the ones they know as Tony Cox and Tanya Clayton. We the ones you have placed there to work for The Darkness. They were the ones Lisa was handed over too for her induction into ATONEMENT."

"You do not have to remind us who works for The Darkness. Wait while we confirm your claims. Be careful you're not trying to deceive The Darkness."

It wasn't long before the winds had confirmed the most damning of allegiances had been negotiated.

* * * *

Lisa, Emma and I, managed to reach Mickey's Vauxhall Corsa laboriously as I was passing out and coming to, like the flickering of a light bulb. I was becoming convinced my light would soon extinguish and grow cold forever. Maxie shouted that he would take his vehicle, collect Carla and follow us. The roads were narrow and winding. Apparently, we were heading for a natural beauty spot about two miles away, as it was the only real landmark Emma had been able to direct her brother too. Just when it had been, albeit, silently, agreed by everyone, we had all witnessed enough violence, gun shot and evil intent, to last us a lifetime, we heard more shots being fired behind the car. Lisa had spotted Maxie's car behind us, but there was nobody in the passenger seat, next to Max and yet another vehicle was also following Max'. The race seemed to be very much on!

DEVILS DYKE ½ MILE - The sign was barely visible, but Emma swerved the car left and up a sharp hair pin bend, toward the historic beauty spot on the South Downs Way. It is named after the huge dry valley that carves its way through ridges of rolling chalk grassland and Emma had reached the car park as if training for formula one. Her brothers car was there and so although it was a weekday and there wasn't a lot of activity in the car park, Lisa had felt a little more secure that, at least, they were now in sight of normal humanity as the pub overlooking the huge cavity in the landscape stood between the valley and the rolling Downs, from where they had came from. "Come on Charlie, try and stick with us. My brother is a doctor. His name is Simon, he can help you. Come on, we need you out of the car so that he can look at you properly." I groaned, I ached in places I thought couldn't possibly hurt that much. I knew I was in shock and I also knew I was slipping away. A doctor was all very well, but, I would have thought by now, I would need a blood transfusion. Emma, Simon and Lisa dragged me out of the car and lay me on the dry grass about ten yards from the edge of the massive drop in the landscape. Simon administered a needle into my arm and a drip was inserted. Emma was told to hold it above my head and I wondered why these people, were going through so much trouble and how Emma had managed to find, either the time or the ability to communicate to her brother while we had been so busy fighting off Rev. Jed and Camille.

Emma was standing over me and Lisa had drifted over to catch some clean air by the side of the gorges edge. The black Audi screeched into the car park and Maxie flew out, before the car had halted properly. He knew that every millisecond counted and a very great danger was approaching fast."Lisa, move. DJ's on his way in the Range Rover. Move, quick, run."

"Where's Carla?. "He's got her and he………."
DJ's Range Rover came to an abrupt halt and Lisa could see that he had Carla by the hair. Lisa

was desperate to run, but her loyalty to Carla was still surprisingly still intact. I was being patched up and being administered fluids and an anti-biotic. I was starting to feel like I was in the middle of a film set around me, as the tension grew. DJ was approaching Lisa, holding Carla close and threatening to shoot her in the head if Lisa didn't come to him. Maxie was standing a little way off and although he still had his firearm, he wasn't about to risk hitting Lisa or Carla, to take DJ out. Emma and Simon seemed totally removed from the drama unfolding before them. "Cum on bitch, you're cumin wit me girl."
"Let her go DJ. LET HER GO."
"You know that ain't gonna happen bitch."
"Well, you're goin to have to shoot us both then, cos, god knows I ain't coming with you, ever again, NOW FUCK OFF."
Two walkers were rounding a bend about thirty yards away from the sight of DJ holding Carla by the hair. Max was standing in the car park, holding a gun, Lisa standing on the edge of the sheer drop toward the valley below and I was lying flat out, being worked on by a doctor and his nurse in attendance. It was obvious that they were approaching a less than controlled scene; yet, the two walkers continued to walk toward us all. Lisa had noticed them, but had no idea why they seemed unaffected by the scenes unfolding just a little way ahead. Max too had noticed and was similarly confused at their lack of concern. "You listnin to me girl, look it'll be different

okay, I'll treat ya right. I jus want you wit me okay, now stop puttin your friend in danger. I gonna throw her off this ridge if you don't start movin soon. You know I mean it, you know I do.""DJ, there is no way okay, look there are people coming. Someone's gonna call the cops sooner or later, so you better get wise DJ. It's over, now let Carla go and get away. Just go, leave us all alone." With that DJ turned, still holding Carla close to him and shouted at the approaching couple."Turn away, you, turn away, there ain't anythin here for you." He motioned for them to move away, gun in his waving hand. They continued to approach, not even acknowledging DJ's remonstrations. They had almost reached the curious group and stopped about ten yards away. That's when it dawned on Lisa "Oh my God."

"Wat up Lisa?" Max was still standing in the car park, gun pointed at DJ, he was now edging closer, but was cautious, as it was apparent, DJ's head was more out of whack than normal.

"It's them, them that tied me up in there." Lisa didn't know what to do with herself, or where to point. Her index finger was moving frantically between pointing at where they had come from over the hilly expanse and at the couple standing in front of DJ, Carla and herself. Lisa, who had backed off so far and was dangerously near the edge of the grassy drop, decided to divert her attention to Carla.

"You betrayed me Carla, you lied to me."

"Listen Lisa, we were planning, I promise. We were tryin to think of a way to get you out. Mickey was scared that's all. They had him beaten, hurt him, cut him. Honest girl, I love you. There's no way we would have hid forever. Look Mickey was scared shitless bout bein discovered.""What do you mean, *was?* And where did you fuck off too?" "They took me too Lisa babe. They held me and told Mickey, that unless he brought you back, they would do for me. You know what they're like."

"Oh great, so he's willing to bring my ass back to save yours is he?" "Lisa, babe, he wanted to save us both. They fucked with his body and his mind. For gods sake, he's just fuckin killed Regis in the woods. He got fucked up babe, didn't know what he was doin in the end. I know he loved you. I know he wanted to save you." "Why do you keep talkin like he's dead, Carla. Where's my brother?""He's gone babe, there was all sorts of chaos in the woods, while you were tryin to escape from that house."

Lisa didn't have the strength in her to hate anymore and gave her friend a look of resigned acceptance, indicating that forgiveness was being offered. Carla started to sob.

Lisa suddenly realised where she was positioned and looked over her shoulder. The beautiful countryside gave way to a drop of, at least a hundred and fifty feet. Below them all, was a fearful drop that led down to the gravelly salt base below. Max was trying to reassure Lisa,

which wasn't an easy task, with DJ standing no
more than a foot away from her, waving a gun
around and hurting her girlfriend.
"Who is it Babe, who is it?" He tried to keep his
voice calm, as to convince Lisa that he had
everything under control.
"Them, them, fuckin Tony and fuckin Tanya.
"MAXIE, I NEED TO GET OUTA HERE."
Lisa was now trapped between Tony and Tanya
on her right and DJ and Carla on her left. Tony
looked at DJ and Tanya moved slowly in sync
with him as they walked to face DJ and Carla.
 DJ was clearly thrown, not comprehending why
passers by would be so interested in the events he
was desperately trying to control. Lisa wondered
how on earth Tony and Tanya had managed to
move so fast, as to appear as walkers strolling
along the National Trust landmark, all the way
from Fairways Haven so quickly.
"Wat the fuck man, now listen, listen good, you
come one step further and I'll throw, this bitch
over there and shoot you two inta the bargin."
Tony and Tanya, simply kept going, walking
nearer and nearer to DJ. He sent out a warning
shot and neither of them even twitched or blinked
an eye lid. "Okay, I'm warnin you."
Lisa was looking over at me. The bond we had
formed over past events caused genuine concern
and I too was fighting to stay conscious, just so
that I could make sure she was okay and free
from danger. They kept coming and so, DJ shot
Tony. The bullet hit the left side of the shoulder

and blood spurted from the wound. Tony kept coming, the impact had slightly jolted his body but again, not even a flinch, from a face set like flint toward his purpose. DJ emptied five more bullets in quick succession into Tony's chest. Tony gave a slanted smile and kept approaching. Lisa screamed as the bullets were released into Tony, witnessing the blood starting to literally pour from his wounds. DJ panicked and took one step to far backward. Lisa looked to her side and saw DJ and her friend disappear in a moment. As if in slow motion over the grassy precipice, the couple simply disappeared in front of the shocked on-lookers'. DJ had gripped Carla so tightly; she had toppled over easily with him, clutching at him as if he were a life raft caught in mid-air. They were both gone and all that could be heard was a desperate fading squeal coming from Carla. Lisa was now sobbing furiously, fully expecting the evil twins to turn on her. Instead they briefly looked at her, turned and continued to walk along the ridge path, as if the events of the last few minutes had been nothing more than a mere distraction. Emma turned to Simon."At least we know two things now." "Yes," said Simon. "More deaths, on account of the human, lying here they're also being aided by The Darkness. Max rushed over to Lisa and immediately wrapped her up in his giant frame, holding her delicate head in his massive hands. She felt safe for the first time, in a very long time and that made her sob even more. Max reassured her that it would all be okay now and tried to lead her off. Lisa however had other concerns and screamed out at Simon to make sure I made it through. I remember being overwhelmingly touched by her concern. Simon in the meantime, didn't look at all confident. I saw genuine fear in his eyes, which was a surprise to me, as I had assumed Doctors would be used to losing patients. I could have expected to see concern or even anguish, but this was fear and with the mental energy I had, I wondered why. And, who the hell was the darkness?

"He's too weak and we have to be careful we don't interact with anymore humans. It's impossible, he needs a hospital and we can't risk it Emma. Its way above what we've been asked to do." "We were asked to make sure he didn't die and he's dying Simon." "I know, but if any of us interfere anymore, we'll only have a bigger mess to clear up. We have to let him go and see what the others have to say. I can't go running around the Earth, interacting with even more of them who might also get infected by this event." The strange use of language was slightly confusing, but I put it down to the fact I was dying. I even thought that my brain might well have been playing tricks on me, as it started to close down. "Okay Simon, I have to submit to your seniority. But, this is the most serious move away from an intended path, I have ever witnessed.""How long have you existed Emma?" "Let's say, I was overseeing when the kind of

297

slaughter we have seen here, on the Earth today, was common practice among humans. And still, this mistake has affected many more lives than I have seen in my time either, as one who is assigned, overseeing, or since I've been able to move freely upon the Earth."

"Yes, I wouldn't want to be the ones involved, either assigned, or overseeing, on this one!"

"We must leave now, before we are detected."

"Yes, peace and provision, to you Emma, you have served well.""Peace and provision, to you Simon and thank you. Just remember, it could always be worse. We could have ended up as human." With that they were gone. I however, remained, having just heard that I had no chance of survival and that I had been nursed by someone who had been knocking around England, when the Druids were running around most of Anglesey and Cornwall. I felt very peaceful and had no desire to hang on to life. It felt a lot different from the first time I'd attempted to thrust myself into the abyss. For one thing, I'd been so anxious on that occasion, to get it right, the whole sorry event must have looked like some sort of old British Carry on film. I was rushing around, looking for pills and enough alcohol to knock out an African Elephant, for a month. I smiled at myself, as I thought of the farce it must have looked like. A romp, involving, pills, booze and razor blades flying around my bathroom. I could have sold tickets! Oh yes and since I'd learned that if you cut lengthwise down the vein, instead of across, you produce much more of a productive gush, it would have been quite the spectacle. Oh god, there was lots and lots of blood. I remember the stench of iron emanating from my very own life source, filling the flat and becoming even more overwhelming than the reek of whiskey fumes. I thought of Tommy and felt sad and suddenly very lonely, wishing desperately that he was there, with me. The pain had now vanished from my side and my muscles and I was ready to be taken to a better place. Little did I know, they weren't ready for me and that a better place wasn't guaranteed. Lisa ran back to my side tears pouring from her beautiful big blue eyes, but my eyes were blurry as they faded and I was sorry I couldn't see her more clearly. She was surely, one of the most stunning sights, of my whole miserable existence. "Charlie, please don't die. You're the only person on this god forsaken planet that has ever tried to really help me. I'm so sorry I robbed you. Please don't leave me, please don't go."

Max sidled up to both of us. "Hey bro, you gonna go an die on us, just as we startin to get acquainted?""Yeah, I'm tired my bro.""We all tired man, come on, can't you see yourself clear to tryin to stay alive?""Nah, I got no blood left. Look after Lisa mate.""No worries bud. Sleep well, you did gud by Lisa and Emma, in this affair and in dat house. An that gotta count for sumink in the bigger house up top."

Lisa was inconsolable and the people who had finally decided to creep out of the pub near the car park, were starting to show the curiosity that would have been a little more helpful much earlier. Now, it was too late, much too late. Max gently led Lisa away. She looked back, blew me a kiss and I was gone.

* * * *

"Hello Charlie. You are back. My goodness you've caused chaos around here.

Epilogue
The Verdict's

There were those who had been in service for The Power for so many ages, they had consequently witnessed the beginning of time itself and yet; had still never been privy to a more sobering event, than that which was now in session! The assembly had considered every account, report and often what they had considered to be monumentally flaky, pieces of evidence and rationale, for what had occurred in the case of Charlie Becker.

The verdicts were presented clinically; with one who served The Power announcing sentence with a rapid intensity, pausing only to ensure clarity and to allow her peers to pass the relevant 'Notices of verdict' that were duly distributed amongst the heavenly host.

One by one the verdicts were presented to the

anxious winged servants of the only being in the known universe, whose decision was irrevocable. Those who were assigned to Charlie Becker were addressed first; "Dina and Gavreel – As you are novices – You will escape the fires of annihilation – You will be reassigned and remain as those assigned to new subjects. However, be warned; Dina; your nature is to learn! Ensure that you do. There will be no other reprieve, should you appear before this assembly in disgrace a second time. Gavreel; your nature is to create peace and yet your lack of wisdom has created chaos! You will also suffer the ultimate penalty, should you appear in disarray to this place in the future. Micah and Rashnu – You were assigned to inspire divine plans through wisdom and understanding.

Yes! And judgement as you has demonstrated in ages past, your ability to judge between whole nations in regard to righteousness and justice. We are surprised you have survived. However, due to your exploits in previous missions, survive you will! The verdict is – That you will both remain as those assigned to Charlie Becker – This will be after a period of reconditioning. This, as you know, is not an easy process – Now; leave this place and join your tutors in the place they will purge you from this folly."

It was now the turn of those who were overseers to Charlie Becker;

"Urim - Angel of Light - Zuriel - Angel of Harmony and Murial - Angel of Emotions – You have all been found negligent and yet not entirely informed of essential information only your fellow overseers were in possession of – You are now all demoted, with immediate effect – It has not been decided how far you will be required to fall; and so, you too will undergo a period of reconditioning – Your tutors will assess whether you will ever be trusted as overseers in the future – If the assessment is not favourable, you may well find yourselves facing us again – The pronouncement on your fate will be heard at a later date, after your testing through reconditioning – Leave this place now and yearn for the mercy of the one you have so poorly served. The atmosphere turned even more morbid as the one who served continued pronouncing, what amounted to a dismal collection of decisions, based upon the actions of what had transpired after just a few unfortunate hours in the life of one subject on Earth in just one solitary trickle, in an ocean of surrounding time.

"Omniel - Angel of Oneness & Mihael - Angel of Loyalty – You have submitted inconsistent reports that have resulted in the discovery of conclusive evidence that you conspired together to keep certain information hidden from your leader Nathanial and your peers in this team of overseers! – Namely, the knowledge that both Micah and Rashnu attempted to contact those who were overseers; before they settled upon their decision to send the subject back to Earth – Considering your natures and the blatant movement away from those most pure and trusted of attributes, your actions were negligent in the extreme – You did not demonstrate the essential teamwork that would have created the oneness needed to successfully offer a collective steer to the subject, nor indeed the loyalty needed at this level of operation – We cannot begin to reflect to you the degree of anger that was displayed to us; as we took this information back to The Power – You will be taken from this place to the fire that causes permanent destruction to the essence of your being – No part of you will live on – The verdict is therefore, ANNIHILATION! – Be gone!" As the accused were starting to gradually be led away, thus thinning the congregation somewhat; it had become apparent to some that not all of the required parties were in attendance. The assembly immediately went silent at the ruthless dismissal of the previously condemned. Nathanial went as cold as it was possible for an angelic being to petrify. The voice of his accusers rang out and although sounding a little disappointed, those who were serving The Power were emphatic with the tone of their address. "Nathanial – Angel of fire! How distressing it is, that you of all of our kind should now have to face the fire that you yourself helped the Power to create at the beginning of all known creative existence – You were both responsible for this group and accountable for their actions – You too are now utterly condemned this day! – The

Power did not utter but one morsel of anger as we brought news of your failure – Instead, he has asked us to convey his utmost regret, as well as instructing us to ensure minimal degrees of suffering as you take the ferocious fires into your essence – We will indeed be obedient to his divine edict – Nevertheless the verdict is; ANNIHILATION! – Take him!"

There then followed a lengthy and extremely pregnant pause before the angels sent to serve the assembly continued.

"Many of you may have noticed the rather confusing activity that has surrounded The Place of Decisions again recently. You may have heard rumours that the subject, Charlie Becker returned; once again without permission to do so. I have a statement from those who advise The Power, please bear with me." The angel conveyed the message with no little degree of hesitance.

Regarding Charlie Becker!

The subject - Charlie Becker returned to the Place of Decisions after his spirit left his body after being injured by the subject known as Mickey Baker. Once again; it was not the appointed time or approved destiny that saw him return to us again. The Power has decided, after much advice and consultation, to allow him to return to his body; again! – Please don't interrupt, I will convey all I know about this matter – Due to the progressively degenerative state of the body in which he resided and the fact

304

that there were a number of other subjects that had witnessed the demise of Becker; he has been returned retrospectively to a time a little earlier in his life on Earth – He will return at the age of what they refer to as; forty years old. It is five of their years earlier! The Power has expressed the desire to understand why, after his first sojourn to our realm, he suddenly started to adjust his character toward a greater good? There are a number of other questions The Power is demanding answers to! For example; will he do better a second time at the precise point in history he really started to, shall we say; give up on the essential virtues, such as, goodness, hope, his marriage vows and the preservation of his own body and soul. We have also been given a directive, instructing us to find out why his interaction with the subject known as Lisa Baker was so influential in the process that is rapidly being referred to as Charlie Becker's awakening! Also - to put all other speculation into the realms of reality; Yes - it is true that The Darkness has been alerted and will now dispatch huge reinforcements to ensure Becker repeats his historical folly – And – Yes - Sofiel The prime Angel of Nature – has gone missing! Of course that is having a de -stabling effect on the Earth's environmental health. And Yes – Although we have tried extensively to locate the soul of Mickey Baker – It remains missing – We simply do not know where he is."   To be Continued